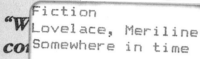

"W
co

Aurora drew a deep
years from now."

Lucius stared at her for a long, silent moment.
"Are you blessed by the gods, then? Have they
given you immortality?"

For a moment Aurora was tempted to claim
divine power. But a sober recollection of what
had happened to the so-called witches in Salem
made her hesitate.

At his frown, she shrugged. "Trust me, I'm
human." Her chin rose. "And as such, I insist
that you release me. I offer no harm to you or
to Rome. You have no reason to hold me."

"Oh, I have good reason."

"What, for Pete's sake? Why do you keep me?"

"For my pleasure."

Dear Reader,

Once again, we're proud to bring you a lineup of irresistible books, something we seem to specialize in here at Intimate Moments. Start off your month with award-winning author Kathleen Eagle's newest American Hero title, *Defender*. In Gideon Defender you'll find a hero you'll never forget. This is one of those books that is bound to end up on "keeper" shelves all across the country.

Linda Turner completes her miniseries "The Wild West" with sister Kat's story, a sensuous treat for readers everywhere. Award-winner Dee Holmes once again demonstrates her skill at weaving together suspense and romance in *Watched*, while Amanda Stevens puts a clever twist on the ever-popular amnesia plotline in *Fade to Black*. We have another Spellbound title for you this month, a time-travel romance from Merline Lovelace called *Somewhere in Time*. Finally, welcome new writer Lydia Burke, who debuts with *The Devil and Jessie Webster*.

Coming soon—more great reading from some of the best authors in the business, including Linda Howard, whose long-awaited *Loving Evangeline* will be coming your way in December.

As always—enjoy!

Leslie J. Wainger
Senior Editor and Editorial Coordinator

Please address questions and book requests to:
Silhouette Reader Service
U.S.: 3010 Walden Ave., P.O. Box 1325, Buffalo, NY 14269
Canadian: P.O. Box 609, Fort Erie, Ont. L2A 5X3

SOMEWHERE IN TIME

Merline Lovelace

Published by Silhouette Books
America's Publisher of Contemporary Romance

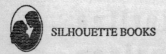

SILHOUETTE BOOKS

ISBN 0-373-07593-6

SOMEWHERE IN TIME

Copyright © 1994 by Merline Lovelace

This edition published by arrangement with Harlequin Enterprises B. V.

® and TM are trademarks of Harlequin Enterprises B. V., used under
license. Trademarks indicated with ® are registered in the United States
Patent and Trademark Office, the Canadian Trade Marks Office and in
other countries.

Printed in U.S.A.

MERLINE LOVELACE

As a career air-force officer, Merline Lovelace served tours of duty in Vietnam, at the Pentagon and at bases all over the world. During her years in uniform she met and married the world's sexiest captain, who subsequently became the world's sexiest colonel, and she stored up enough adventures to keep her fingers flying over the keyboard for years to come. When not glued to the word processor, Merline goes antiquing with her husband, Al, or chases little white balls around the fairways. Merline also writes historical romances for Harlequin Historicals.

To my sister, Mary,
who also wore air-force blue—
with all my love.

Chapter 1

Captain Aurora Durant understood that flying was a dangerous occupation. Every time she taxied her sleek air force jet down the runway and launched it into the sky, she accepted the fact that someday she might not be able to bring it back down safely. What she couldn't accept was that this was the day.

"Looks like the weather front stretches clear up to the Saudi border!" her copilot shouted over the rattle of thunder and crackle of static electricity in their headsets.

"We can't get above it!" Aurora yelled back. She struggled with the wheel as winds buffeted her C-21. The small six-passenger jet that the air force used to haul cargo, as well as people, bucked under her hands. "We'll have to try to go around!"

"Check. Just don't take us too far off course. I wouldn't want to stray into Iraq's airspace. Those folks are a might touchy since the Gulf War."

Aurora flashed the lieutenant a quick grin. "No kidding. I heard one of our F-15s got a radar lock last week, and—"

Her grin faded as another violent wind shear flung the craft sideways. Sucking in a quick breath, she fought to level the plane.

There'd been no indication of a storm in their flight path when they took off a half hour ago. After dropping off the congressmen who'd come out to see and be seen with the UN peacekeeping forces in Saudi, Aurora had anticipated a quick run back to Ramstein, their home base in Germany. Their only cargo was a half-dozen crates of communications equipment being sent back for emergency repair. But fifteen minutes out of Saudi, one of those freak desert storms she'd heard so much about and hoped never to experience had suddenly enveloped them.

Aurora flinched as lightning flashed out of the dark clouds to their left and arced earthward. She eased the plane farther and farther east, keeping its nose to the wind. Charlie adjusted his earphones and tried once more to raise ground control, but turbulence in the airwaves defeated him.

Just when the winds had calmed and Aurora thought the worst might be over, lightning split the sky in front of them. A blinding white light filled the cockpit. Keeping one hand on the yoke, she threw up her other arm to shield her eyes. Charlie yelled as static reverberated through his headphones in a high-pitched screech that could be heard even over the sound of the skies splitting.

The force of the lightning knocked the plane sideways. It tumbled like a wounded bird through the skies. Aurora's head, protected only by her flight cap and her thick, curly hair, cracked against the side window. Desperately she blinked back tears of pain as unconsciousness dragged at the edges of her senses. For a timeless moment, darkness closed over her, and her mind floated free.

Slowly, painfully, the storm's violence brought her back to full awareness. As if from a distance, she saw her white hands gripping the wheel. Fighting the pounding ache in her head, Aurora pulled at the controls.

"Charlie," she shouted hoarsely. "Help me stabilize the plane. The instruments are going berserk. I can't tell what's been hit."

She struggled with the controls as the small Learjet plunged through the heaving maelstrom. Tearing her eyes from the writhing darkness, she looked over to see Charlie slumped back against his seat. Blood was running from his ear.

Sheer panic sliced through Aurora. She would have to fight the malevolent forces of nature herself. Using every ounce of strength she possessed, she battled the pull of gravity. With the plane's electronic systems knocked out, she had only training, instinct and sheer guts to rely on. Planting both feet against the floor pedals, Aurora sawed back on the wheel. Still the plane spiraled downward.

Panting, squinting against the pain stabbing through her head, Aurora fought on. Her legs ached with strain. The muscles in her arms quivered with stress. Controlling the panic that drummed in her veins, she ran through every emergency procedure she'd ever learned. Still the plane dived.

Dizzy now, sure that the earth would reach up to crush them into oblivion at any moment, Aurora worked the pedals and controls. Her conscious mind told her it was no use, that she couldn't pull this speeding cylinder of steel out of its suicidal dive. She set her jaw. The flier in her wouldn't give up. With the last of her reserves, she hauled back on the wheel.

Imperceptibly at first, then more noticeably, the uncontrolled spin began to slow. With a sobbing cry, Aurora forced the wheel back farther. The small plane responded. Its nose lifted a couple of degrees. She held on with grim determination. The nose came up a few more degrees. In the enveloping blackness, with no instruments to guide her, Aurora had no idea where she was flying her plane, but she was flying it. She glanced out of the cockpit, desperately searching for some light, some sign of the horizon, to let her get her bearings.

Far to the right, she thought she saw a thinning in the smothering blackness. Holding her breath, she tried a banking movement. The plane quivered, but responded. Air rasped in her throat as she gulped in relief. For what seemed like hours but she knew was only minutes, she raced toward the patch of dimness ahead. Suddenly, like an arrow shot from a crossbow, her small craft burst through the wall of gray into blinding sunlight.

Aurora gasped in sheer terror. The desert sand was less than two hundred feet below her hurtling craft. Another couple of seconds in that dive, and they would've augered in. Swallowing the acrid bile that threatened to choke her, she leveled off and skimmed the shuddering plane along the earth's surface. Heart pounding, she scanned the barren landscape for some sign of civilization, some airport where she could attempt a landing. Only low, shifting sand dunes, and a narrow road stretching into the far distance, filled her vision.

Aurora wasn't certain how much damage her plane had sustained, but she knew she had to land it, fast, before it fell apart in the air. The long, lonely road would have to serve as an emergency landing strip. With aching arms and feet, she worked the throttle back and applied the air brakes. A shudder racked the plane when she pulled the manual release for the landing gears. Slowing her airspeed, she dropped lower and lower, until the wheels just skimmed the road. Surprised at its narrowness, she looked for a spot where the dunes were back far enough from the pavement for the Lear's forty-foot wingspan. Praying that a truck or a tourist-laden bus wouldn't suddenly appear over a hill, she put the plane down on the narrow road.

The tires bounced along its uneven surface. Aurora fought the stick, trying to keep the craft on a straight line. Her disbelieving eyes saw what looked like cobbles flash by under the craft's nose. Cobbles! Of all the places in the world to put down a crippled bird, she had to pick a damned cobblestone road, probably left over from the last millennium. At least that explained the lack of traffic, she thought grimly as she struggled for control.

One wheel bounced into a jagged hole. The sleek bird skittered sideways, and Aurora felt fear close her throat as the right wing dipped dangerously. The plane bounced forward a few more yards, then skidded off the cobbles. Sand flung up by the engines beat against the windshield, obscuring Aurora's view. Blood drummed furiously in her ears. Her hands ached as she fought the wheel. After an endless, heart-stopping moment, the plane slid to a shuddering stop with its wheels buried in soft sand. Stressed metal creaked and groaned as it settled with the wing tanks just touching the desert surface.

Resting her head against hands still wrapped around the wheel in white-knuckled desperation, Aurora wanted to sob with relief.

Instead, she took deep, gasping breaths and waited for the blood to stop roaring in her ears. The sound of her plane creaking and snapping and settling in the sand penetrated her consciousness, and brought with it the knowledge that she had to get the hell out of there. And take the unconscious Charlie out with her. Leaking fuel or shorted electronics could spark an explosion at any moment.

Years of training kicked in. Aurora unlatched her seat belt and pushed her way out of the tilted seat. Noting that the blood had stopped flowing from Charlie's ear and his pulse seemed steady, Aurora grabbed her copilot under his arms and dragged him backward. Once she had Charlie clear and she was sure there'd be no explosion, she'd come back to check the damage and put together a survival pack. It could be hours, or even days, before rescue arrived. She kicked a path through the scattered crates of communications equipment and backed toward the rear hatch, panting from the effort. For someone who looked like the long, tall Texan he always bragged he was, Charlie packed a solid weight.

Pushing open the heavy door, Aurora jumped down and planted her feet firmly in the sand. She reached up with both hands to drag her copilot's limp body over her shoulder in the fireman's carry she'd learned in survival school. The hold was supposed to allow smaller people to carry weights much larger than themselves, but Aurora found herself staggering through the low dunes. If— *when*—they got back to Ramstein, she would definitely have to talk to Lieutenant Charles Everett about a diet.

Aurora tried to ease her burden off her shoulder gently. The soft, sucking sand, and his deadweight, proved too much for her. Her rubbery legs gave way, and she tumbled down in an awkward heap. Charlie landed square atop her. One of his knees slammed into her stomach, knocking the wind out of her with a *whoosh*.

Aurora lay pinned under him, dizzy from exertion and residual fear. Her arms trembled, too weak from the strain of fighting the plane and hauling Charlie out to push him off. Hot, burning sand slid down the neck of her flight suit as she tried to wiggle out from under his crushing form.

Her movement only burrowed her deeper in the enveloping sand. With an exasperated grunt, she forced herself to relax her trembling muscles. For a moment, Aurora was tempted to just lie there while the rest of her fear and pumping adrenaline drained away. But then Charlie's body twitched, as if he were awakening to pain, and Aurora gathered her strength for another try.

Over his shoulder, she saw that the sun now burned low on the horizon, all evidence of the storm gone. Closing her eyes against the glare, she braced both arms to heave Charlie up. Red spots danced behind her lids as she took a deep breath. Suddenly Aurora felt a cooling shadow block the painful light. Her eyes flew open in stunned surprise to see a black silhouette outlined against the flaming red sun a few yards away.

Her first reaction was relief, blessed relief.

"Hey, over here!" she yelled. "I need help!"

When the figure towering over her didn't move, didn't speak, Aurora's relief turned to caution. Eyes narrowed against the sun's glare, she tried to make out his features. All she could see was the outline of a lean, sun-bronzed face. The long swirl of material hanging from his shoulders made her think he must be a desert tribesman, wearing a loose, cooling burnoose.

The thought didn't reassure her. In the months she'd been flying in and out of Saudi, she'd heard tales of the fierce Bedouin tribes that roamed the Arabian peninsula. They weren't exactly known for their hospitality to strangers, especially since the Gulf War had ravaged their tribal grazing areas. Remembering the pistol still buried in debris inside the cabin, Aurora stifled a groan. Still, this guy was the only help available at this moment.

"Please," she called out, her throat dry and raspy. "My friend's been injured. Help me lift him."

She pushed at Charlie's shoulders, miming her need.

The figure above her didn't move.

Aurora swallowed her nervousness and tried again. "Please. Help me." Wriggling her hips, she tried to slide out from under the crushing weight.

Finally, the tribesman stirred. Striding forward, he lifted Charlie with a smooth, easy movement and laid him on his back.

Aurora dragged in the first lungful of air she'd had since the lightning hit her plane. Still shaken, she lay sprawled in the sand. But when the stranger took a step toward her, she scrambled backward and pushed herself up onto unsteady legs.

"Thanks, but I'm okay."

He folded his arms across his chest and subjected her to a piercing scrutiny.

She pushed her tangled hair out of her eyes with a shaky hand and returned his assessing stare. He had an impressive face, she admitted to herself. All planes and angles, with a square, determined chin, and a nose that looked like it had taken a punch or two in its day. From the neck up, he looked exactly like what Aurora feared he was—a fierce desert warrior. From the neck down, however, he looked like no one she'd ever seen before—at least not outside of a museum.

What she'd assumed was a burnoose was in fact a red swirling cape that draped across his chest. Red? she wondered wildly. Here, in the desert? Under the cape, he wore some kind of upper-body armor. Its burnished surface gleamed and glinted in the sun's setting rays. Below that... Aurora blinked. Below that was a short white tunic that stopped about midthigh. After four years at the air force academy and five years of military service, Aurora had seen her share of male thighs. But none quite as long or as tanned or as roped with sinewy muscles as these. The thought flashed through her mind that in other circumstances she might have appreciated the sight, but she was too shaky to do so now.

Dredging her memory for the country briefings she'd received when she first started flying in the Middle East, Aurora tried to remember the section on desert tribes. With so many different peoples in this part of the world, it was hard to recall individual characteristics. Still, try as she might, she couldn't remember any mention of tall, golden-skinned people with dark, curling hair who wore short skirts and red capes and—her eyes narrowed incredulously—swords! Was that really a sword she saw strapped to the man's waist? She took another step back in sheer surprise.

"*Qui es? A qua venis?*"

Aurora tore her eyes from that long, lethal-looking implement. "I'm sorry, I don't understand. Uh, *no comprehende.*"

He glanced from her to the plane, then back again. Dark brows drew together over a long, aquiline nose. "*Ubi equi sunt?*"

Aurora started to shake her head, then stopped. The word *equi* triggered a memory from her high-school-Latin days. *Equi, equine.* Something to do with horses, she thought. Her wariness lessened. Maybe the man was speaking a form of Italian. Aurora knew the European powers had carved the Middle East into their own spheres of influence during the previous century. Maybe this tribe roamed land that had once been part of the Italian colonial empire. The guy could be offering to get horses, to take them to the nearest town or village.

"Yes, *equi.* Bring *equi.*"

At the man's frown, Aurora guessed her answer was less than satisfactory. The fierce look on his lean, sun-bronzed face made her distinctly nervous. With his powerful build, he wasn't exactly the type she wanted to get crosswise with. He was solid muscle, and a good four inches taller than her own five-foot-five. Now that she was over the shock of the crash and her wobbly legs were starting to regain their strength, she could handle him. Probably. If she had to. But she'd just as soon not have to.

Smiling, she tried again. "Uh, *equi.* Horses."

His frown deepened.

What was this guy's problem? She waved one hand in the air. "We go. You know, *arrivederci?*"

Wishing she'd taken some language courses along with her double engineering major, Aurora made a walking motion with her fingers. "To town. *Villa. Urbana.*"

His eyes narrowed to dark, glittering slits.

Exasperated, Aurora placed both hands on her hips and made a sashaying motion.

His frown faded, and, incredibly, he smiled. One corner of his mouth drew up in a slow, crooked grin, softening the sharp planes and angles of his face.

Aurora's own mouth fell open in astonishment. His grin was so blatantly masculine, and so reminiscent of some of the cocky, self-assured fighter pilots she'd dated, that for a moment she forgot she was standing with her plane sunk in soft sand and half the desert trickling down the back of her flight suit.

When he spoke again, in his low voice, Aurora pulled her scattered wits together. This time she didn't catch even a glimmer of a meaning. She shook her head, and his grin faded. Stepping forward, he reached for her arm. Aurora stepped sideways. No way she was going to let this hulking stranger take hold of her, thighs or no thighs, grin or no grin.

"Cool it, big guy. Look, I'm American. United States Air Force." She pointed to the U.S. flag sewn on the left shoulder of her green one-piece flight suit. "Americans. Friends. *Amis.* Buddies."

He issued an unmistakable, growling order. Aurora had been in the air force long enough to know an order when she heard one. But even if she'd understood the words, she wouldn't have had any intention of following any instructions this fierce-looking individual issued. Not until they came to an understanding. She gave her head a firm shake.

Before she quite realized his intent, the man lunged across the small distance separating them. Taking Aurora's arm in an iron grip, he pulled her against him.

Startled, she struggled to regain her balance. When he turned and began to haul her behind him, she managed to find her feet. Infuriated at being caught off guard like some gutless wimp, Aurora yanked her arm free and took a couple of quick sideways steps. Her chin shot up.

"Watch it, pal. You're starting to irritate me, big-time. Now get this straight. I'm not leaving. Not without my friend."

He snapped something at her. Aurora shook her head in stubborn refusal.

When he reached for her again, she was ready. Taking a firm grasp on the his upper arm, she used his own forward momentum to flip him neatly, head over heels, onto his back. He hit the sand with a satisfying thud.

Standing over him, hands splayed on hips, she measured each word in slow, distinct syllables, as if the force of her determination could make him understand. "Read these lips! I . . . will . . . not . . . leave . . . my . . . friend. . . ."

Sprawled at her feet, the man stared up at her in blank astonishment. Aurora savored his stunned look. A smug, self-satisfied grin tugged at her lips. Just as she was congratulating herself on the neat takedown, one sandaled foot whipped out and knocked her right leg out from under her. She landed on her rear with a painful thump.

In the space of a heartbeat, she found herself flat on her back, his full weight sprawled over her. For the second time that afternoon, Aurora was pinned to the ground by a man. This one, however, was definitely conscious, and thoroughly enjoying his brief dominance—if his grim, mocking smile was any indication. She sucked in a furious breath. The scent of wool and hot, sweat-streaked male filled her nostrils.

"Okay, you've had your fun. Now let me up."

His hips shifted. One knee wedged between hers. A hard thigh pried her legs apart.

Shocked, Aurora searched his eyes. What she saw in their gold-flecked brown depths made her pulse leap and her heart skip at least three beats.

"In your dreams, big guy," she ground out through clenched jaws. She brought up her knee with all the force she could muster.

As fast as she was, her attacker's reflexes were even faster. Before her knee could connect with his groin, he rolled to one side and deflected her thrust. To her fury, amusement flashed in his brown eyes.

So the bastard thought this was some kind of game, did he? Aurora curled her fingers into her palm and prepared to smash the heel of her hand into the nose just inches above her face.

As if reading her intent, the man caught her wrist. In a quick, lightning movement, he snagged the other. With both wrists banded together, Aurora could only arch her back and heave, trying to dislodge him. His grin widened as he rode her bucking body, and he made some comment she was glad she didn't understand. Furious, she writhed back and forth in the sand, struggling to break his bone-crushing hold. After several thrashing, futile moments, she recognized that she was just wasting her strength. Dragging in deep gulps of air, she stilled.

With a sure, lithe grace, he rolled to his feet. Then he yanked Aurora to her feet, still holding her wrists with one hand. The other fumbled at the buckle of the wide leather belt that held his sword. Ignoring Aurora's vehement protests, he swung her around with a jerk. Within seconds, the leather bound her hands painfully behind her back. With a hard hand on her arm, her captor began to pull her with him.

Sure that he was going to drag her to some distant encampment or town, Aurora began to panic. She couldn't leave Charlie alone and injured in the desert. She stumbled after him for a few paces, then dug her heels in once more. She could almost feel that long sword slicing through her throat when he turned, exasperation etched clearly across his high cheekbones.

"Please. My friend. *Mon ami*. Uh, *mon amour*." She had no idea what the word for *friend* was in Italian. Desperate, she nodded toward Charlie.

As if weighing whether to give in to her pleading, he pursed firm, molded lips. Finally he raised his head and gave an ear-splitting whistle. Aurora nearly jumped out of her flight suit.

The distant jingle of a bridle carried over the dunes. At least, Aurora thought it was a bridle. Never having been on a horse in her life, she wasn't too sure. The faint sound of the approaching horse grew louder. Of course, it could be a camel jingling along behind that sand dune, Aurora thought, or even a donkey. She tried to picture this formidable man on a donkey, deliberately clinging to the ridiculous image that filled her mind. Somehow it made her captor less frightening, more human.

The jingling grew louder, then fractured into separate and distinct pieces. She could hear several different bridle bits, muffled hooves hitting the ground, and a man's echoing command. To her utter amazement, a troop of mounted soldiers rose out of the shimmering sand a few seconds later. The setting sun glinted off their armor and red-plumed helmets and, unbelievably, shields.

Wondering wildly if she'd stumbled onto the set of a remake of *Ben Hur,* Aurora gaped at the disciplined troop. They moved with the ease of professionals, their ranks rigid, their mounts stepping lightly through the sand. One trooper rode at the head of the column, leading a huge, prancing horse. Even to Aurora's untrained eye, the animal appeared magnificent. Midnight black, and wearing a strange wooden saddle with four pommels, the stallion—yes, he was a stallion, she decided after a quick look, sure she knew that much about horses, at least—danced to a stop a mere yard in front of her.

Her mind whirled in confused, chaotic thought. A dozen improbable ideas flashed through her head, only to be discarded on the spot. Nothing made any sense. Her intellect refused to accept the images her eyes presented. Numbness filled her, slowing her thought processes, clogging her brain cells. That crack she'd taken when her head hit the window must be causing her to hallucinate, she decided at last.

A blond giant in burnished armor slid from his horse to offer Aurora's captor a stiff closed-fist salute. He stood close enough for her to see the sweat beading his face. This was no hallucination, her mind screamed. This was real. Aurora felt her knees buckle.

The grip on her arm tightened, jerking her upright. With a quick nod, the man holding her sent the blonde and a squad of men toward her plane. Aurora watched, breathless, as they drew their swords and approached the open rear door. After peering cautiously into the dim interior, the blonde edged sideways through the open door, his sword at the ready, as if he feared attack at any moment. A moment later, a second soldier followed him inside, then a third.

Aurora prayed they wouldn't find her sidearm, not before she had a chance to get to it. She didn't know where she was or who these clowns were, but she'd feel a heck of a lot better if she had a pistol in her hand when she found out.

One of the soldiers appeared at the hatch, carrying a wooden crate. He tilted the box, spilling communications components packed in static-resistant protective plastic into the sand.

"Hey, watch it!" she croaked involuntarily. "That's government property."

The men ignored her and continued rummaging through the broken crates. A few moments later, the blonde returned, holding the motherboard from a satellite-signal receiver in one hand. He passed it to the one Aurora now understood was the leader of this...this horse patrol. Keeping a firm hold on her arm, the tall, broad-shouldered warrior examined the small circuit board.

He turned it over and over, then glanced up, shrugging. Aurora strained to catch some word, some phrase, she understood in the conversation that ensued. Fragments of words jumped out.

Equus meant *horse,* she was sure of that much. And *Deus* was the word for *God,* she remembered from Sunday mass. It took a few seconds for the significance of the connection to sink in.

Good grief, these men were speaking Latin! A language that had been dead for nearly two thousand years. When her captor gestured to Charlie and said something that included the word *amat,* Aurora jumped.

"Amo, amas, amat," she recited hoarsely. Every beginning Latin student learned to conjugate the verb *to love.*

At her raspy words, the leader speared her with a hard look. He barked some question, to which she could only shake her head in response. Desperately Aurora raked through her memory for long-forgotten phrases. An image of her seventh-grade Latin teacher shimmered in her mind. Thin, tiger-faced Sister Mary Joseph had fought valiantly to pound conjugations and declensions into the heads of two generations of Durant children, without notable success. In sheer desperation, Aurora clung to the image of the steely-eyed nun. Her former teacher was more real, more concrete, at this moment than the bristling soldiers surrounding her.

As if in a trance, she watched two men lift Charlie and drape him over the broad back of a horse. With quick efficiency, they ran a rope under the horse's belly and tied her copilot's ankles to his dangling hands.

The man beside her said something. She looked at him blankly. Disdaining to repeat himself, he moved to his mount, pulling her along with him. Hard hands reached out to hold her as he swung onto the horse with a fluid, graceful movement. Leaning down, he wrapped an arm around Aurora's waist, then lifted her bodily to sit sideways before him in the wooden saddle. She wanted to protest, but the words stuck in her throat. She wasn't quite sure what to protest against—his rough handling, or the unreal images filling her disbelieving eyes.

Strong, tanned arms closed around her. Steadied her. Restrained her. The red cloak swirled as her captor spun his horse in the sand and headed it toward the stone road.

Swathed in the enveloping heat of the woolen cloak, Aurora fought down a wave of sheer panic. She stared at the cobbled road stretching endlessly before them. Where did it lead? Where was he taking her? Who *was* he?

Chapter 2

Lucius Antonius, senior centurion, Commander of the Twentieth Cohort *Palmyrenorum*, eased back against the pommels to give himself and the creature he held more room. With a little grunt, she slipped sideways and fell against him. Her hip ground into his groin. Grimacing in the gathering darkness, Lucius righted her yet again. At this rate, she would unman him completely before they reached camp.

Muttering something in her incomprehensible dialect, she shot him a venomous glare. She dug a shoulder into his breastplate and struggled to seat herself. Her full hips settled once more across his thighs. Lucius let out a slow breath.

By the gods, she rode as though she'd never been on a horse before. For the past half hour she'd bobbed and bounced in the saddle like a half-full sack of grain. He'd had his hands full with the constant effort to subdue her fitful attempts to break free and keep her in her precarious perch at the same time.

Glancing down, Lucius studied his captive in the gathering dusk. His gaze lingered on a sweep of thick black lashes. A begrimed cheek. Tangled hair the color of dark red wine. As he watched, she hunched one shoulder, then the other, obviously trying to ease the discomfort of her bound arms. She caught her lower lip between even white teeth, biting back what he suspected was a groan of pain. Admiration rippled though him at her endurance, followed swiftly by a twinge of regret at having to bind her so cruelly. But after her surprising attack when he'd first approached her, Lucius was taking no chances.

Not for the first time since a deafening roar had cut through the black, storm-filled skies and he'd led his patrol to investigate, he wondered just who or what it was he'd captured this day. She sported the curly tresses and soft mouth of a woman, but the curious green covering that swathed her body from head to toe was like nothing he'd ever seen. Moreover, her mysterious presence in the desert confounded him.

When he topped the rise and saw her lying intertwined with the other captive beside the huge silver-skinned vehicle, Lucius had thought at first that he'd stumbled on some strangely dressed natives coupling in the sand. Then the woman had twisted her head, and her wine-hued hair had spilled out across the sand. Eyes the color of a storm-tossed winter sea had met his.

Across the low dunes separating them, Lucius had felt the impact of her gaze to the soles of his leather sandals. He'd stared at her, drawn by the shimmering, swirling depths of her incredible gray eyes. At that moment, with the setting sun beating hot upon his back and sand swirling at his ankles, Lucius had known he would have her.

Then the woman had called out to him in her unintelligible tongue and tried to shift the man's limp body off her. Wondering if she had drained the life force from her lover with the strength of her loins, Lucius had gone forward to pull the man aside. Only then had he seen the dried blood smearing the side of his face. She must have tried to escape him, Lucius had decided. She'd probably struck him when he brought her down. The gods knew she had the skills to do it.

He shifted in the saddle and glanced down once more at his captive, remembering how this same female had subsequently caused him, a seasoned Roman legionary, to stumble and fall into the sand. He wanted to believe it was an accident, but her smug, gloating grin had told him she'd engineered the fall somehow. He'd soon wiped the grin off her face, but that she'd brought him down at all was extraordinary.

Lucius frowned, searching for an explanation for the woman in his arms. For her strange garb and her sudden appearance in the desert. For her huge winged chariot. 'Twas like none he'd ever seen, even in the most elaborate spectacles in Rome's arena, when senator vied with emperor to delight the crowds, staging parades and fanciful recreations of the tales of the gods...

A low groan carried above the rhythmic clip-clop of iron-shod hooves on cobbles, interrupting Lucius's disturbing thoughts.

"Captain. The man wakes."

Lucius reined in his mount. Before the beast had even slowed, the woman had begun to twist and turn, craning her neck to see over his shoulder. Her voice harsh and urgent, she called out to her companion.

"Char-Li! Char-Li!"

Lucius swore under his breath as her hip ground into his groin once more and her booted foot kicked against the stallion's withers. The huge steed snorted and skittered sideways across the road. Lucius fought to contain his fractious mount and the wiggling, twisting creature in his arms.

"Be still, woman."

Ignoring his low-voiced command, she shouted to this Char-Li. Her feet flailed as she tried to break free of his hold.

"By Jupiter, cease your struggles," he ordered through clenched teeth. One hand gripped the reins, and the other tightened around her middle, deliberately, cruelly.

Her breath shortened to gasping pants. After a few moments, she stopped struggling. She stared up at him, her eyes gleaming like molten silver in the glow of the moon's light. For a timeless moment, they measured each other. Her quick, uneven breaths washed against his cheek. The acrid scent of sweat teased his nostrils, his own from the long, hot ride he'd endured this day, hers from the heat and, Lucius suspected, from a fear she refused to show. 'Twas no small matter, after all, to challenge a Roman commander.

"Captain, do you need assistance?"

As if from a distance, Lucius heard his deputy's low voice. Slowly he relaxed his rigid hold. The woman slumped and drew in painful gulps of air.

"I'm not yet to the stage where I need assistance with a mere female, Quintus," he drawled, sliding from the saddle.

"Is she truly female?"

Lucius pulled the woman from her awkward perch, then turned to answer the hesitant question. "She's female," he replied calmly, holding her up with a strong hand.

"She's dressed so strangely, 'tis impossible to tell."

A smile tugged at the captain's lips. "I can tell. Her rump has rubbed against my manhood for the past half hour and more. She has woman's flesh beneath this green covering, firm and ripe and warm."

His knowing grin, and the possessive pat he bestowed on the firm, ripe flesh under discussion, earned a reluctant smile from his deputy and a furious sputter from the female. The younger man relaxed his rigid stance, although Lucius could see doubt still etched across his face.

"That huge chariot she was traveling in," Quintus said slowly. "I've never seen anything like it. How did they drive it, do you suppose, with no axle, no shaft or harness?"

"I know not, but I intend to find out."

"And the roar that trumpeted across the sky just before you found her! It sounded as though Jupiter himself were flinging thunderbolts across the heavens." The lieutenant leaned forward, lowering his voice. "What if this creature we've captured is a spirit, sent from the gods?"

"Nay, she's flesh and blood."

"The gods often take human form. Dare we hold her and risk the gods' wrath?"

Both men glanced toward the one under discussion.

She frowned at their assessing stares, then lifted her chin and shot them a fierce look. The hulking deputy, a head taller and half again heavier than the female who faced him, took a quick step back.

Lucius felt a grin curve his lips. What the woman before him lacked in stature, she more than made up for in spirit. She was so fiery, so unlike the doe-eyed women of this region, who hid behind their veils and shied away from any contact with men outside their families. 'Twas certain she wasn't from this part of the Empire. His smile faded as he again pondered her origins. Where had she come from, in that strange vehicle? Was she truly of this earth?

Lucius understood his deputy's fears, even if he didn't share them. At least not completely. He was as much in awe of the gods as the next man. He knew, as did every soldier in his command, that offending a deity could mean a lost battle, an arm lopped off by an enemy sword, disease from an unclean woman. No legionary with any sense would knowingly court the disasters the gods had been known to visit on mere mortals for interfering with one of their own.

But this creature was no goddess, Lucius told himself firmly. No spirit or demon sent by the denizens of the heavens. She was human. He'd felt the heat of her body next to his, smelled her scent, heard her soft pants as she struggled against his hold. When he covered her body with his and pinned her to the sand, her smoky eyes and flame-filled hair had stirred his desire.

Ruthlessly suppressing his last lingering doubts, Lucius addressed his deputy. "Keep an unruffled mind, Quintus. She is naught but a woman, a—"

A low, tortured groan interrupted him.

The female surged forward, heading toward her companion. "Char-Li!"

Lucius caught her arm. "You will stay here. I'll speak with him."

She shook her head and tried to shoulder him aside. His mouth thinning, Lucius pinned her back against his mount.

"Stay here."

With a curt gesture, he signaled to Quintus to guard her. He left the two eyeing each other warily and strode toward the rear of the patrol. At his nod, two legionaries cut the ropes binding the captive's hands and feet. Hauling him off the horse, they laid him on his back in the sand. Lucius knelt, buried one fist in the man's short-cropped hair and lifted his face to his.

"Who are you? What do you here?"

Eyes wide and uncomprehending in the moonlight, the man made no answer.

"Who are you? Whence do you come?"

Pain etched deep grooves in the man's face. His lids fluttered shut.

Lucius lowered his head to the sand. Propping one arm across a bent knee, he studied the supine figure. He saw no visible signs of injury, no twisted limbs betokening broken bones, no blood other than that which had trickled from his ear. But 'twas obvious the wound to his head had addled the man's senses.

Curious, Lucius skimmed the male's length with his eyes. He wore coverings identical to the female's—heavy black boots and a tough outer garment that covered arms, legs and torso. Questions tumbled through the captain's mind as he fingered the strange garment. What animal had yielded this green hide? What tribe had cured it to such a supple thinness? Where were these two from? What business did they have here, deep in the vast, half-conquered desert territory Lucius administered in Rome's name? As Rome's representative, he had the responsibility to find the answers to these tantalizing questions.

The man groaned once more. His long limbs twitched in the sand as his eyes opened. He fixed them sightlessly on Lucius and muttered something in an unknown dialect.

Lucius responded in Latin, then in the Greek still used by the upper classes of the region, before switching smoothly to Aramaic, the language of the fierce desert tribes. After receiving no response, the captain gave up. Whatever he learned of these travelers, he would have to learn it from the female. As Lucius rose and brushed the sand from his tunic, anticipation tightened his loins. 'Twould be an interrogation he much enjoyed.

They rode for hours through dark, starry night. For the first part of the ride, Aurora felt panic threatening with every breath. Where were they? Who *were* these guys? A hundred explanations crowded her mind, each more improbable than the last.

Maybe... maybe they were some kind of lost tribe, like the Stone Age people discovered a few years ago deep in the Philippine jungles. Maybe they'd passed the centuries in some uncharted, undiscovered desert oasis. That would

explain their archaic dress and their old-fashioned but lethal-looking swords.

The moving mountain disguised as a horse hit an uneven cobble and dipped its powerful shoulders, sending
Aurora into her captor's bronzed cuirass with bruising
force. Biting back a gasp of pain, she sagged in his hold.
His arms closed around her, offering strength and warmth.
For a long moment, she was tempted to lean against him,
to let him cradle her in a cocoon of dark intimacy that shut
out her fears and churning thoughts. But almost as soon
as she became aware of the urge, Aurora pushed it aside
and struggled to sit upright once again.

Damn it, she wasn't some weak-kneed wuss. She was an
officer. A captain in the finest air force in the world. As
aircraft commander on this mission, she was responsible
for her crew. Wherever they'd landed, whoever held them,
it was up to her to find a way out. And she would! She'd
spent two hellish months going through survival school.
She'd been trained in hand-to-hand combat. She'd been
tested before, under incredibly adverse conditions, and
she'd always come through.

Maybe that was it! Her agile mind latched on to an improbable thought. Maybe this was some kind of... of se-
cret training unit. Maybe the Saudi Special Forces had set
up this unique unit in the desert, to test their military's
endurance and survival skills. To take them back to the
most primitive times. Maybe the US government even
knew about it. Hell, the CIA had probably financed the
whole thing.

Aurora managed a wobbly smile and reined in her wildly
escalating imagination. When they arrived at their desti-
nation, she'd find someone she could communicate with,
someone who'd see that Charlie got care. She'd establish
some ground rules for their treatment. She began to repeat the phrases of the Code of Conduct for U.S. Fighting Forces. Every soldier, sailor, marine and airman

studied the Code in basic training. It governed their conduct if taken as prisoners of war.

Aurora swallowed. Okay, so she was a prisoner. But of what war? And who fought a war these days with swords and shields? The events in Somalia had shown that even countries with whole populations dying of starvation could still arm themselves to the teeth with AK-47s and grenade launchers. These bronzed, red-cloaked warriors must be the only combatants left on the face of the earth who still relied on muscle power instead of firepower.

Aurora felt bubbles of fright rise in her throat at the thought that she might be in the hands of some primitive warlord. Resolutely she forced them down. She'd deal with one situation, one fact, one event, at a time. Right now, she had to concentrate on keeping her back straight and ignoring the growing soreness in her rear. Shifting on the hard wooden saddle, she tried to find a comfortable position. With every jouncing step of the horse, a front pommel rubbed against her right hip, another against her right buttock. She refused to think about what was rubbing against her left hip. The captain's short white tunic didn't leave much to the imagination.

After what seemed like an eternity but was probably about two hours, the troop topped a slight rise. Aurora sucked in her breath at the panoramic vista below. Thousands of flickering fires dotted a black-velvet background. The sound of dogs barking drifted across the starry night, and a reedy flute filled the air with a sad, thin keening.

A town. People. Help.

Aurora shifted from one tender buttock to the other in anticipation of parting company with the hard saddle. The commander nudged his mount forward and began a long, slow descent. Aurora scanned the distant scene for some familiar sign. Car lights, maybe. A flash of neon, or the glow of streetlamps. Anything! When they entered the outskirts of the city, however, she saw that the small, round huts they passed were illuminated from the inside by glowing hearth fires. If there was any electricity in this town, it hadn't made it to the suburbs. Trying not to let her panic well up once more, Aurora forced herself to concentrate as the small patrol wound through the narrow streets.

The huts soon gave way to more substantial buildings. She stared in dazed wonder at the tall, graceful structures that rose on either side. Gleaming white in the starlit night, they were girded by rows of elegant columns. Crowded along the bases of these majestic buildings were what looked like shops. As the troop clattered past, men and women in long robes spilled out of brightly lit, open-fronted stores to shout greetings, while children squealed and ran alongside. Aurora caught a glimpse of firelight flickering on glistening animal carcasses hanging from a beam inside one stall. The sounds of drunken voices raised in song poured out of another.

She tried to assimilate the sights flashing past her and the sounds reaching her above the clatter of horses' hooves. Despite her desperate efforts, nothing seemed familiar, nothing was recognizable. When at last the troop approached a pair of gates set in a massive wall, her eyes were aching from the strain of staring into the strange street scenes. A horn sounded behind Aurora, and she almost slipped off the saddle in startled surprise. Only the commander's strong arms kept her upright. He muttered something under his breath and settled her across his thighs once more.

The gates swung open with ponderous, thundering slowness. As they rode past, sentries stood at stiff attention, arms raised in salute. From the soldiers strolling the wide streets, Aurora guessed that they'd entered the enemy's camp. Her mind skittered away from the word *enemy,* but at this point she had to assume the worst.

A wide cobbled boulevard led from the gates straight through the camp. Ahead, Aurora could see what had to be the headquarters. A row of colorful pennants flanked the entrance to the building, illuminated by flaring torches. The banners rippled in the night breeze, reminding Aurora of the banks of flags outside the headquarters building at Ramstein. The familiar military panoply gave her a curious sense of relief, as if she were coming home. That momentary ease fled when the troop halted and the commander slipped out of his saddle. Placing a firm hand on either side of her waist, he lifted her down.

Aurora felt a rush of shame when her knees buckled under her. Stiff from unaccustomed hours in the saddle, she would have crumpled to the ground if the leader hadn't caught her just in time. He slid one arm under her knees, the other under her back, and lifted her against his chest. His red cloak flared out behind him as he mounted the steps.

"Hey, wait a minute." Aurora struggled in his arms. "Wait. I stay with my copilot. Charlie!"

Slumped against the man in front of him, Charlie didn't look back as they led him away.

Furious, Aurora twisted her body, trying to free herself and watch the direction the patrol took at the same time. If the commander even noticed her frantic wiggling, he gave no sign. He carried her through the echoing halls, his hobnailed sandals ringing against the marble floors. Soldiers and servants in flowing robes stood gaping at the spectacle as Aurora twisted and shouted until she was hoarse.

She lost both her voice and her bearings in the maze of corridors. When he stopped before a sturdy wooden door, a guard leaped to open it. Striding into a small, cell-like room, the commander dumped Aurora on a pile of straw in one corner. She landed awkwardly on her bound arms.

Her boots scrabbled for purchase in the thick straw as she pushed herself up on one knee.

"You creep!" she panted. She got her other knee under her and rose.

He watched her impassively, his dark eyes gleaming in the dim light.

"Look, Captain, or Colonel, or whatever you are, I'm going to..."

Whatever useless threat she would have uttered faltered when several men crowded into the small room behind their leader. Aurora recognized the blonde who had searched her plane, but none of the others. One of them lit torches set high up in the walls. In the sudden light, she saw rampant curiosity and wonder in their stares.

"Go ahead, take a good look," she muttered. "I'll just bet you Neanderthals haven't seen a woman officer before."

At her taunting words, a low, excited exchange took place between the milling men. Aurora heard them question the commander repeatedly, heard his flat responses. Although she understood none of the words, she sensed the leader's gathering impatience. He shook his head more than once.

Finally, his jaw set, he barked an order and held out his hand. One of the men slipped a dagger into it.

When he took a step toward her, Aurora gasped and backed away.

Knife in hand, he stalked her. His eyes were fixed on her face, telegraphing a message she was too shaken to understand. Stumbling, she backed away. His face grim, he followed. Cold stones pressed into her shoulder blades, and she could move no farther.

Aurora studied his expression as he closed the distance between them. In the flaring torchlight, he looked intent, but not murderous. Maybe he just wanted to cut the leather binding her wrists. Aurora took a deep breath. Twisting sideways, she offered him her hands.

The knife snaked out and caught the tough fabric at her shoulder.

"What the—"

Aurora tried to pull back, away from the knife, but it was caught in a seam. Designed to protect a pilot's body from such minor unpleasantries as fire, freezing water and animal bites, the tough Nomex of her flight suit refused to give.

Grunting, the commander caught her around the waist and held her steady. The muscles in his arm bunched as he sawed, upward, away from Aurora. The stubborn reinforced seam held.

"Wait! Wait!"

The furious desperation in her voice got through his utter absorption in his task. He held the blade steady, its point still half buried in the fabric. His dark brows drew together in an unmistakable question. The other men clustered around them, their voices raised in wonder.

"Don't . . . don't cut it," Aurora gasped. "I'll show you how it works."

She wasn't about to stand there while this idiot skinned her. He'd probably take off her arm along with the flight suit. Nodding, she nudged herself out of his hold. The commander's eyes narrowed, but he let her put a little distance between them.

Lowering herself to one knee, Aurora twisted and strained until she could just reach her other ankle. Each leg of her flight suit had a zipper that opened to allow her to pull it off over her boots. With awkward fingers, she tugged the metal tab upward.

The men around her murmured in surprise. The commander hunkered down, his powerful thighs bracketing Aurora. His fingers brushed hers aside and grasped the little tab. Frowning, he worked it up and down, up and down.

"There, you see?" Aurora sneered. "Even a cretin like you can figure it out, given time and the proper training."

His head snapped up.

Meeting his narrow-eyed look, Aurora realized that she'd made a mistake. A big mistake. He might not have understood her words, but he certainly understood her derisive, mocking tone. The man was no dummy, she decided, edging away from him.

He bent, wrapped a strong hand around her ankle and tugged. Off balance, Aurora tumbled back into the hay. Pulling her foot high in the air, he unzipped the green fabric as far as it would go. A good three inches of bare calf showed above her boot top.

"Okay, okay," Aurora bit out. "Now that you know how it works, how about letting go?"

He did, only to grasp her other leg and work that zipper, as well. Aurora felt his rough-tipped, callused fingers slide down her bare skin. The gentle abrasion seemed to set her nerves on fire. Her pant leg flapped in the air as she kicked furiously against his hold. His fingers tightened for a moment, then released her. Aurora pushed herself up on her hips and scooted backward.

Eyes gleaming, he stared at the zipper on her chest.

"Now just a minute!"

She realized his intent an instant too late. Before she could scramble out of his reach, his hand whipped out and grasped her ankle once more. Ignoring her indignant squawk, he tugged her toward him. One strong, blunt-fingered hand reached for the metal tab at the neck of her flight suit.

"Don't! Don't you dare! Damn it!"

With one swift pull, he exposed her from her chest, in its regulation green T-shirt, to her hips, in their decidedly unregulation hot-pink panties. Eyes gleaming, he reached for the hem of her T-shirt and dragged it upward.

Panting with rage and embarrassment, Aurora lay in the straw. Her bare breasts heaved with the emotions coursing through every nerve in her body. When cool air washed over her nipples and made them pucker involuntarily, Aurora let loose with a string of colorful and highly explicit curses picked up during five years of flying the line.

The bastard sat back on his heels, a satisfied grin on his face.

"Femina," he stated, as if pronouncing some scientific wonder.

"Of course I'm a woman," she ground out through clenched jaws. "What the hell did you think I was?" The other men crowded around to peer over his shoulder. Aurora felt a wave of heat stain her face.

"Amazon," one of them muttered.

Yeah. Right. Amazon.

"Nay," the commander said in his deep voice. His hand brushed her bare nipple. *"Femina."*

Before Aurora could react to that fleeting, electric touch, he had rolled her over. Her stomach knotted in sudden fear. She lay facedown in the hay, biting down on her lower lip until the coppery taste of blood filled her mouth. Her heart thumping, she tried to prepare herself for the worst.

His hands fumbled at the belt binding her wrists. Her arms fell free, to lie useless and numb at her side. He rose, one foot straddling either side of her hips.

Aurora kept her nose buried in straw, a deep-seated feminine instinct warning her of what was to come. She tensed her muscles, expecting at any moment to feel his hands pull the flight suit down over her shoulders. Drawing in a deep breath, she prepared to twist and turn and kick.

For a long moment, nothing happened. Then hob-nailed sandals clattered against the stone floor.

The door slammed.

A heavy bolt dropped into place.

Absolute silence descended.

Chapter 3

Lucius poured a goblet of wine from the chilled pitcher his orderly had left and settled his long frame in a wooden chair. A stack of dispatches sat on the campaign desk tucked in one corner of his private chambers, but he was too restless to take them up right now.

For a little while he toyed with the idea of going to the baths for a massage to relax his tense muscles. At this hour, however, the bathing chambers would be filled with men and women gathered there to socialize as much as cleanse themselves. Lucius didn't doubt that the gossip that flowed as freely as the waters there would be centered on the captives. Word would have spread through the camp about these strangely garbed prisoners and their great silver chariot within minutes of their arrival. Before he dealt with more doubts and questions about his captives, Lucius had to sort through his own confused thoughts about them. Particularly the female.

Her forward manner and unusual dress fascinated him, almost as much as her flame-kissed hair and smoky eyes.

An image of small, pink-tipped breasts filled his mind, and his fingers tightened around the stem of the silver goblet. His ploy of disrobing the female, of displaying her womanly attributes, had lulled his officers' superstitious fears. It had also strained his control almost to the breaking point.

Lucius shook his head, surprised at the lust that still gripped his loins. By the gods, he was not some untried pup, some young stag in rut. He was past his thirtieth summer, a seasoned veteran, a senior commander who exercised the strictest discipline over himself and his men. He couldn't remember the last time his blood had raced like a runaway chariot at the mere sight of a female.

Stretching out his legs, Lucius rested the goblet on the flat plane of his stomach and considered how he should handle his exotic captive. His first duty was to discover who she was, and what her sudden appearance portended. If she was not some messenger of the gods—and after feeling her flesh rub against his during the long ride back to camp, Lucius did not believe that she was—then she had some other reason for being in the territory he administered in Rome's name. And there must be some explanation for the hollow, silver-skinned conveyance she'd obviously arrived in.

Unbidden, the story of the siege of Troy sprang into his mind. The Greeks had gained entry to the beleaguered city by hiding themselves in a hollow wooden horse. Was that the answer? Had this woman thought to breach his camp's fortifications in this winged vehicle? Had he unknowingly fallen in with her plan by bringing her here? Was she spy, or seductress, intent on enticing the men who captured her to commit reckless acts, as had Helen of Troy?

A lazy grin lifted his lips. Nay, this one was no Helen. Not with that stubborn chin and grubby face. And her belligerent manner held not the least hint of seduction. Although fear had darkened her mist-filled eyes at times, she'd challenged him repeatedly. She'd showed no awe of Rome's might, no respect for the representatives of the empire that ruled the world. His grin deepened wickedly. He would enjoy taming this one, Lucius decided. He'd soon teach her respect. And when he was through, it wouldn't be fear that darkened her eyes.

For a brief moment, he considered having her brought to him to begin her training this very night, but he discarded the idea almost immediately. Despite the woman's defiance and mocking tone, Lucius had seen that she was near the end of her endurance by the time they arrived at camp. He'd felt the tremors that racked her during the long ride, and had held her slumped against him more than once. Moreover, it had been obvious she was unused to riding. His lips twitched as he recalled the way she'd jolted up and down in the saddle like the rawest recruit. He had no doubt she would ache mightily on the morrow. Nay, 'twas best to wait. To let her work the soreness from her muscles, before he exercised them anew.

He'd see to the dispatches, he decided, setting aside the wine. He'd attend to work this night, and attend to the woman on the morrow. When she'd had time to ponder her plight and accept the fact that she was now under Rome's domination. When she'd had time to realize that she was now his to command.

Like one putting off the first bite of a sweet, the more to enjoy it, Lucius purposely delayed visiting his captive the next day. He was too conscientious a commander to put his personal interests before his duties, and too skilled a tactician to rush his next meeting with the female. Besides, a few hours pacing her cell would do her no harm.

He left his quarters just as the clarion call of trumpets sounded through the camp, summoning the men to morning parade. The sun cleared the camp walls in a flaming red ball while the company commanders called the roll, then the adjutant read out the orders for the day and issued the new watchword. In a loud, clear voice Lucius shared the latest bulletins from legion headquarters, approved work details, and took the men's oath of obedience.

Having officially sanctioned the start of the duty day, Lucius joined his officers in the mess for breakfast. Although his well-appointed villa boasted its own kitchen staffed with cooks eager to please, he always took the early meal with his officers. He knew well that more information flowed with the morning ale than ever showed up in official reports.

As expected, the talk this morn was of the captives. The deep rumble of conversation died as Lucius entered the mess, but not before he had picked up several references to Amazons and winged chariots. Seating himself on a low couch, he waited while slaves served him bread, cheeses and fruits, then turned to his senior medical officer.

"How fares the male?"

The graying, bushy-haired physician rubbed a hand across his chin. "He has bruises on his back and shoulders. The blood that flowed from his ear indicates he's sustained some injury to the head. I thought to bore in and drain the putrid humors from the skull, but he awakened this morning, so I chose not to operate."

"Is he lucid?"

"Nay, not as yet. His eyes hold pain and confusion, and he doesn't respond to my words. I've packed his ears with a poultice of plaintain root, and put him on a diet of peas and lentils until his strength returns."

Lucius nodded, then turned to his deputy. "When he recovers, put him to work to keep him out of mischief. House him separately from the other slaves."

He paused, thinking of the man whose body had covered the woman he now held captive. The woman he now claimed for himself. "Provide a female to see to his needs, and have her report to you. Advise me daily on his behavior and attitude."

The men leaned forward, eager to learn of their commander's plans for these captives in coverings the like of which no one had ever seen before.

Lucius turned to his deputy. "Do you still include that Greek tutor among your household slaves, Quintus? The one you bought to school your sons?"

"Aye, Captain. I doubt he pounds much knowledge into the boys' thick heads, but my wife says at least he keeps those two imps from Hades out of her hair for most of the day."

"Please present my apologies to your wife, but I would like to borrow the tutor for a few weeks."

"For the prisoner?"

"Aye."

"Do you think to instruct him in our ways?"

"Not him. Her."

Lucius grinned at the astonished looks on the faces around him. "The male may not recover full use of his senses for some weeks," he explained, "but this female has a sharp tongue on her. Although I understood not her words, she doesn't fear to speak out. With a little tutoring, she can learn to communicate, and we can learn whence she comes."

Lucius didn't miss the quick glances the men gave each other. After a few seconds, the grizzled medical officer ventured to voice the doubts hovering in their minds.

"What if she tells of unknown places, of peculiar happenings?"

"'Tis but a woman we speak of, after all," Lucius replied easily. "I proved as much last night. And since she is a female, I doubt not whatever 'happenings' she speaks of will be peculiar to us."

Masculine laughter, tinged with relief, greeted his dry comment.

Lucius nodded to a middle-aged officer sitting across the table. "Take a team of engineers out to the place where we found these two and retrieve their vehicle. Centurion Quintus will give you an idea of its size and shape."

The senior engineer nodded, his eyes bright and eager. Lucius knew that his inventive mind was itching to examine the conveyance.

"I'll go out this day, Captain, and do a site survey."

"Good."

The officers returned to their breakfasts. Lucius noted that the conversation centered on the captives for a while, then, gradually, turned to more familiar matters—work details, plans for the upcoming festival of Mars, the intelligence reports on raids by the desert tribes.

"Do you wish the tutor to come now, Captain?" Quintus asked as they rose.

"Nay, later. I must preside at the municipal court this morning. The city councillors have a rack of grievances to address. Unless you wish to take the session?"

Quintus hastily declined the honor. "I would not deprive you of the privilege. Besides, I have to oversee the quartermaster's grain inventory."

Lucius smiled, well understanding the deputy's reluctance to deal with the affairs of Dura-Europus. This rich city on the banks of the Euphrates was a melting pot of cultures. Founded by the great Syrian dynasty of the Seleucids some four centuries ago, it now wore Rome's mantle but lightly. The upper classes still spoke the Greek of Alexander, although the desert peoples used their own flowing blend of Aramaic and Arabic. The diverse population embraced a host of laws and philosophies, including the Oriental mysticism brought from lands far along the caravan routes. Such sophistication made for a vast array of festivals and feast days, but also for painfully long judicial sessions. Every grievance was discussed and examined and weighed against a host of laws. Presiding over the court was grueling duty, one Quintus hated to perform when Lucius was absent.

Lucius, who had spent many late nights reading the literature of these people since his arrival in the area six months ago, actually enjoyed the sessions. They exercised his mind, just as the daily drills and rigorous physical training he participated in exercised his body. Still, as he waited for his driver to bring around his ceremonial chariot, he couldn't prevent a sudden, swift stab of anticipation at the thought of what awaited him when he returned.

Aurora woke slowly to stifling, suffocating heat. Groggy, disoriented, still half-asleep, she turned her head to see sunlight streaming in through a small window set high in a stone wall. Dust motes danced in the glaring light filtering through the bars. Bars?

Frowning, she pushed her tumbled hair out of her eyes with a shaky hand. Her stiff fingers combed through the tangled mass. Bits of straw fluttered out of the reddish strands and settled on her cheek. Her frown deepened. What the heck was she doing on the floor, in a bed of foul-smelling straw?

Memories of the night before came flooding back. Aurora sat up abruptly, then gasped as her bottom connected with the stone floor. Good grief, she felt as though she'd bailed out of her plane without a parachute, and landed square on her backside. With a low groan, she rolled onto her hip and struggled to her feet. Rubbing the afflicted area with both hands, she turned slowly, her eyes fixed on that high, barred window.

It hadn't been a dream. The storm. The near-crash. Charlie. She swallowed convulsively. Dear Lord, it hadn't been a dream. She was really here, in a stifling little cell, the prisoner of...

She swallowed once more. Surely that much at least had been a... a hallucination of some sort, a delayed reaction

to the shock of the near-crash. She *had* to have imagined
that lean, muscled warrior in his crazy red cloak. She *must*
have fantasized the way he'd banded her to him in a hard
hold as they rode through the night. She took an agitated
step, then groaned and rubbed her bottom once more. No,
she hadn't imagined that ride.

Fear sped through her bloodstream. Her anxious gaze
roamed the small cell. Her breath shortened to shallow,
painful pants. As frightened by her near-hysteria as by the
slowly growing conviction that the storm had sent her
plane tumbling through time, as well as space, Aurora
drew in long, slow breaths.

"Get a grip here, lady," she muttered sternly.

She wasn't the type to fall apart in a crisis, she reminded herself. Not after five years in the air force. Not
after her grueling years at the academy. And certainly not
after growing up with four older brothers whose favorite
sport was testing their sister's temper and endurance every
chance they got. The thought of her brothers and her parents brought another flash of panic. What had the air force
told her family about her missing plane? What would her
mother think?

Stop it! Just stop it! she admonished herself. She
couldn't do anything about things beyond her control. She
could only focus on the here and now. Wherever and
whenever that was. She could handle this bizarre situation, she told herself firmly. She could handle one muscle-bound, hawk-faced...warrior.

Aurora paced the small cell, trying to bring some order
to her confused thoughts. Gradually her mental consternation gave way to a physical one. She paused in midstride to search the barren room. It contained not a stick
of furniture, no creature comforts other than the pile of
straw she'd slept on. There wasn't anything that even
faintly resembled sanitary facilities. No jug of water to
wash with. No bucket to...

A small trench in the stone floor along one wall caught her attention. Green slime clinging to the sides of the trench told her the water flowing through it wasn't for drinking. At least *she* didn't intend to drink it.

It took a few moments longer for Aurora to realize the trench was some kind of rudimentary sewer system. She hesitated, one eye on the cell's door, one eye on the sluggishly flowing water. The bizarre thought that this whole crazy setup might be some kind of endurance-training center flashed into her mind once more. Pivoting slowly on one heel, she searched the stone walls for hidden cameras.

When she realized what she was doing, Aurora shook her head. "Get real, Durant," she murmured. Moving toward the trench, she took care of her most pressing need.

Feeling infinitely better, Aurora settled on the stone floor. With a thick pile of straw to cushion her sore bottom, she crossed her legs and decided to inventory her zippered pockets. She wasn't sure whether she'd have to talk or barter or fight her way out of this place, but she'd need to know just what she had at hand to use in any case.

In one pocket she found a comb and a tube of Scarlet Caress lipstick. Aurora twisted the tube experimentally. The lip color had melted to a shapeless blob. Sighing, she set it aside. From another pocket, she retrieved her crushed dark blue flight cap, with its silver braid and shiny captain's bars. Tucked inside the flight cap were her keys.

Great, Aurora thought with a surge of disgust, just great! Somewhere among the debris in her plane was a whole arsenal of modern survival equipment. Her nine-millimeter Beretta. A flare gun. A shatter-resistant compass. A supply of beef jerky, and some vitamins. And here she sat with just a blob of melted lipstick and a bunch of keys.

She fingered the bits of metal, wondering if she'd ever again open the door to her comfortable, messy rooms at the Ramstein bachelor officers' quarters. If she'd ever again slip into her sleek, two-seater sports car and open her up on the German autobahn. The little car was her pride and joy, her escape when she wasn't in crew rest or flying. Aurora loved the feel of air rushing through her hair, the sense of barely leashed power in the Daimler engine. Damn, she hoped one of the guys at the squadron would think to start up her car occasionally and drain the oil if she didn't get back soon.

She would, Aurora swore fiercely, her hand closing around the keys. She would get back. She struggled to her feet and paced the cell once more. Frustration and a sense of being shut in grew with every passing minute. When the heavy wooden door swung open some hours later, she swung around to face her captor with something close to eagerness.

Eagerness turned to dry-mouthed fear as the reality she'd been trying to deny all morning came crashing down on her. This wasn't any modern-day warrior masquerading in a fancy get up. This guy *was* right out of the first or second century A.D.

Black spots danced in front of her eyes, and for a few seconds the tall, lean figure in front of her blurred. Drawing on every ounce of strength she possessed, Aurora willed her panic to subside. Slowly, deliberately, she forced herself to meet the steady gaze of the man who stood before her.

Seen in the full light of day, he was even more commanding than she'd remembered from the night before. A good half foot taller than Aurora, he sported wide, powerful shoulders, and strong arms that rippled with well-toned muscles. One hand had rested on his sword hilt with casual menace. Aurora noticed a long scar, dulled by age but clearly discernible amid the dark hair on his arm, running from wrist to elbow. He wore a red mantle across his shoulders, and a white tunic with a ridiculous short skirt. Although... Aurora swallowed the dry lump in her throat.

She had to admit the skirt didn't look ridiculous on him. Her eyes slid down the strong columns of his thighs, to the leather thongs wrapped around his calves. No, on him that skirt looked just the other side of awesome.

Irritated at the direction of her thoughts, she snapped her attention back to his face. Under his close-cut black hair, his face was lean and tanned. Brown eyes glinted as he surveyed her with the inbred arrogance of a conqueror whose armies ruled the world.

Aurora lifted her chin. His country might have ruled the world at one time, but hers had a pretty good handle on it now. She wasn't about to let some guy in a skirt intimidate her.

Lucius smiled to himself. 'Twas obvious her confinement had not subdued the woman's spirit. Although she'd paled when he first entered the small cell, defiance now radiated from every inch of her lithe body. She folded both arms across her chest and met his assessing look with one of her own. The metal fastening of her green covering was closed to the neck, and only her high cheekbones and wildly curling reddish hair proclaimed her womanhood.

Lucius knew, however, that other evidence of her femininity lurked under that green hide. Sternly he banished the memory of her small, soft breasts from his mind. He would savor them and her other hidden delights, later, when he finally peeled that covering from her.

He advanced into the room. "I am Senior Centurion Lucius Antonius, Commander of the Twentieth Cohort *Palmyrenorum.*"

Her dark brows drew together.

Lucius repeated the words slowly, tapping his chest.

She drew in a deep breath, then tried to echo his words. "Lu...Lucius Antonius. Palmy...Palren..."

"*Pal-my-re-no-rum.* Of the Third Legion Gallica. Who are you, and what do you here?"

At her frown, he pointed to her and raised his brows in obvious question.

She straightened her shoulders. "Aurora Durant. Captain Aurora Durant, United States Air Force."

She strung some other phrases after that first, something about her companion, the one called Char-Li, but Lucius didn't understand them. The fact that this female bore a Roman name intrigued him. Aurora, goddess of morning, gave her name to many girl children within Rome proper. Had this woman been adopted into a Roman family? Sold into servitude in a Roman household? Mayhap she'd been given the name by a male protector. He studied the woman, trying to place her origins. Trying to decide whether her presence in the territory under his command boded good or ill.

She pointed to the small striped emblem on the shoulder of her covering and uttered a string of words.

Lucius shook his head. If she was trying to identify her land or her tribe, it was none he'd heard of before.

Her chin lifted. She spoke again, with some haughty demand that made his brows snap together and the guards behind him gasp in surprise. They might not understand her words, but there was no mistaking her tone. By Jupiter, the woman dared address a Roman centurion as if he were some low-ranking lackey. Lucius took a step forward, intending to cure her of that habit forthwith. That was one aspect of her training he would begin immediately.

A commotion at the door halted him in midstride. One of the soldiers pushed a slight, graying man through the doorway. The old man peered around the dim cell. When he saw Lucius, he bowed nervously.

"I am Theodorus, Captain. My master said you wished my presence."

"Aye, tutor. Enter."

His arms full of scrolls, the old man edged inside. Clearly *he* had a healthy respect for Roman authority, if a certain dirt-streaked female did not. Lucius waved toward the one called Aurora. "I would that you teach this woman our language."

The man's mouth dropped open as he looked from the captain to the glaring creature at the far end of the cell.

"This man is here to teach you," Lucius informed her in a hard, flat voice that brooked no argument. That same tone had been known to make hulking soldiers blanch and wonder what rule they'd broken, what task they'd left undone.

To his surprise, it made the woman lift her head and spear him with a cold look from her gray eyes. By all that was holy, this looked to be a long and interesting taming.

"You will listen to this man and learn from him. He was much honored in his native Greece, before gambling debts forced him to sell himself into slavery. You will not harm him, nor will you try to escape while under his tutelage. The guards are right outside, and will watch your every movement."

He paused, letting his voice drop to a warning growl. "Rome's punishment for recalcitrant prisoners is most unpleasant. I would not wish to see your skin broken by the lash or your bones broken as you're dragged behind a chariot."

The deliberate menace in his voice and his intimidating stance produced the desired effect. Wariness replaced the defiance in her wide, black-fringed eyes. She took a step back, away from him. Satisfied, Lucius turned to the goggling tutor.

"I'll be back later to check her progress. By this night, I want her able to identify the foods she eats and the contents of this room. By next week, I want her able to discourse freely."

The old man's jaw sagged. "But, master..."

"I sense that she's not stupid, but I suspect she'll be stubborn. You'll have to exercise all your skills. Do you accomplish this task I've set for you, I'll purchase you from Centurion Quintus and grant you your freedom. Her name is Aurora, by the way. Lady Aurora."

With that, he turned and left.

Aurora watched her captor's broad back disappear through the door with a sense of mounting outrage. Who did this guy think he was? He swept in here, announced he was Lucius Something Something in a tone that implied she should bow or kiss his feet, growled a few threatening sentences, and swept out again! Just like that! Her hands curled into fists.

A nervous cough behind her made her spin around.

"What do you want?" she barked.

The old man's bony knees shook visibly. After emitting a high squeak, he swallowed and let loose with a spate of words.

Frowning, Aurora tried to make sense of his hurried speech. The only phrases she recognized were *Domina Aurora* and *praeceptor.* The commander had referred to her as *domina,* so she assumed it was some sort of title. And she'd had a preceptor in grad school, who'd tutored her in a particularly difficult aerodynamic structural engineering course.

So this little guy was here to instruct her. Aurora leaned against a stone wall and folded her arms across her chest while she considered this new development.

If she really was caught in some bizarre time warp—and Aurora was slowly accepting the idea that she was—she needed to learn all she could about this time and these people. At the very least, she needed to be able to communicate with them. Particularly with a certain arrogant soldier.

As senior aircraft commander, she was responsible for her crew. It was up to her to ensure that Charlie got care. Dragging in a long, slow breath, Aurora nodded.

"Okay, let's get on with it."

The little man jumped at her gruff command.

Sighing, Aurora softened both her voice and her expression. "Come. We'll begin. *Instituto*. Oh, hell, sit down."

She sat cross-legged on the floor and patted the rough stone beside her.

Hours later, Aurora straightened her aching back and slanted her erstwhile instructor a look of reluctant admiration.

"Ted, old boy, I thought Sister Mary Joseph was one tough teacher. You've got her beat hands down."

The tutor frowned and responded in Latin. To her amazement, Aurora understood most of his short sentence.

She couldn't believe how quickly the words had come back to her. Either the good sister had pounded more into her recalcitrant students' heads than Aurora had ever given her credit for, or Latin wasn't quite as dead a language as everyone supposed. Once she remembered to tack masculine, feminine or neuter endings on to every noun and sorted through a few conjugations, she recognized more words and phrases than she'd have thought possible.

Theodorus had become so excited at her progress that he rushed to the door and ordered the astonished guards to bring writing implements. To Aurora's surprise, they'd complied. The thin, almost transparent sheets of paper and charcoal sticks helped tremendously. Once she saw, as well as heard, the words, they stayed with her.

Old Ted's excitement had secretly amused Aurora. If he thought relearning Latin was tough, he ought to try air force flight school. After those grueling months of absorbing every principle of aviation known to man or machine, this business of reacquainting herself with long-forgotten conjugations was a piece of cake.

They worked through a lunch of meat cooked in a savory garlic sauce and some unidentifiable vegetables. After the meal, the tutor spread some of the scrolls he'd brought with him out on the stone floor. They soon abandoned all attempts to get Aurora to understand what looked like lines of poetry. She wasn't ready for that yet. The tutor clucked and shook his head. Sorting through the scrolls, he rolled out what was obviously a map.

Aurora snatched it out of his hands. At last, something that could give her a clue where they were.

"Domina!" His black eyes reproached her.

"Sorry, Ted old boy," Aurora mumbled, scanning the parchment. Her brows drew together at the unfamiliar borders and the Latin names, but she was sure she recognized the shape of the Mediterranean Sea and the Italian boot. And a land mass at the eastern end of the sea that had to be the Middle East. "Where are we? Um... *Ubi...* *ubi sumus?"*

The tutor beamed as if she'd just recited the entire Pledge of Allegiance in Latin. With a blue-veined finger, he pointed to a mark on the map that represented a fortified town.

"Dura-Europus."

With an engineer's passion for precision, Aurora scanned the distance from the spot Theodorus indicated to the coast. Superimposing twentieth-century borders over the land area on the map, Aurora gave a silent groan. Although she wasn't absolutely positive, it looked like she'd landed smack in the middle of Iraq. Great. Just great! Nothing like putting her plane down where escape and rescue would be difficult, whatever century she was in. Refusing to give in to the tide of panic that threatened to swamp her, she focused on the map.

"What . . . what is this?" She pointed to a gold crest in the right hand corner.

In slow, careful syllables, he explained. "'Tis the emperor's own seal, mistress. Marcus Aurelius. He who rules this empire."

The map crumpled under Aurora's fingers. Well, she'd wanted to know when and where she was. Now she knew. She was sitting in a cell in the ancient Roman city of Dura-Europus, staring at the seal of an emperor who had ruled the world almost two thousand years ago.

"Domina Aurora, do you . . . do you wish to rest?"

"Wh-what?"

"Do you wish to rest?"

The tutor's voice dragged at her, pulled her back to the present. Or the past. Wherever.

"Nay! Nay, I don't wish to rest," she said fiercely in fractured half Latin, half English. "I wish to learn. As much and as fast as I can."

Chapter 4

The sound of the bolt being drawn back broke into their intense concentration some hours later.

"The captain!" Theodorus squeaked, scrambling to his feet. He shot Aurora a pleading glance, as if begging her not to disgrace his efforts.

Aurora rose more slowly, her heart pounding.

Captain or Centurion Lucius Something Something ducked his head and entered the cell.

Aurora lifted her chin.

His eyes flickered for a moment. Aurora could have sworn she saw amusement in their gold-flecked depths before he turned to the old man.

"*Ave*, tutor. How does she?"

"*Ave*, Captain," Aurora responded before Theodorus could stammer out a reply. "She . . . she does well."

His gaze swung back to her face. One dark brow rose. "You learn quickly," he murmured.

Aurora's brief bubble of self-satisfaction deflated immediately when he uttered a string of incomprehensible sentences. Frustrated by her lack of understanding, she shook her head.

He tried again, more slowly.

She caught only a couple of familiar words. With both hands flapping and his chin quivering, the tutor helped translate. Aurora finally understood that the soldier wanted to know where she was from, and what she did here.

He wouldn't believe her, Aurora thought grimly, even if she had the words to tell him. Instead of attempting a response to his question, she struggled to remember the phrases she'd drawn from Theodorus earlier. "How fares my friend? My...my companion?"

The stark planes of the captain's cheeks became more pronounced. "Worry not about this one you call Char-Li," he told her in his deep, harsh voice. "Worry instead about yourself."

Aurora slanted him an angry glance. "Look, Captain Lucius Something Something, we need to settle a few matters between us. I demand to—"

"Speak in the Roman tongue," he ordered, clearly not impressed with either her firm tone or her mangled verbs.

Aurora's mouth thinned. "I would if I could."

"What are your needs?"

"What?"

"What do you need?"

Good Lord, what didn't she need! Soap, water, a telephone, Charlie, freedom, a one-way ticket to the twentieth century. Realizing that she wouldn't be able to communicate any but the first items on her list with her limited vocabulary, she pantomimed washing her hands. At least she could get rid of the sand ringing her neck.

"Water. I wish water to wash with."

"Lavatio?"

"Yeah, *lavatio.* I wish to lavatio."

A golden gleam entered his eyes. He studied her for a moment, as if trying to come to some decision. After a moment, he shrugged and motioned her forward.

"Come."

Wary of that sudden glint in his eyes, Aurora stayed put.

"Come! I will take you to the baths."

She folded both arms across her chest. "I don't need 'taking,' big fella. Just send some hot water, and I'll do fine."

Theodorus pushed at her with a wrinkled hand. "Go, lady. To the baths. *Lavatio. Aqua.*"

Aurora hesitated, torn between a fierce desire to be clean and an instinctive reluctance to obey any order issued by her arrogant captor.

"Come," he ordered, in a voice that brooked no disobedience. "At once."

Aurora shot him an evil look, then marched toward the door.

Her heart thumping, she followed him down the halls she had been carried through the night before. A small escort of armed guards fell into place behind her. After a bewildering series of twists and turns, they finally reached the entrance. When the captain stepped outside, sentries snapped to attention.

Hard on his heels, Aurora followed him into the dazzling sunshine. Suffocating heat surrounded them like a blanket. Searing white light blinded her. She threw up an arm to shield her eyes and stumbled against the broad back in front of her. He turned and took her arm in a firm grasp. When Aurora recovered her balance and tried to yank free, his fingers tightened warningly.

"All right, already," she muttered.

The relentless grip loosened, but he kept his hold on her arm.

At the captain's side, Aurora walked down a flight of shallow marble steps and out onto a broad, cobbled boulevard. Her mouth sagged as she got her first full glimpse of life in an honest-to-goodness Roman camp.

The streets were filled with soldiers, marching in small squads or striding past on some duty or another. Several mounted troops clattered by, their horses' iron-shod hooves ringing on the cobbles. Marble statuary lined the broad thoroughfare, drawing her wide-eyed gaze. Women with tall jugs balanced on their heads and gauzy veils across their faces gathered at fountains. Dogs barked and growled, while goats added to the din with bleating cries. Noisy vendors hawked an assortment of foodstuffs. Long skewers holding chunks of meat and vegetables sizzled on charcoal braziers, filling the air with a tantalizing aroma. The scent of fresh-baked bread made Aurora's mouth water.

As they passed, men and beasts alike parted to let them through. The men saluted their commander respectfully, although it seemed to Aurora that she was the focus of all eyes. The children gaped and pointed at her. Women whispered behind their veils. Men gawked openly. Thinking that she must be a whole heck of a lot dirtier than she'd realized, Aurora reached up self-consciously to brush her hair out of her eyes.

After a couple of turns, they approached a huge building with a curving, vaulted roof. Its massive wooden doors swung open, and Aurora felt her jaw sag in surprise. For a stunned moment, she thought she was back at the base gym, where she took aerobics classes whenever her flying schedule permitted. Men with bulging, glistening muscles worked out on a variety of sports equipment. Their biceps strained as they lifted weights and pulled themselves up on rings hanging from the high ceiling. Others wrestled, while companions called out encouragement. Grunts and groans filled the air, and the acrid scent of raw sweat made Aurora's nostrils twitch.

But this gym wasn't exactly like the one at her base, she saw after a moment. The weights were of stone. The tumbling mats were of rope, not rubber. And the men were all naked. Completely, unselfconsciously naked. Splendidly naked, she noted in one or two spectacular cases. When they stopped their activities to stare at her, Aurora tried, unsuccessfully, not to stare back.

Her eyes on the interesting display, she stumbled through the crowded hall after the commander. Two turbaned attendants met them at another set of large double doors and bowed them into the bathing chambers.

Dank, frigid air hit her face like a wet blanket. Aurora barely had time to note the curious expressions of a half-dozen men and women in a large, marble pool before Lucius Something barked an order. Attendants surrounded her like a swarm of bees. One knelt to fumble with the laces on her boots, while others plucked ineffectually at her flight suit. She slapped at their exploring hands and backed away.

"Allow them to disrobe you," the captain said—or words to that effect.

Aurora shot him a quick look, prepared to put him in his place once and for all. The words died in her throat. A similar crowd of slaves had surrounded him and deftly removed his clothes. He stood before her, legs spread, hands on hips, superbly and unselfconsciously naked.

Aurora gulped.

His muscled body put the specimens in the exercise room to shame. There wasn't an inch of fat on his lean frame. It was covered with a light mat of black, curling hair and tanned in places she'd never realized could absorb the sun's rays. When Aurora stood motionless in reluctant admiration, he stepped forward and reached for her zipper.

"Hey, hold on, bud!" She backed away, both palms raised. "We're not into communal bathing where I come from."

He shook his head at her unintelligible words and pushed aside her protesting hands.

"You wished to bathe, lady," he said, or so Aurora thought. "You will bathe." He pulled the zipper halfway down.

Aurora caught his hand in both of hers. Biting down on her lower lip, she quickly assessed the situation. Aside from the fact that it galled her to give in to this man, she desperately wanted a bath. Fear, desert heat and several long days in her flight suit had given it a less-than-pleasing bouquet. She let out a long breath and nodded. When in Rome...

Lucius Something—Luke, for short, she decided—stepped back and motioned for her to continue.

"Okay, okay, hold your horses."

The phrase struck Aurora as incredibly ironic. She almost giggled as she tugged the front zipper the rest of the way down. When she'd peeled off the flight suit and stood exposed in black boots, hot-pink panties and green T-shirt, she felt as ridiculous as she knew she must look. She knelt to untie her bootlaces, only to have the attendants rush in to finish the job.

Within seconds, she had shed the last of her clothes and was shivering in the cool air. A low murmur rose above the gurgle of water as the pool's occupants eyed her avidly. The rush of whispered comments brought a tide of heat to Aurora's face. Her body might not be in the same league as Cindy Crawford's, but it had never caused snickers or low, murmured comments when she appeared in public before. Of course, she'd never appeared in public naked before.

Lifting her chin, Aurora ignored the staring bathers and met the commander's eyes. An inscrutable smile tugged at his lips as he ran his gaze slowly down, and even more slowly up, her body. The heat in Aurora's face spread to her neck, and then to parts south.

"Take a picture, big guy, it lasts longer."

Her mocking tone brought his black brows together. Their eyes clashed and locked in a battle of wills, until Aurora had to fight the urge to raise her arms and cover her breasts. At last she realized he would keep her standing in the dank air, goose-bumped and shivering and naked as the day she was born, until one of them signaled surrender. Drawing in a deep breath, she let her gaze drop.

He gave a small, satisfied grunt and headed for the pool. With a splash, he plunged in. He surfaced a few feet away, muscles quivering in an involuntary reaction to the cold water. He shook his head, sending a spray of silver drops arcing in all directions, then motioned to her.

Aurora took a deep breath and stepped off the edge.

Her mouth opened in shock as icy water closed over her head. Sharp, searing needles of cold penetrated every square centimeter of her skin. She floundered, her arms flailing, her feet slipping and sliding on the slick tiles. Finally she found her footing on the frigid floor and surfaced, sputtering and gasping. The water settled just below her breasts. Aurora wrapped both arms around her chest and glared at the captain. He grinned, then turned to respond to a low, murmured question from a man nearby.

Teeth chattering, Aurora watched in amazement as he fielded a host of queries, obviously about her. The men in the pool cast her wary looks and pelted the captain with questions. The women kept their distance, clustering in one corner as they whispered behind their hands. Aurora could understand how she and Charlie might have caused some consternation, arriving from out of nowhere as they had, but she was getting tired of everyone whispering and staring at her as though she were something from the lower end of the food chain. Especially when they did it in a blasted refrigerator.

She'd just decided she had enough when Commander Luke hauled himself out of the pool and reached a hand down to help her out. As she stared at his tanned hand, Aurora was tempted. Lord, she was tempted. A firm grasp, a quick pull, and a certain obnoxious soldier would tumble head over heels into the icy water.

Putting aside the delightful, if childish, impulse, Aurora allowed him to pull her out of the water. Servants swarmed around her, wrapping her clammy skin in thick, rough towels. She tried to clutch the material around her, but the attendants whipped it away and bowed.

Flesh tingling, face flaming, Aurora progressed through what she soon understood was an elaborate, well-orchestrated bathing ritual. After the icy pool came a lukewarm one. Then another army of attendants, armed with abrasive boards, attacked them, rasping off her dirt—and half her skin, Aurora was sure. Finally the captain led her into a vaulted chamber dominated by a hot, steaming pool.

Aurora submerged herself in the hot water with a long, slow sigh. This was more like it. She floated for a few moments, letting tension and fear and confusion ebb and flow with the soft ripple of water against her body.

She protested halfheartedly when the captain pulled her out of the pool sometime later and led her toward a small room filled with marble tables and waiting attendants.

"These chambers are for females. You will stay here and let the attendants do their women's work."

Aurora struggled to understand his clipped words. "What—what women's work?" she asked suspiciously.

"I will await you without."

"What women's work?"

"Do not think to run or escape," he warned her as he turned to leave.

"Hey, what women's work?"

Aurora eyed the attendants who surrounded her. They returned her look nervously. Shrugging, she allowed them to lead her to one of the marble tables. Skilled hands began to knead her legs and arms, then the muscles of her aching bottom. Swallowing her deep embarrassment, Aurora surrendered to the magic wrought by the masseuses. By the time they finished, she was a boneless, spineless mass.

When an older attendant came into the chamber, a pile of clothing in her arms, Aurora sat up. She eyed the soft linens with a frown.

"Where are my clothes?"

The woman shook her head and reached forward to wrap a strip of light, almost transparent linen, around her breasts.

Aurora pushed her hand away. "My underwear. My..." She pulled on an imaginary pair of pants. "My flight suit. My boots."

The woman shook her head once more.

Jaws tight, Aurora realized she had no choice but to submit. It was either that or wander around naked in search of her clothes. Fuming, she stood while the slaves finished wrapping the linen around her breasts, then tucked the ends under her arms. A similar strip covered her loins. The fabric felt awkward, but at least it was clean. Until she recovered her own underthings, these would have to do, she decided.

The attendant helped her pull on a soft linen shift that reached just below her knees, then an ankle-length tunic of flowing cotton in a pale blue color. Although Aurora would never have admitted it if asked, the cotton felt wonderful against her skin after the hot flight suit. The final touch was a scarf or shawl of some gauzy purple material that draped over her arms. Feeling awkward in the long, clinging robes, she plucked at the skirts.

The older woman smiled, then pointed to Aurora's wet, wildly curling hair.

In a military profession in which the standard uniform was a unisex flight suit and heavy, black boots, Aurora's one concession to feminine vanity was her hair. A tad longer than allowed by regulations, it hung just past her shoulders in a thick mass of mahogany-colored curls. Knowing it would be a relief to have it off her neck, Aurora nodded.

She was led to a small antechamber crowded with scattered chairs, stools and tables littered with pots and jars of every description. Aurora blinked, realizing that she had just stepped into the Roman equivalent of a beauty salon. This was unreal. Totally unreal. The lines between the world she'd left and the world she now inhabited blurred. The chasm seemed to lessen imperceptibly.

Some things were eternal, Aurora decided after a breathless moment. They spanned time and place. Things like love. War. Death. Beauty salons.

Bemused, she let the attendant lead her to a low stool.

When the senior bath attendant finally brought the one called Aurora out into the courtyard, Lucius felt his breath catch somewhere in the vicinity of his belt buckle. The woman who came toward him bore little resemblance to the dirty, sweat-stained female of a scant hour ago. Her shining, high-piled hair caught streaks of dark fire from the afternoon sun. Subtle shadows highlighted the gray mist of her eyes. Her skin glowed like a babe's from the oils rubbed into it.

By the gods, he'd captured a beauty. No, Lucius corrected immediately. Not a beauty, at least not by Roman standards. Her limbs were too long and lean, and her body was too slender, for true womanly munificence. But what flesh she carried, by Jupiter, she carried well.

She was like the horses of the Arabian desert, he thought, all sleek, elegant lines. Her head, with its thick mane of silky hair, rose above a long, graceful neck. Smooth shoulders carried the clasps of her robe with casual elegance. The folds of material were draped to fit the shape of her breasts—small, perfect breasts that had quivered and crowned in the icy air of the *frigidarium*.

Seeing her then, Lucius had desired her. It had taken every ounce of his rigid control to keep from displaying it to the interested spectators, but he had definitely desired her.

Seeing her now, he felt desire harden into a fierce, aching need that he didn't trouble to disguise. It swept through him, tightening his muscles, stiffening his rod.

Drawing in a deep breath, he turned to the attendant. "My compliments. You have wrought wonders."

"Nay, my lord," the woman said with a smile, tucking the coin that Lucius passed her into her girdle. "This one flies on her own wings."

"Has she all she needs?"

"All except shoes. There were none at the market that would fit her."

Lucius glanced down at the toes peeking out from under the hem of her robe. "I will attend to the matter later."

Much later. She'd not need shoes this night, he decided, nor for many days hence. Once he got her home, she'd have little use for the clothes that covered her, either.

'Twas too soon, Lucius thought as they walked toward the gate. He'd not yet ascertained who she was or why she was in this land. Nor had he put to rest the wild rumors that still circulated about the prisoners. If he had any sense, she'd be in chains or in a cage on public display to satisfy the camp's curiosity. Only then, when the rumors had died away and he was certain she could cause no harm, should he pursue his own interests. With sudden decisiveness, he decided he could pursue them and work the other matters at the same time.

He shrugged, understanding, if not excusing, his uncharacteristic lack of discipline. Even the gods found it hard to love and be wise at the same time. And he intended to love this one well ere the night was through. With a firm hand under her arm, he guided her through the camp.

She picked her way carefully over the cobbles, her bare feet slipping and sliding on the stones. When they approached the commander's quarters, she halted and threw a puzzled glance across the street at the array of flags in front of the headquarters. "Do... do we not go there?"

Lucius understood the gist of her halting Latin. "Nay, we do not. We go there." He pointed toward the villa that constituted his private quarters.

She frowned, suspicious of the change.

Only this particular captive would balk at giving up a small, squalid cell, Lucius thought with an inner smile. At the thought of what else she would soon give up, Lucius tightened his hold on her arm and led her through the portico.

His predecessor, the son of a wealthy senator fulfilling his military duties in this far-flung province, had leveled the old commander's quarters and constructed a new building to his own design. The pleasure-loving aristocrat had ensured that he would live in all the luxury this trade-rich province could produce. Shaped like a large, open rectangle, with a courtyard in the center, the twenty-room villa offered every amenity its sybaritic designer could think of. Colorful frescoes of the gods sporting in the heavens decorated the walls. Mosaics tiled the floors, and every room boasted furniture inlaid with gold and ivory.

Although the opulence was not to his taste, Lucius understood well the impact of this visual symbol of Rome's power and wealth. His position often required him to entertain visiting dignitaries. He'd left his predecessor's work intact for the most part to impress visitors, even if his more ascetic soldier's soul winced on occasion at the unabashed luxury around him.

As he led the way through marble halls, Lucius felt his lips twist in a sardonic smile. It always amused him to remember that his petulant, spoiled wife had divorced him some years before because she refused to endure any longer the hardships of military life on the Empire's remote frontiers. He might not have been so lucky had she seen this villa.

They had reached the inner courtyard when a breathless, panting soldier overtook them.

"Captain! Centurion Quintus begs you come at once."

Lucius turned, his eyes narrowing at the soldier's grim expression.

"What is it?"

"An outrider has just arrived. He brings word that the caravan en route to Palmyra has been attacked by raiders."

"Casualties?"

"Ten legionaries massacred, and the others taken as prisoners."

Outraged mutters arose from the soldiers who had escorted them from the baths. "These desert rats grow ever more bold," one of the men snarled.

Lucius waved him to silence, his mind racing. "Inform Centurion Quintus that I'll be there immediately. Have him assemble the senior staff, and call the first and fourth century to arms, if he has not already done so."

"Aye, Captain." The soldier gave a quick salute, then whirled and ran out.

"Legionary!"

The young trooper Lucius addressed snapped to attention.

"Summon my orderly. At once. At this hour, he should be at his supper."

"Aye, Captain."

"The rest of you, report to your companies."

The dismissed escort left in a clatter of hobnailed boots and low, angry comments about the fierce, scavenging desert raiders.

His mind already churning with plans for the line of march, Lucius gave the woman a curt order as he turned to enter his private chambers. "Come."

The keen interest in her wide gray eyes stopped him in his tracks. Suspicion coursed through him like a swiftly flowing river.

"Do you know aught of this attack?"

She frowned at his harsh question and shook her head in either denial or lack of understanding.

Lucius took hold of her arms and hauled her up until her face was just inches from his.

"If you value that soft skin of yours, you'll tell me now whether you know aught of this matter."

She gave an angry squeak and kicked his shin. The squeak turned into a gasp of pain when bare toes connected with bone.

"By the gods, I have not time to curb this belligerence of yours. But you may be assured I'll do so when I return."

Flinging open the wooden door to his chambers, he pushed her inside. She stood in the middle of the room, rubbing one foot across the toes of the other and shooting him malevolent looks while he pulled his armor from the rack that held it.

The rack was one of the few pieces of furniture in the austere room. Here in his private chambers, at least, Lucius had imposed his own tastes. He'd had his predecessor's ornate furniture removed and brought in only his campaign desk, a chair carved especially for his long frame, a chest to hold his gear, and the rack for his armor. And his own bed, firmer and less splendid by far than the carved and gilded one that had dominated the chamber before.

Lucius cast the bed a rueful glance as he strapped on his gear. He'd not use it this night.

The woman frowned, watching his actions with mistrustful eyes. She started when his orderly, a hulking sergeant with twenty years and more of service under his belt, pounded through the door.

"Have you heard the news?" Lucius asked.

"Aye, Captain."

"I will be absent some days. You will see to this lady's needs while I am gone."

The orderly rushed forward to assist the commander, giving Aurora a dubious look as he passed. "But...is she not the one who came from the skies? The one who belongs to the gods?"

"She belongs to me," Lucius snapped, dipping his shoulder so that the orderly could tighten the straps that held his breastplate together. "You will guard her as you would my person."

"Aye, Captain."

"Her name is Lady Aurora. She will occupy the room next to mine while I'm gone, and you will sleep here, in my chamber. None may visit her, except Centurion Quintus and the tutor, Theodorus. Do you understand?"

The veteran nodded, then stood to one side while Lucius surveyed the small room adjoining the main chamber.

'Twas not the best arrangement, but 'twas better than the cell. Here at least she'd have a measure of comfort. Here she'd be away from prying eyes. And here she'd be isolated from all possible contact with outside sources. Satisfied that the woman was as safe and secure as he could arrange, Lucius motioned to her.

"Come, Lady Aurora."

Frowning, clearly not understanding what he was about, she shook her head.

Lucius bit back an impatient sigh. By the gods, did this stubborn female never do anything without argument? He wished heartily he had time to deal with her lamentable tendency to disobey orders right here, right now.

Not willing to waste any more time, he swept the woman off her feet, carried her into the room, and dumped her on the orderly's cot.

The door slammed on her indignant shouts.

Chapter 5

"Do you think it's the work of the one called al Azab?"

Lucius glanced up at his deputy. "I know not, Quintus. But the fact that the soldiers escorting the caravan were gutted, then slowly strangled with their own intestines, while the others were carried off, suggests bitter vengeance against Rome."

One of the officers in the group gathered around the commander's desk swore. "By the sword of Mars, these people are savages."

"The indignities Rome wrought on this al Azab's father were no less savage," Lucius remarked.

"That was different," the man offered. "'Twas done in Rome's name, to show these peoples what occurs do they dare challenge our authority."

"It matters not the uniform," Lucius said absently, his attention on the map spread out before him. "Man is ever a wolf to man."

His eyes thoughtful, Lucius studied the thick, oiled parchment. As much as Quintus, he suspected that the vicious attack was the work of the desert chieftain whose father had been captured and executed by the previous Roman commander. For all his pleasure-loving ways, the senator's son had possessed a vicious nature. He'd delighted in public prolonged and painful executions of any who dared interfere with the precious cargoes of silks and spices and exotic slaves that wended their way across the desert to the Mediterranean. It mattered not that these nomadic desert tribes had lived for centuries off their plunder from the caravan trade. He'd been determined to wipe out the raiders, tribe by tribe.

When Lucius assumed command some six months previously, he had inherited the bitter enmity of the roving desert peoples. An even hand and a measured response to their attacks had lessened both their frequency and ferocity. Except for those by the one called al Azab. The son, according to all reports, was determined to avenge the death of his father and drive all Romans from the land.

"The attack occurred here, halfway between Dura and Palmyra." Lucius pointed to a spot on the map in the middle of the barren desert. "'Tis the second attack in that area in the past few months."

"'Tis unusual for these wandering raiders to strike twice in the same spot," Quintus volunteered.

"My thoughts exactly. Usually the attacks on the caravans are scattered, random. That these two took place in such close proximity may mean that he whom we seek has built a camp, a base from which to foray out."

"If he's done so, 'twould be most strange," the intelligence officer offered. "These people are wanderers, without roots. They roam at will across the desert."

"So they do," Lucius concurred, rolling up the parchment. "But if my instincts are right, and this al Azab has established a camp, we will find it." He flashed his men a wolfish grin. "And when we do, heads will roll."

* * *

Aurora spent the next week alternately cursing Captain/Colonel Lucius Something, fuming at his continued absence, and dreading his return.

At least the small room she now inhabited was an improvement over her previous cell. It had been furnished with a rope bed frame covered by a thin straw mattress. A low table for eating, a carved wooden chair and a chest with an oil lamp atop it constituted the only other furnishings. Light filtered in through two large, shuttered windows. Water running through a marble-lined trench provided sanitary facilities, and the stocky, rock-faced valet brought hot water each morning and evening for washing. Through wooden window slats, Aurora could see bright flashes of a garden filled with green plants and colorful flowers.

The unfriendly blond deputy came daily to check on her. Neither of them enjoyed the visits. Quintus, as she discovered he was named, still eyed her with a mixture of suspicion and hesitation, as if she were some exotic, dangerous creature that might bite his hand. He stubbornly refused to give her any information about Charlie, and always left her feeling caged and furious.

Good ol' Theodorus provided the stimulation that kept her from going stir-crazy. The tutor showed up each morning carrying scrolls and tablets and stacks of thin, oily paper. With nothing else to occupy her mind, Aurora threw herself into her studies. Within days, she had a working vocabulary. Within a week, her tongue no longer tripped over sentence structure. The same determination that had won her top honors in every school she ever attended made Theodorus's eyes widen in appreciation of her quick mind. They moved from simple primers to geography and philosophy and history.

Aurora had particular difficulty with dates. The Romans measured every event *ab urbe condita,* from the date their city was founded. She had to struggle constantly to translate years marked A.U.C. into B.C. and A.D.

"So tell me again," Theodorus asked patiently. "In what year did Marcus Aurelius become emperor?"

"Didn't he follow Julius Caesar?" Caesar at least Aurora knew. He'd lived around 50 B.C. or thereabouts. The poor guy had cocked up his toes on the Ides of March, stabbed by his best buddy, if Shakespeare was to be believed.

The old man put a paper-thin hand over his mouth to hide his laughter at her ignorance. "Nay, lady. Caesar Augustus has been dead for two centuries and more, as measured by his own calendar."

Scratching out a series of numbers on a scrap of parchment, Aurora decided the current year must be around 160 A.D. When she saw the stark black numerals against the white parchment, her lunch of steamed fish and mushrooms swimming in a rich sauce rolled in her stomach. She swallowed hastily. Even after a week, Aurora still had difficulty accepting the fact that she and Charlie had flown into their own version of the Bermuda Triangle and landed in another century.

"Look you, mistress, here is an easy way to remember which emperor follows which. There is an anagram schoolboys use. 'Tis slightly naughty, but—"

Theodorus broke off with a start as the door to the small room banged open. Aurora rose and pressed her fingers into the surface of their worktable to hide their sudden shaking.

Her captor stood framed in the doorway. Late-afternoon sunlight gleamed dully on his armor, and he looked every inch the warrior Theodorus had described. Senior Centurion Lucius Antonius. Commander of the Third Legion *Gallica's* twentieth cohort, a detachment of one thousand men. Hero of the Parthian campaign. Honored by the emperor himself for his valor and his consummate leadership skills in the field. Although a layer of dust coated his red cloak and fatigue etched fine lines beside his eyes, he looked every bit as intimidating as Aurora had remembered him.

Lifting her chin, she met his assessing gaze.

Amusement seemed to glimmer for an instant in those brown eyes flecked with gold.

Amusement? Aurora stiffened.

"*Ave, Domina Aurora.* I hope you have fared well in my absence."

"*Ave,* Captain. I have fared well," she responded, in smooth, flowing Latin.

One dark brow rose. "You've been most diligent in your studies, I see."

"'Tis best to learn what one may of one's enemies."

His brow inched up another notch, but he declined to comment on her deliberately provocative response. Instead, he nodded to the old man. "You've done well, tutor."

Theodorus bowed. "I but stretched her agile mind, Captain. It has been a most successful pedagogy." He gathered up his books and scrolls. "I hope your mission went as well."

Aurora strained to catch the answer. Theodorus had told her of the desert raids that harassed the caravans, the lifeblood of Dura. He'd told her, as well, of the rumors circulating the camp about the one called al Azab. According to the tutor, this fierce tribesman had almost supplanted Aurora herself as a topic of consuming interest within the camp.

"My mission was most successful," the captain replied with a sudden, slashing grin that made Aurora blink. "Although the fox himself slipped out of the snare, we caught a goodly number of his men in the trap. 'Twill be a while before he challenges Rome again."

Theodorus chortled. "The camp's walls will wear a host of heads this night, I take it?"

"Aye, they will," Lucius replied easily. "Come and see me on the morrow, and we will settle the terms of your contract."

When they were alone, the captain propped himself against the wall and gave Aurora a considered, leisurely inspection.

She felt the touch of his roving eyes from the tips of her sandaled toes to the silver pins holding her robe together at the shoulders.

"You look and sound much different from our first meeting," he finally commented.

No kidding, Aurora thought. She had a fleeting vision of how she must have appeared to this ancient warrior the first time they met. The soft, violet-hued robe that now draped from her shoulders in graceful folds was a far cry from her green flight suit and boots. Which reminded her of the list of grievances she'd been waiting to present.

"Let us dispense with informalities, Captain. I demand that you release me immediately. And that you bring my companion to me at once. I wish also to have my clothes returned, the ones I arrived in." She stumbled once or twice, but managed to get her rehearsed speech out without too much difficulty.

Even white teeth gleamed as his lips lifted in an amused grin. "By what right do you demand anything?"

"By law. I've learned you Romans lived by codes. You've set them down in stone and parchment. These laws say you must protect my rights, and those of my companion. Tell me how he fares."

The captain shrugged. "Your lover lives."

"Lover?" Aurora sputtered.

"But you mistake the matter of rights," he continued, ignoring her interruption. "Neither you nor he can claim protection under Roman law unless you can also claim citizenship." His eyes narrowed imperceptibly. "Are you of Rome?"

"Nay." She drew in a deep breath, preparing to tell him just where she'd come from, but he forestalled her.

"Then you have no rights."

"Look..." she began in English, then took a deep breath and started again, this time in Latin. "Despite my hasty words earlier, I am not your enemy, Captain. You need not confine me or my companion."

"Rome does not hold women of sufficient worth to be considered enemies," he responded mildly.

Stung, Aurora slipped back into English. "Oh, yeah? Seems like I recall someone named Cleopatra who gave you guys a run for your money."

He caught the name. His brow arched in a silent query. "Are you from Egypt, land of this queen?"

"Nay, I'm from a place much farther away—one you know not."

"What do you here?" For all his relaxed stance, his eyes gleamed intently.

"I, uh, came here by accident. Out of the sky."

"Out of the sky," he repeated slowly.

"Yes, damn it." Aurora tapped her foot in frustration. "I know it's hard to believe, but it's true. My plane... the craft I was traveling in... was struck by lightning. I don't know how it happened, but somehow we were thrown back through time."

He stared at her through hooded eyes.

"Do you believe me?" she asked with a touch of desperation.

"Nay." He held up one hand to still her sputtered protest. "But neither do I disbelieve you. I've been stationed in too many lands, seen too many things for which the philosophers have no answer or explanation. I'm willing to be convinced. Tell me, if you have the power to fly, why are you still here? Why have you not flown away?"

His tone set Aurora's teeth on edge. He sounded as though he were reasoning with a child. "Believe me, I'd fly this coop if I could."

He frowned at her unfamiliar words. "So you can no longer travel through the sky. What time is it you have come from?"

Aurora drew in a deep breath. "Some two thousand years hence."

He stared at her for a long, silent moment. "Are you blessed by gods, then? Have they have given you immortality?"

For a moment, Aurora was tempted to claim divine power. The tutor had told her that half the camp still believed she'd descended from the heavens. But a sober recollection of what had happened to the so-called witches in Salem made her hesitate. She wasn't sure what measures the Romans might use to test the powers of demigods, but she wasn't taking any chances.

"Nay, I ache, and hunger, and... and have to use the john just like other mortals."

At his frown, she shrugged. "Trust me, I'm human." Her chin lifted. "And, as such, I insist that you release me. I mean no harm to you or to Rome. You have no reason to hold me."

"Oh, I have good reason," he responded at length.

"What, for Pete's sake? Why do you keep me?"

"For my pleasure."

With that, he straightened and left the room.

Aurora gaped at the open door, translating and retranslating his words in her mind. Surely she misunderstood him. Surely, he didn't mean pleasure, like in... pleasure.

She stood stiff and silent for long, anxious minutes. He didn't reappear, nor did he shut the door between her small room and his chamber. Aurora heard him moving about, heard his orderly's murmured words, and the clank of armor being removed. She listened to the sound of the outer door closing. A few minutes later, she heard a splash, then a deep, drawn-out groan of contentment. His voice called out, low and commanding.

"Come, take wine and speak with me."

Biting her lip, Aurora debated what to do. She certainly wouldn't learn much of his intentions regarding her and Charlie if she didn't speak with him. On the other hand, he'd made at least one of his intentions pretty clear a few minutes ago. She didn't like the thought of just tripping lightly into his bedroom like a mouse walking willingly into the cat's paws. On the other hand... if they were alone, maybe she could overpower him and make her escape.

"Come, woman."

The guy was starting to get on her nerves, Aurora thought. Squaring her shoulders, she marched toward the door. Just over the threshold, she stopped and looked around curiously.

This was the first sight she'd had of anything other than the four walls of her little room in more than a week. Despite bribes, demands, harsh commands and outright pleading, the stone-faced orderly hadn't allowed her to stick so much as her big toe out the door. Frustrated, she'd eyed his solid form, waiting for an opening, calculating how she would take him down. But the old soldier had been around the block once or twice. He never got within arm's reach. He'd unlock the door, wait until she was seated in full view at the far end of the room before he entered, then set the food trays or water jugs down, just inside the threshold, and depart.

Aurora's hungry eyes now welcomed a change of scene. She drank in every detail. The captain's room was as sparse as she remembered, in stark contrast to the quick glimpses she'd had of the rest of the villa. She glanced around the spacious room and wondered at the man who, according

to Theodorus, commanded the wealth of this rich city, yet
lived so austerely in private.

"There is wine on the table. Bring it."

The peremptory command set her hackles up. Stiffening, she looked around for the source. Lucius Antonius
was stretched out in a shallow bath built into an alcove off
the main bedroom. Hot water swirled around his upper
torso and sent tendrils of steam drifting up toward the
ceiling.

Aurora darted a quick look at the door. This could be
her chance.

"There are guards posted outside. You would not get
far."

The amusement and condescension in his voice added to
her mounting irritation. She counted to ten and took a
deep breath before walking over to the table. Picking up a
small silver jug and two drinking bowls, Aurora headed for
the bathing alcove. If he wanted to talk with everything
hanging out, it was fine by her.

She settled herself on a low, padded stool beside the
sunken tub, wondering why he didn't use the public baths.
Aurora had learned from Theodorus that the bathing ritual was as much a social experience as a cleansing one for
the Romans. It had certainly been a social experience for
her, she thought sardonically.

The memory of her first and only visit to the baths, and
of her first sight of this man unclothed, brought a slow
stain of heat to Aurora's cheeks. Carefully keeping her eyes
above his waist, she handed him a shallow bowl of beaten
silver filled with wine. He took it with a smile of thanks
and leaned back against the marble tub, eyes closed. The
white lines of fatigue around his mouth and eyes stood out
in stark relief to his tanned skin.

It was just curiosity that sent her gaze skimming along
the length of his long, lean body, Aurora told herself. She

just wanted to see if he really was as . . . in shape as she remembered.

He was. He certainly was. Aurora swallowed, impressed despite herself by his superbly muscled torso. As any one of her several lively nieces would say, the guy was awesome. A major stud muffin. Totally rad. The swirling water did little to conceal his long legs or his reclining body. Her gaze filled with dark, curling hair, tanned skin, and thick muscles. *Very* thick muscles. Aurora's eyes snapped up from just below his waist to his face.

His mouth lifted in a mocking grin. "Why do you redden? Does your man have such a puny root that mine disturbs you?"

Damn straight it disturbed her. Aurora hadn't ever seen quite that much . . . root before. She kept her eyes on his face and her tone cool. "If you speak of the one who accompanied me, he is not my man. He is my companion, my comrade-in-arms. I would know how he fares, and where he is."

Ignoring the main thrust of her words, he inquired casually, "If he is not your man, to whom do you belong?"

"I belong only to myself."

"You're too old to be still under your father's roof. You must be married—or were you sold into usage?"

"Where I come from, those aren't the only choices for a woman," Aurora told him dryly.

"I do not understand. What other choices are there?" The big man leaned back against the marble backrest of the bath, his brown eyes regarding her with interest.

"In my time, women may choose their—" Not knowing the word for *profession*, she substituted. "They choose their ways in life. They teach, practice medicine, raise families. Some of them even drive trucks and fly airplanes," she muttered, half under her breath.

At his questioning look, she amended, "They drive large horseless chariots."

"Like that which lay near you in the desert?"

"More or less."

Aurora hesitated, wondering if she should try to explain airplanes and cars and the twentieth century to this naked, semiaroused male. While she debated with herself, Lucius returned to the original topic.

"Roman women do these things, as well. They teach, they are skilled in herbs and medications, they manage properties and raise children. But they still do so under the mantle of their father, or husband, or owner."

Aurora gave him a condescending grin. "You'll just have to take my word for it, big guy. Things are different where I come from. I belong to no man."

His dark brows lowered at her flippant words. "I mislike your tendency toward disrespect. You will watch your tone when you address me."

His curt order reminded Aurora that she was dealing with a senior military officer. Either that, or the men of this world weren't used to women who spoke their minds, despite his reports of liberated Roman matrons. She bit back a sharp retort, and repeated, in an even voice, "I belong to no man."

He rose with a slosh of water and reached for a towel.

"You belong to me now."

Aurora was so fascinated with the way his broad back tapered to a narrow waist and the neatest set of buns she'd seen since *Dances with Wolves* that she almost missed his casual words.

"What?"

"You are mine now."

Aurora jumped up and followed the naked man into his bedroom. "Listen here, Senior Centurion. I'm an officer in the United States Air Force. A captain, like yourself. Well, not quite like you. More like one of your lieutenants, I think. I demand that you accord me the privileges and respect due my rank. Let's not have any more of this 'belonging' crap.''

Her words tripped out in a sputtered mixture of Latin and English, but some must have penetrated. Lucius looked up from the loincloth he was wrapping—thankfully!—around his lean hips and gave her a hard look.

"Officer? Captain? What do you speak of?"

"I *am* an officer. My skills are in war-fighting." So she was stretching the truth a bit. So transports weren't exactly frontline combat aircraft. He didn't need to know that.

"You claim to be a soldier?" Incredulity battled with amusement in his voice.

"Yes," she snapped. "Well, not a soldier, exactly, but a warrior."

A wide grin spread across his face. "Men have been telling tales of Amazons for eons. Despite all the stories of women who cut off their breasts so that they do not interfere with the drawing of a bow, our armies have never encountered such female fighters. And I know from personal observation that your breasts are small, round, and entirely intact." He waved a dismissive hand. "Women warriors exist only in legend."

"Is that a fact?"

Aurora wasn't sure which angered her more—his slighting reference to her physical endowments, or his amused refusal to take her seriously. She forgot his injunction to mind her tongue and rocked back on her heels, hands planted on either hip.

"Just because you haven't encountered them doesn't mean such women don't exist. I hate to be the one to break this to you, Luke ol' buddy, but Rome doesn't encompass the entire universe."

He frowned at her cocky mixture of American slang and fractured Latin. "Speak slowly, and use words I know. And watch your tone."

The low, growled order made the hairs on Aurora's neck stand on end. She knew she was playing with fire, but her week of confinement and the man's arrogance overrode her caution.

"I am an officer," she said with slow deliberation. "A soldier. Do you think an untrained woman could have thrown you to the sand so easily?"

He paused in the act of pulling on his tunic. "That was an accident."

Aurora gave him a mocking grin. "Wanna bet?" At his scowl, she searched for the Latin words. "Nay, it was no accident. It was the result of much training and practice."

The tunic settled over his hips. Lucius picked up his belt, shaking his head. "It was an accident," he repeated.

"Would you like another demonstration?"

His dark head tilted to one side as he eyed her consideringly. "Do you think you could do it again?"

"I not only think so, I know so."

"You could not."

"Would you care to wager on it?"

Golden-brown eyes gleamed as he surveyed her from head to toe. "What do you have to wager?"

"If I take you down, my companion and I go free."

"Nay." He turned away, reaching for his sandals.

"Are you afraid?" she taunted, infuriated by his flat denial.

"I do not fear you, woman. But you are a prisoner of Rome. It would fly in the face of my duty as commander were I to let prisoners loose before I was satisfied as to their intentions."

Furious, Aurora stared as his dark head as he bent to strap on one sandal. Her intentions right now were definitely lethal. She was tempted to bring her knee up and add a lump or two to his nose, but with two guards outside the door, she knew an unprovoked attack wouldn't do her any good. As a matter of fact, it would probably do her a whole lot of harm.

"Okay, okay. How about if I win, you let me see my companion, let me speak with him?"

Lucius lifted his head to stare at her with narrowed eyes. For a long moment, neither of them moved. Finally, he straightened.

"Agreed."

Elation washed through Aurora. "Do we return to the gymnasium? To the wrestling mats?"

He shook his head. "No gymnasium. We will play this foolish game here. Now."

Aurora glanced down at the colorful tiles decorating the floor, then shrugged. "It's your head, fella."

Hitching up the long skirts of her robe, she tucked them into the gold cord around her waist. She took a few experimental steps to make sure she had the freedom to maneuver, then lifted herself to the balls of her feet and beckoned to him with one hand. "Okay, you're on. Come and get me."

He didn't move, except to flash her a wide, amused grin. "We have not settled the stakes. I have agreed to what you would get if you win. What will I get if I win?"

Aurora's heels thumped back down on the tiles. "I . . . I have nothing, except the clothes I arrived in. Those you already have."

She scoured her mind for something to wager. She couldn't lose this chance to see Charlie, to touch base with reality for the first time since the storm that had landed them in this crazy place.

"I have knowledge of events and places beyond your experience. I would share them with you."

He dismissed her offer with a casual wave. "You will share them, in any case, as time progresses. That is not a meaningful bargain." He paused a moment. "I will take your promise not to struggle when I bed you," he finished casually.

"What?"

"If I win, you will not fight me when I take you to bed."

Not *if*. Aurora fumed. *When* he took her to bed. The arrogant, lecherous, slimy, chauvinistic— Her teeth snapped together. "Agreed!"

His grin widened into a wicked, predatory leer that Aurora recognized instantly. She'd been around enough men to recognize good old-fashioned lust when she saw it.

"In your dreams," she jeered, back up on her toes now.

They circled each other, Aurora in a half crouch, her arms up, her fingers beckoning. Lucius moved with the slow, sinuous grace of a panther. He balanced easily on the balls of his feet, thigh muscles bunching, shoulders tensing.

Aurora waited for him to make the first move. She wasn't stupid enough to tackle his solid mass of muscle and bone. She'd have to use his own strength against him. Warily, she watched him. Lucius murmured something she didn't catch, something taunting, but she refused to rise to the bait. Suddenly, he lunged.

At the sound of a crash and a startled grunt, the bedroom door flew open, and two helmeted soldiers rushed in. Their eyes bulged when they spied their commander sprawled on the tile floor, and Aurora standing just out of his reach, in an unmistakable wrestler's stance. Drawing their swords with cold, deadly efficiency, they rushed at her.

"Hold!"

The captain's harsh command stopped them halfway across the room. He pushed himself up on one elbow and shook his head.

"Leave us."

"But, Captain, this woman attacked you."

He picked himself off the floor and gave Aurora a rueful glance. "She but defended her virtue. This one will take some taming. Get you gone. Do not reenter unless I call you."

Knowing smiles spread across the two soldiers' faces as they looked from the commander to Aurora and back again. "Aye, Captain."

The door closed behind the leering men.

Aurora turned to Lucius in disgust. "That was not well done, Senior Centurion. Are you ashamed to admit I bested you in combat? Need you make it something sexual?"

"Don't be stupid. Had those two thought you had really attacked me, your head would even now be rolling across the floor." Straightening his tunic, he bent his legs into a crouch. "Come, show me how you did that."

Aurora stared at him. "We had a deal. A wager."

"You will see your companion tomorrow," he told her impatiently. "Now show me these movements."

The scowl on his face gave her a distinctly pleasurable glow. Commander Luke didn't like getting tossed on his back, not one bit. Well, he wanted to learn her moves. He'd learn them the hard way, Aurora decided. By practical experience.

She used every trick in her repertoire. On the next pass, she rolled onto her back and lifted him with her legs. He flew over her body and hit the floor with a thud that echoed off the walls. For a moment Aurora half feared, half hoped he might have cracked his skull on the hard tiles, but he landed with a wrestler's twist that ensured that flesh, not bone, took the shock of impact.

"Have you studied with the Greeks?" he asked as he rose, shaking himself off.

"Nay, with my four brothers," Aurora answered, a cheeky grin on her lips. "And with one of the meanest, ugliest, nastiest instructors ever to wear an air force uniform. You better watch yourself, big guy."

When he tried again, she grabbed his outstretched wrist, ducked under his arm, and used her shoulder to tip him off-balance. He slammed into the tiles once more, then picked himself up slowly, jaws tight. Aurora's grin widened.

She had to give him credit, though. By the next pass, he'd learned that she was using his own weight and momentum against him. He came at her again, but this time he checked his lunge just as she snaked out a leg to wrap it around his calf. Instead of contacting solid flesh, her leg flailed at the air and she was thrown off-balance. He helped the process by knocking her other foot out from under her. Aurora landed on her bottom with a thump.

"Think you're pretty smart, don't you?" she grumbled up at his grim face.

"Nay, not smart, or you would not have thrown me on my head thrice already. None has ever done so." He reached down to help her up.

Aurora ignored his hand and scrambled to her feet. "You mean a mere woman was the first to toss you in the dust?" she gibed, resisting the urge to rub her tingling rear cheeks.

He shrugged. "Sometimes even the excellent Homer nods off."

Aurora stared at him. "Homer? Homer who?"

"The poet."

She searched her limited store of knowledge. "The guy who wrote about Ulysses? How did he get into the conversation?"

"It's a saying," he explained. "A maxim. Even Homer produced some bad poetry. Thus it follows that man cannot be right, or correct, or win, every time."

"We have such a saying in my land, as well," Aurora said after a moment. "You can't win them all."

He let loose with one of those roguish grins that did funny things to Aurora's pulmonary system. She stared at him, mesmerized.

"Nay, you cannot win them all," he agreed. "Not now that I understand your moves."

"Izzatso?" She couldn't resist the challenge of that cocky smile. "Do you wish to try once more?"

The fleeting glimmer of satisfaction Aurora saw in his eyes made her pause. Before she could decide what it meant, Lucius lunged again. She had no time to raise her arms. His weight carried her backward. He twisted as they tumbled to the floor, so that his body absorbed the impact. Before Aurora could break his hold, he rolled over, pinning her to the tiles, and captured her arms between their bodies.

She gasped, trying to suck back into her lungs the air that surprise and his solid bulk had forced out. With every breath, her breasts pressed against the hard planes of his chest. His brown eyes hovered just inches above hers, gleaming with smug triumph.

"Okay," she panted. "So even Homer sleeps sometimes. Let me rise."

Chapter 6

"Nay, little one. I find this pillow too much to my liking to toss it aside just yet."

Lucius savored the feel of the woman beneath him. Her breasts pushed against his chest with her every gasping breath. Her stomach quivered under his thighs. He felt blood, hot and thick, surge into his loins as he absorbed the movements of her body into his flesh.

The one called Aurora stared up at him in confusion and gathering consternation. Lucius read the expressions that flitted across her face, and anticipated her next move easily. When she twisted her lower body to gain some leverage, he insinuated his knee between hers. Slowly, deliberately, he pushed her legs apart and settled himself at the juncture of her thighs.

Her eyes widened until thick black lashes framed pools of swirling mist.

"Captain!"

She struggled to get the word out against the press of his weight. Lucius shifted imperceptibly, taking some of the burden off her chest. As a result, his root buried itself in the soft flesh of her belly. He bit back a groan when her stomach muscles tensed, giving him an involuntary, and totally erotic, caress.

"Captain, you must let me rise. I . . . I am an officer, remember? I proved I've been trained."

Her breath beat against his lips in soft little pants and made his own catch deep in his throat.

"Aye, you've been well trained. You may be as you claim, but you are also a woman. One I desire."

He could see that his blunt words shocked her. For the space of a second, Lucius wondered if her wild claim of belonging to no man meant that she was yet a virgin. Nay, he decided as he stroked one hand along the curve of a womanly hip. Her ripe mouth and fire-kissed hair bespoke passion, not timid maidenhood. The very sight of her parted lips inflamed him. With the arrogance of a conqueror taking his plunder, he lowered his head and covered her mouth in a hungry, driving kiss.

Sheer surprise held Aurora motionless. That, and a startled acknowledgment that the man knew what he was doing. For a barbarian, Captain Luke had a pretty sophisticated technique. Despite the weight pinning her down, despite the hard tiles tormenting her shoulders and hips, she felt the force of his kiss in every inch of her body. A fist tangled in her hair to hold her head still while his lips molded hers, possessing, shaping, tasting.

After a long, breathless moment, the fierce pressure eased. Sweet torment followed. His tongue ran along the inside of her lower lip, teased at her teeth, then arrogantly demanded entrance to her mouth. When she opened to him in dazed wonder, he engaged her own tongue in a sensuous battle. He tasted of wine. Of cloves. Of hot, hungry male.

Aurora had kissed a respectable number of men in her life, but none whose warm lips and predatory tongue had sent her into a tailspin like this. She shivered with the sensations shooting through her. Her body dared her to see where these incredible sensations might lead. Her mind screamed that she'd better stop him, fast.

His hand slid up, over her hip, along her waist, to shape her breast—her *small* breast, he'd said. He seemed to find enough there to keep his interest, Aurora noted through the darts of pleasure wrought by his hand. Brushing aside the cotton folds of her robe with a sureness that told her he knew well how to get around women's garments, he insinuated his fingers under the linen band binding her chest. They closed over her nipple, tugging the sensitive tip into a turgid, aching peak.

Twisting her head aside, she managed to suck air into her tortured lungs. "Wait," she panted. "Wait."

His dark head lifted. "For what? I am as a rock for you. And you are ready for me." To give emphasis to his words, he slid his hand down her belly and buried them between her legs.

Aurora stared up at him, her senses whirling. It took a moment, but she managed to shake her head. "No, no, I am not ready. I don't want this."

Well, part of her wanted it, Aurora acknowledged silently. A wet, aching part of her. But this man was her enemy, her captor. Her self-respect was already in shreds from her initial, startled response to his kiss. She would not allow it to disintegrate further.

Dismissing her words as though they were the token protests of a woman who wanted to be coaxed, Luke buried his face in the juncture of her shoulder and neck. Desperate, Aurora refused to acknowledge the fire that shot from his nipping teeth, along the length of both arms, to her very fingertips.

"Is this how Romans remain true to their word?" she gasped. "Is there no honor among the officers of the Empire?"

Once more his head lifted. "What honor do you speak of?"

"You promised not to force me if I won our contest."

His hand loosened its grip on her hair. The other hand, Aurora noted, regained its possessive hold on her breast. Her *small* breast.

"Nay, woman, I promised to let you visit your companion should you win. You shall see him tomorrow."

"But... but I agreed not to fight you if I lost. I did not lose."

"So you may fight me."

Aurora's arm wedged itself against his massive chest as he bent over her again. Her muscles trembled with the effort of holding him off.

"I do not wish this, Roman."

Aurora congratulated herself. Most of the breathy quality was gone from her voice. She waited in tense anticipation. Various self-defense moves flitted through her mind as the captain stared down at her. To her relief, amusement glimmered in his eyes, and he rolled off her body. Aurora gulped in deep, steadying breaths. This time, when he reached down, she took his arm and allowed him to help her up.

When he took her to her small room, Aurora found that it suddenly looked much less like a prison and more like a haven.

"An escort will come for you in the morning," he told her, turning to leave.

Aurora bit her lip, then called out to him in a low voice. "Thank you, Roman."

He glanced back, a dark brow quirked. "For the visit, or for not taking you this night?"

She lifted her chin. "For the visit. You will not 'take' me, this night or any other."

"Ah, little one, I will. And soon. As the pundits say, hunger but adds spice to the beans."

"Beans? What beans?"

The bolt slid into place behind him.

"Hey! What beans?"

The next morning Aurora rose early and paced her room with long, impatient strides. She listened intently to the sounds of the captain rising with the dawn, heard his orderly's murmured voice as he dressed. Half fearful, half hopeful, she wondered if Lucius/Luke would open the door between them, and wondered what she would say to him if he did.

He didn't open the door. He didn't even bother to call out a greeting, or acknowledge her presence in any way. Not that Aurora wanted him to. Still, it was disconcerting to be living within a few yards of a man who boldly stated his desire, then ignored her very existence.

Aurora strode around the small room, refusing to think about how she'd lain awake most of the night, trying to erase the feel of his hand from her body and the taste of his lips from hers. Wondering if he'd try to finish what he'd started. She'd been a mass of nerves by the time light began to streak the darkness outside the shuttered windows. And this long wait wasn't helping.

Too keyed up to eat the simple breakfast the orderly brought, she continued her pacing. Finally, when the sun had climbed halfway up the shutters, she heard the sound of voices in the outer chamber. Her door opened to admit a grizzled, gap-toothed soldier.

"*Ave*, Lady Aurora. I am the sergeant of the household guard. The captain has ordered me to provide you escort."

Aurora surveyed the double rank of legionaries in the outer chamber. "You and all of them?"

A tinge of red mottled the sergeant's leathery cheeks. He shrugged, then gave her a sheepish look. "I would be sure I have sufficient men to... to restrain you. Tales of your, uh, confrontation with the captain circulate the halls. 'Tis said you have unearthly powers.''

"Unearthly?" Aurora's eyes lit with genuine amusement. "You think I have unearthly powers, just because I tossed big, bad Commander Luke on his head?"

The sergeant struggled to translate her words. "Nay. Because you did so and lived to see the light of day."

Feeling pleased with herself, Aurora sauntered out of the captain's chamber. The escort fell into step behind her. After a series of turns and hallways, she stepped out onto the portico fronting the villa, into bright, dazzling sunshine. Hot air swirling with fine, stinging particles of sand enveloped her.

Aurora eyes adjusted slowly to the glare. Except for the filtered sunlight coming through her locked shutters, this was the first daylight she'd seen in over a week. Her foot caught on the trailing hem of her robe, and she would have pitched headfirst down the shallow stairs if the sergeant hadn't caught her arm.

As if reassured by the feel of solid flesh and bone, he flashed her a crooked grin, showing wide spaces and a broken tooth in front. His nervousness seemed to fade, and he answered Aurora's questions with gruff good nature as they walked past rows of long barracks.

"Nay, lady, these are not officers' quarters. The men live here."

Aurora peeked through an open portal as they passed. The small two-room apartment she saw, with sleeping quarters at the back and a living and cooking room in the front, was a heck of a lot roomier than the cubicles airmen shared at her home base, she noted with some interest. The sergeant pointed out hospital buildings, granaries, busy workshops and majestic temples. The camp was an orderly, self-contained, bustling unit.

"'Tis not as well laid out as most," he explained, almost apologetically. "This city is old, and constrained by the bend of the river. We inherited buildings constructed centuries ago, by Greeks and Parthians.'' He launched into a detailed description of what a really well-laid-out camp would contain that fascinated Aurora as much as his rapid Latin confused her.

By the time they reached the rows of long, low stables, she was overwhelmed by details and halfway to admitting a grudging respect for this army whose stocky, superstitious troops ruled the known world.

Her budding respect died the instant she stepped into the stables. The first thing that hit her was the overpowering odor of manure and warm horseflesh. The second was the sight of chained, scarecrow-thin slaves shoveling out endless rows of stalls. A few uniformed troops worked with the horses, but it was the slaves who drew her horrified gaze.

These creatures were nothing like the house and bath servants Aurora had seen. Those had worn soft robes and had looked well fed, if timorous. These men wore rags at best, and many were completely naked. Their ribs showed in gaunt detail, and more than one back carried livid, blood-encrusted weals. As Aurora stared, one of the slaves bumped into a soldier backing a horse out of its stall. With a muttered oath, the soldier swept out a brawny arm and sent the slave clattering to the floor with a jangle of leg irons and chains.

''Why are they in chains?'' Aurora demanded. ''How can they work that way?''

The sergeant shrugged. ''These tribesmen are fierce fighters, and good with horses. Were they not restrained, they would be gone.''

Aurora swallowed at his callous unconcern. Her gaze swept the stable again, adjusting to the gloom. She spied a tall figure at the far end of the stable, some distance apart from the others.

"Charlie!" She darted forward, her escort scrambling after her. "Charlie, it's me, Aurora!"

She ran down the long, dim aisle between the stalls, toward her friend. Toward sanity, toward a link with reality in this unreal world. Brushing past a guard lounging against a wooden post, she reached for Charlie. A sob caught in her throat as she noted the fading, mottled bruises on his back and shoulders and the iron collar around his neck. Her hands grabbed at his sweat-slicked arm.

"Charlie, are you all right?"

He jumped like a startled rabbit at her touch. Jerking away, he cowered against the stall. Wide, frightened eyes stared up at her. His look held no welcome, no relief, not a glimmer of recognition.

"Charlie, it's me, Aurora."

She lowered her voice, trying to coax the confused fright from his face. Her foot squished in the dirty straw as she took a step forward. Charlie's fear spilled over into low, unintelligible mumbles, and he backed even farther into the stall, his chains clanking with every step.

"My God, Charlie," she cried softly, "don't you know me? Please, it's Aurora."

The uncomprehending, cowering figure stared back at her blankly.

Hot, scalding tears blurred Aurora's vision, and a mixture of pain and outright terror lanced through her. All this time she'd clung to the thought of Charlie, to the thought that she had an ally somewhere in this time and place. As she stared into his wide, confused eyes, a feeling of loneliness washed over her, so intense that it twisted her soul. She almost gave in to it, almost crumpled to her knees beside Charlie in the reeking straw, almost let the sobs tearing at her throat find an outlet. For long, aching moments, she stood still, fighting tears. A black, empty darkness seemed to stretch between her and her only friend in this strange world.

"Lady?" The sergeant's tentative reaching hand brought her back from the void.

"Do not touch me," she snarled, whirling on him.

He snatched his hand back, startled. Swallowing, he tried again. "Lady, he does not know you."

Aurora stared at the stolid sergeant. Slowly she forced her panic down and her tears back. "Aye, I see that." Straightening her shoulders, she turned to the guard standing between her and Charlie. "Remove his chains. At once!"

The guard gaped in surprise and looked to burly sergeant for guidance.

The grizzled veteran shook his head. "My lady, my instructions were to bring you to him, not to release him."

"I don't give a damn what..." Aurora took a deep breath and started over, this time in Latin. "I care not what your orders were. This man is ill and needs care. Release him at once."

"Nay, lady, I cannot."

"Get Senior Centurion Lucius Antonius."

His mouth dropped open in sheer astonishment. "Disturb the commander? For a prisoner? Nay, lady."

"Very well. I'll go to him myself." She turned back, calling softly to the figure huddled in the far corner.

"Charlie, come with me. I'll help you." Her voice low and soothing, she stepped toward her friend once more. He shook his head violently. Panic filled his hazel eyes and wrenched at Aurora's heart.

"Okay. It's okay," she whispered. "I won't force you. Just...just hang in there, until I get some help."

Fighting down the pain that nearly swamped her, Aurora stumbled into the sunlight. After the dark, fetid atmosphere of the stables, she sucked in fresh air greedily. She had no interest in the passing scenery on the return trip. Her mind was filled with Charlie, and the creeping feeling of despair that threatened with every step.

By the time they reached the headquarters building, she'd managed to still the trembling in her hands. She barely noticed the array of flags on their wooden standards, or the golden statues that graced the central rotunda when she stalked through the front entrance. As she waited with her escort outside a set of tall wooden doors, her chin lifted and a healthy, healing anger coursed through her. Lucius Antonius would answer to her for his treatment of Charlie.

"The commander will see you now, lady."

"You bet your little pointed head he'll see me," Aurora muttered, following the soldier through a wide, spacious outer office into Lucius's inner sanctum.

She stopped in midstride as a circle of faces turned to her. Her startled gaze took in a dozen or so officers seated around a long, polished table, observing her with varying expressions of curiosity, wariness, and outright male assessment. She recognized the deputy, Quintus. His golden brows were drawn together in a scowl, and his fingers tapped impatiently on the table. Maps and parchment scrolls littered the table. Someone who looked suspiciously like a company clerk sat on a low stool, taking notes.

A staff meeting! She'd interrupted a damn staff meeting! A bubble of hysterical laughter rose in her throat at the astonishingly familiar scene, one she had participated in on countless occasions in the past. The only difference was that the men here wore white tunics and embossed armor, not blue air force shirts with metal rank insignias on the collars.

With the instinctive disdain of all operational officers for staff pukes, as they were lovingly known, Aurora ignored the assembled men and turned to the leader seated at the far end of the table. "I wish to speak with you, Senior Centurion."

"So I've been informed," he responded dryly. "A matter of some urgency, such that the sergeant of my household guard would disturb this meeting."

"Very urgent. I demand that my companion be released immediately."

His brows snapped together, making Aurora wish she'd tempered her hasty words and arrogant tone just a bit.

"Leave us."

His low command to his assembled officers didn't reassure her. Nor did the disgusted look on the deputy's face. The captain waited until the door shut behind the last man, then rose and strolled forward.

His sheer size and intimidating look almost made her step back. Even without the added bulk of armor or thick red cloak, the man's shoulders blocked out the light from the row of high open windows at the far end of the office.

"I have told you once, and will not do so again. You will keep a respectful tongue in your discourse with me."

"Or what?" she asked, amazed at her own nerve. "Or you will put me in chains, as you have my companion?"

His stern features softened as a flicker of amusement deepened the gold flecks in his eyes. "The idea holds a certain appeal."

Aurora bit her lip to hold back the retort that sprang up.

"That's better." He leaned his hips back against the table and folded his arms across his chest. "You say you were an officer in this different time you claim to come from, yet words spill thoughtlessly off your tongue. Were you allowed to speak thus to the senior commanders in your world?"

"Yes! Well, no. Not always."

Aurora bit her lip, remembering the pile of demerits she'd collected at the academy, and the irate looks her squadron commanders had given her on more than one occasion. Okay, so she tended to be a bit impetuous. So she was a bit outspoken at times. Big deal.

"If you can do so with proper dignity, you may speak."

Aurora ground her teeth. Letting her unruly temper loose wouldn't help Charlie, but at that moment nothing would have given her greater satisfaction than to knock the captain's leg out from under him so that he slid off the table onto his duff. She managed to keep her voice even— barely.

"Why is my companion in chains, when I am not? Why is he treated so?"

Lucius shrugged. "He is of no use to me in his present confused state, except for menial labor. You are. I have plans for you."

Aurora's stomach lurched. She stared at him, her eyes wide. It was one thing for him to talk of taking her to bed in the dim privacy of his chamber. To have him refer to it so openly, in the bright light of day, with the litter of a staff meeting all around them, took Aurora's breath away. The urge rose in her throat to tell him just what he could do with his plans, but his cocked, warning eyebrow, and a sudden vision of Charlie's bewildered face, made her temper her response.

"You must afford my companion better treatment. He is an officer, like me, and worthy of respect."

"You are not the warrior you claim, if you believe captured soldiers, whether officers or not, deserve much respect," Lucius told her with a lifted brow. When she would have argued the point, he held up a hand. "This man fares better than most captives."

The image of Charlie's bruised back and cowering figure huddled against the stable wall filled Aurora's mind. Her fingers curled into fists at her side. Lifting her chin, she met the Roman's eyes.

"Captain, I...I beg you to see that he has medical attention."

He straightened. "You waste my time, lady, and yours in these pleas."

"Wait!" Aurora grasped at his arm. His flesh felt warm and as unyielding as steel under her fingers. Before she could give herself time to think, Aurora made a last, desperate plea. "Last night you said you would lie with me, whether I fought you or not. I will not fight you, if you ensure my friend receives proper care."

His brown eyes narrowed. "You would bed with me, willingly, to spare this companion? This man you say is neither lover nor husband?"

"Aye." Aurora kept her chin high. "I have nothing else to offer that you would deign to accept. In exchange, you will see that Lieutenant Everett receives medical attention, as well as proper food and shelter."

Behind the thick screen of his lashes, golden lights glittered in his eyes.

"I wish to be sure I understand the terms of your offer. You will give yourself freely if your companion is cared for?"

"Yes. And I must be allowed to visit him regularly."

The gleam in his eyes intensified. "Agreed."

Aurora let out a long, slow breath.

He rose and walked to the head of the table, then sat. "Tell the guard to escort you to your room," he said, his voice even. "We will take the evening meal together."

Shaken now by her rash offer, and more than a little stunned by his blasé acceptance of it, Aurora stood rooted to the spot.

He glanced up. "You are dismissed."

Chapter 7

Aurora paced her small room for the rest of the interminable day. With every turn, she alternated between a simmering indignation at the casual way she'd been dismissed and a growing consternation over what was to come.

Although the Code of Conduct allowed some degree of cooperation with the enemy to ensure the health and welfare of captured personnel, she suspected her agreement with Senior Centurion Lucius Antonius stretched the Code's limits just a tad. Whenever her stomach fluttered with doubt, however, she remembered that Charlie was her only link to her world. She'd do whatever was necessary to save her copilot's life.

Besides, she told herself with ruthless honesty, if the captain's kiss last night was a sample of his bedroom technique, she'd manage to endure, somehow. It wasn't as if she were some frightened virgin. She was twenty-eight, for Pete's sake. She'd been engaged to another pilot for almost a year before separate assignments and dwindling interest prompted her to call it off.

Aurora stopped her restless pacing as she thought about her fiancé. The man's kisses hadn't had half the firepower this Roman's did. She felt more nervous and guilty than ever as shivers of anticipation danced down her spine. Wrapping both arms tight around her chest, Aurora stood at the windows and stared through the shutters, as if seeking both courage and forgiveness from the tiny god dancing atop the bubbling fountain in the center of the courtyard.

"The captain says you are to have use of his chambers to bathe, lady. These women will assist you."

Aurora turned with a start to see the orderly at the door. He nodded to a trio of women standing just outside her room, then stood aside to allow Aurora to exit.

She hesitated, reluctant to move. Once she took that first step, once she bathed and perfumed her body and played the whore, her self-respect would crumble into dust. Her lips trembled with the impulse to renege, to send word that the deal was off. Then she thought of Charlie. Shrugging, she left her small sanctuary.

"*Ave*, lady. You look much refreshed."

In truth, Lucius thought with an inward smile, she looked as nervous as a cat. But a beautiful cat. The oil lamps brought out red lights in her piled hair and made her skin glow like thick, unskimmed cream.

At Lucius's quiet nod, the guard slipped outside, leaving them alone in the villa's spacious, ornately furnished dining chamber.

"Come, seat yourself. I would we partake of the pleasures of food and wine and conversation before we bed."

Her face paled, then flushed a delicate rose at his blunt words. When she lifted her chin in what he now recognized as a prelude to more outrageous conduct, he almost let the amusement simmering in him surface. By the gods, she rose to the bait like a hungry trout. This looked to be a most enjoyable evening.

Settling himself on his side on a long, low couch with bolstered cushions at one end, he gestured to a similar couch across from his.

"Nay, not like that," he said when she perched on one edge, looking as if she might bolt at his slightest movement. "Be comfortable. Recline."

"I don't believe this," she muttered as she draped her robe over her legs and tried to prop the cushions under one arm. Her eyes swept the tall, pillared chamber, lingering for a moment on the painted ceiling. "This whole scene is something right out of the movies."

"What is this 'movies'?" Lucius ignored the swarm of servants who entered and began laying out the first course, concentrating all his attention on his reluctant guest.

She hesitated, then glanced over with a challenge in her eyes. "In my time, we have pictures that move, filled with bright colors. In these pictures I saw scenes of... of Roman orgies. Regular toga parties, in fact." Her tone dared him to disagree.

"We also have such pictures," Lucius told her, blandly ignoring her belligerent reference to orgies. His plans for her included nothing so public, so indiscriminate, as a bacchanal. "Stage players at the theaters undulate painted curtains, making them move. They imitate waves and fire and even winds blowing through the gardens."

"It's not the same," she insisted, taking a bowl of wine from a hovering servant. "The pictures I speak of have people in them that move and speak."

"If so you say." Lucius nodded, his hooded eyes on her long, shapely legs. The pictures moving through his mind at that precise moment had nothing to do with the theater. They were very similar to those drawn on the hide scrolls passed from soldier to soldier in the field, when no women were readily available.

"I do say so," she snapped, lifting her wine to take an angry sip.

"Let us not argue about the shadow of an ass," Lucius said, calming her as he would a nervous young recruit.

She choked on the wine. "What?" she sputtered. "What shadow? What ass?"

He dipped his fingers into a dish set on the low table between them and scooped a healthy portion of savory meat onto his silver plate.

"It is another maxim," he replied. "An admonition not to waste one's energies arguing unimportant matters."

A slow, reluctant grin spread across her face. "In my world, we also have such a saying. We don't sweat the small stuff."

When he gave her an answering grin, she took a hasty sip of wine.

"Tell me more of your world," Lucius prompted.

Shadows darkened the gray mists of her eyes. She slanted him an anxious look from under her lashes, as if daring him to disbelieve her.

"I come from a land far across the seas. Seas your people have not crossed yet."

"I suspected as much." At her quick, inquiring look, he nodded. "If you had come from a land where Rome had touched, you'd not be so quick to pit yourself against its invincible might."

"I wouldn't be so sure about that invincibility business," she muttered. "Every dog has its day, big guy, and Rome's will come a couple hundred years from now."

"Speak in words I understand," Lucius commanded. "Come, sit back and take your ease. Tell me more of this time, this world of yours."

Taking her lower lip between even white teeth, she lowered herself onto the couch. Slowly, hesitantly, she began to describe her home. The minutes lengthened as Lucius listened to halting descriptions of buildings that reached high into the sky, medicines that kept men alive well past their appointed years, weapons that killed with incredibly destructive power. If the world she described existed, and Lucius could not quite bring himself to believe it did, it sounded like a most unquiet, unnatural place.

At least she gave no indication that this land she came from had warlike intentions against Rome. The commander in Lucius relaxed, and he settled back to enjoy her tales. For the first time since he'd plucked this incredible creature from the sand, he began to believe that she had, indeed, tumbled out of the sky into his arms by the sheerest quirk of fate.

As the second course followed the first, her words grew more animated. She took a long swallow of her wine, waved away the dishes presented by the slaves, and let the words tumble forth.

By the third course, her eyes sparkled, and she occasionally reverted to her lamentable, irreverent sarcasm. Magnanimously Lucius decided to ignore her lapses.

When the servants finally set ripe cheeses and fruits on the low table, he signaled to them to fill the wine bowls once more, then leave. 'Twas time to bring the talk back to the present. Wherever this one had come from, whatever time had spawned her, she was here now.

"How came you by your name? Did your parents worship the goddess Aurora, or Eos, as she is known to the Greeks?"

"Not exactly," Aurora drawled. "My father's an engineer. Before he retired, he worked for the railroad, and..." His questioning look interrupted her.

"Oh, never mind. I don't feel like explaining trains right now." She settled back on the couch with a little frown, as if trying to remember what she'd been talking about.

Lucius prompted her. "Your father?"

"Oh. Yes. My father traveled a lot. Mother met him whenever she could. They spent one weekend in a small Nebraska town called Aurora and, um, consummated their love. Nine months later, I was born."

Her eyes clouded, as if she were remembering this family she spoke of. Lucius sought to bring her back to him. "Know you the legend of the goddess Aurora?"

Her troubled expression softened. "Yes, I know the legend."

She lolled her head to one side, letting her hair spill over her shoulder. Oil lamps set on low side tables lit dancing flames in the thick mass. Lucius sucked in his breath as desire shot through his belly, as dark and red as the pinpoints of fire in her mane.

"I looked her up years ago. I mean, if you're going to be saddled with a name like Aurora, you need to have some defense when the other kids make fun of it."

She lifted her wine bowl and stared into it with a dreamy look on her face that made the flame in Lucius's groin erupt into white-hot molten lava.

"The goddess Aurora rode her chariot across the skies each night to extinguish the stars and bring the dawn. She had a love of light, glowing and golden."

Lucius caught the breathless, slurred quality of her voice. Smiling, he leaned across the table to move the wine out of her reach. When she seemed lost in her dreams, he picked up the tale.

"She also had a weakness for mortal men, and took many, many lovers. One day she stole away the son of the king of Troy, carrying him off to the heavens. She begged her father, Jupiter, to give him eternal life, which he did, despite the fact that the young man's abduction caused a great war on earth."

Without seeming to, Lucius watched her carefully. She gave no indication, no hint, that she shared this youth's immortality. His last lingering doubt about her humanity vanished.

"And did they live happily ever after?" Aurora asked, her gray eyes shining, as if sharing in her patroness's escapades.

Lucius swallowed a grin at the universal hunger for romantic twaddle shared by all females, even this strong-willed self-proclaimed soldier.

"Unfortunately, the irate Jupiter neglected to include eternal youth in the arrangement. The man grew ever older before Aurora's very eyes. In time, he became so unappetizing that she locked him away in his room. Many claim you can still hear his feeble cries in the whimpers of old men who ache for a woman, but cannot find the strength to raise their staff." He paused, then added deliberately, "Which problem I have not this night."

At his soft words, Aurora blinked, then jerked upright on the couch. The warm, hazy glow she'd felt in his company drifted away. Her heart began to hammer in an erratic pattern. Her palms suddenly felt moist. This was it, she knew with absolute certainty. The moment she'd been dreading. The moment she'd been anticipating.

All afternoon she'd told herself to just play it cool, simply fulfill her part of the bargain without any histrionics. But the long-drawn-out waiting period, the sensuous ministration of the servants as they'd washed and depilated and oiled her body, this prelude disguised as a private banquet—all had conspired to build a shivering, tingling awareness in her. Healthy, spontaneous passion she could and did appreciate. This preplanned, preannounced sexual agenda made her as nervous as a frightened bride on her wedding night.

She'd stilled most of her qualms as the meal progressed. The wine had certainly helped, as had the captain's attention as she talked of home. But the languor she'd slipped into was gone now. Aurora had only to look at the light gleaming in the man's shadowed eyes to know that he'd deliberately set the stage. He'd lulled her, filled her with wine and spicy foods, and now he wanted her. A wash of disgust at her own shivering passivity filled her. She was damned if she'd let him play on her nerves any longer. She rose, then looked down in surprise when her legs wobbled.

"I can see you've finished your meal. Let us retire, and I will fulfill my promise."

Aurora could have sworn his lips twitched, but she couldn't imagine why. He rose and ushered her ceremoniously out of the room. To her disgust, the hallway tiles seemed to leap up to trip her. His strong hand under her arm held her steady.

She shook off his hold when they entered the bedchamber. Striding to the middle of the room, she waited with swirling, churning impatience while he nodded in dismissal of the ever-present orderly, then leaned his massive shoulders back against the door. All she wanted now was to get the whole sordid thing finished.

"Well, Captain?" Was the man planted against that door?

"Well, lady?"

Aurora clenched her jaw. Obviously he didn't intend to make this easy for her. "Let's get this business over with."

"Proceed," he ordered calmly.

"What?"

"Proceed. Do what you would do in order to finish the 'business.'"

Aurora stood rigid and unmoving for a long, simmering moment. "You got it, buddy," she muttered finally. With a defiant glare, she began to undress. Embarrassed anger sustained her as she untied her sandals. Dragging in a deep breath, she pulled off her outer robe and tossed it to the floor. When she reached for the hem of her shift, her fingers faltered. The linen covering slid halfway up her thighs.

Biting down on her lower lip, she slanted the centurion a quick look. He was watching her disrobe with all the interest of a man observing a circus dog performing its tricks.

Tight-jawed, Aurora tugged the shift over her head and threw it aside. Night air wrapped around her bared flesh, raising tiny goose bumps on her skin. She darted another look at the silent man. Nothing. *Nada. Non est tanti,* as the Romans would say. No big deal.

Muttering a curse that sounded a whole heck of a lot more impressive in Latin that it did in its original, succinct English, Aurora unwrapped her linen breastband. Her breasts, *small* though they were, quivered with emotion. With only a slight tremor in her fingers, she unwrapped the strip of linen banding her hips and let it fall. Her chin lifted , and she stared at Lucius with every ounce of nonchalance she could muster.

"Get in the bed."

Despite her embarrassment, Aurora couldn't restrain the dart of triumph that shot through her at the slight hoarseness in his voice. So old Iron Pants wasn't as in control as he pretended. She ripped back the light bed coverings and climbed onto the sleeping platform. The rope supports were taut and tight, but no stiffer than she was herself. Try as she would, she couldn't force her arms and legs to relax. As if they had a will of their own, they trembled in anticipation.

Refusing to act coy, Aurora watched as the captain stripped off his tunic and sandals. Wearing only a linen loincloth that outlined as much as it covered, he closed the short distance to the bed. The irreverent thought flashed through Aurora's mind that she could make a fortune marketing that particular style of male underwear in the United States. Any red-blooded American woman with half a hormone left would pay big bucks to see her man cupped in a transparent bit of cloth that wound between his legs and up between two trim, muscular buttocks.

Her determination to see this thing through, literally, faltered when he unwrapped the loincloth. A male member about the size of the Washington Monument jutted up, right at her eye level. Aurora sucked in a shaky breath and scooted down, burying all but the tip of her nose under the light cover. Thankfully, Lucius extinguished the oil lamp beside the bed and covered the room, and himself, in soft darkness.

Aurora kept a death grip on the sheet, or whatever this rough, nubby covering was called, as he settled himself beside her.

"You may proceed."

The arrogant command, laced though it was with husky male desire, stilled Aurora's nervousness and sparked her ready temper. As if dousing herself with enough scented oil to choke a streetwalker and stripping for him weren't enough, the man expected her to do all the work, as well. She struggled up from under the confining covers and faced him.

"Look, big guy. The deal was that I wouldn't fight you. Not that I'd make the earth move for you. From here on out, you're flying solo. Well, not solo, exactly, but you've got the stick." Her sputtering mix of English and Latin gave out at his grin. "Oh, hell, you know what I mean," she sputtered, flinging herself down again.

"I understand what you mean, little one."

Laughter rumbled in his chest. Aurora barely had time to absorb either the sound or the minor earthquake he caused on the rope supports. With deft hands, he twisted her body so that she lay with her back to his front, her rear curved into his loins. Or it would have curved into his loins, if Aurora hadn't stiffened at his touch. She lay, rigid and unyielding, while the Washington Monument poked at her backside. Remembering her promise not to fight, she tried to relax, only to jerk once more when he wrapped his arm around her waist and hauled her up against his solid bulk.

"Sleep now."

"What!" Aurora tried to scrunch around. His arm tightened into an iron band.

"Do not move so."

"What is this? More games? More…more spice for the blasted beans?" She struggled in his grip.

"I will have you hot and willing, lady. When you come to my bed and lie not as an obelisk, we will take this further."

Rage rose in hot red waves. Aurora fought his hold in earnest now. She'd stripped and displayed herself like a prostitute, and he didn't even want her. Furious, she butted her hips back against him. When her flesh connected with his, he grunted and threw his leg over both of hers to hold her still.

"You pig," she spit, "Roman pig. You promised. You promised Charlie would get care."

She worked one leg loose and kicked back viciously. Swearing, he rolled her beneath him. It took a few seconds, but he managed to capture both her pummeling hands in a hard hold.

"Listen to me, vixen. Your companion is well cared for. He has been since the day you arrived."

"He's been beaten!" she shouted. "I saw the bruises myself!"

"The marks were on his back when he came here."

"Then why was he so frightened? So scared?"

"Mayhap because he has not heard or spoken since the first day. He has his own quarters, and a woman to tend him, but still he cowers in fright."

Aurora heaved, trying to dislodge his weight. "I don't believe you. He was in chains! He was working with the other slaves in the stables!"

His mouth grim, Lucius transferred both wrists to one hand and buried his other in her hair to still her thrashing head. "Heed what I say! I ordered him chained because in his fear and confusion he tried to flee, to swim the Euphrates. He almost drowned before my men pulled him out. He works in the stables because I know from experience how inactivity rots a man's mind. He seems to find comfort in working with the horses."

"You're lying!"

His hand tugged painfully at her scalp. "I do not lie, and if you value your hide you will not say so again."

His low, icy tone caught Aurora's attention. Her chest heaving, she tried to gather her chaotic thoughts. "I don't understand. If he's cared for as you say, why did you bargain with me? Why did you take my offer of—" She faltered as a horrible suspicion entered her mind.

A mocking gleam replaced the anger in his eyes. "You promised your body if I assured your companion had care. Since I had already done so, I had naught to lose. Think you I would resist such an offer?"

"Oh, God," Aurora groaned. "No wonder you've been grinning like the Cheshire cat all night. You've been stringing me along this whole evening. I can't believe I've been such an airhead, such an utter space cadet."

"In Latin," he ordered softly.

She shortened the translation considerably. "I'm a fool."

The expression in his eyes softened. "Nay, you're no fool. Only impetuous, and loyal to your friend. Would that I had friends willing to sacrifice as much for me."

His words salved her wounded pride, and the golden lights in his brown eyes sent a distinct fluttering through-

out her nervous system. Staring up into the stark, angled
planes of his face, Aurora felt a queer hitch in her chest.

"Is that why…why you do not lie with me this night?"
she whispered. "Because you respect my concern for my
friend?"

He rolled over, fitting her back into the curve of his
body. His breath warmed her ear.

"Oh, I will lie with you this night. But I will not take
you, much as it pains me. Especially when you twitch your
tail so delightfully."

Aurora could hear the smile in his voice, tinged with a
distinct note of wry regret.

"Why not?" Piqued, relieved, frustrated, she let the
breathless question drift on the darkness between them.

"I spoke the truth when I said I want you to come to me
willingly. There will be no bargains, no companions, no
wine fumes between us, when I take you. Tomorrow you
will see your comrade, and tomorrow night we will share
this bed again, as we will henceforth. Tomorrow we will
mate. Now sleep."

Sleep. Right. Sure.

Chapter 8

Aurora awoke the next morning with a headache and a nagging sensation of incompleteness. When she rolled over and surveyed the wide, empty bed, she acknowledged the feeling for what it was—frustration, pure and simple.

Folding her hands under her head, she stared up at the painted ceiling. It was decorated with pastoral scenes of green gardens, blue skies and plump, rosy-fleshed maidens picnicking with gods in various shapes and sizes. Any other time, the detailed paintings and vivid colors would have fascinated her, but this morning they barely registered on her consciousness. Instead, her mind focused on the man in whose arms she'd passed the night.

Aurora stirred restlessly, her nerve endings tingling with the remembered sensation of his flesh pressed against hers. She could still feel the imprint of his arm wrapped around her waist and the brush of his wiry chest hairs against her back. A slow flush heated her skin when she remembered the way his rampant arousal had nestled against her rear. She'd had to fight an insidious urge to curve her bottom against him, to tease and taunt and test his arrogant decision not to take their . . . their relationship further.

Aurora gritted her teeth, staring sightlessly at the cavorting maidens. An inbred honesty forced her to acknowledge that Lucius Antonius, Roman chauvinist first-class, had ignited fires in her blood she'd never before experienced. And the blasted man was taking his own darn time putting the fires out, she thought with a grimace. If Luke ol' boy kept up this sexual cat-and-mouse game much longer, the beans were going to be so well spiced, they'd blow the lid off the pot.

Throwing back the scratchy covers, Aurora stalked to the marble ledge in the bathing alcove that held a covered jug of still-warm water. With a narrow strip of linen for a washcloth and a wedge of scented soap left by the women who'd attended her yesterday, she attacked her treacherous body. The realization that she desired the arrogant, overbearing captain irritated her beyond measure. Especially since he didn't seem exactly overwhelmed by his own stated desire. She was the one who'd lain awake in the darkness, fighting her body's urges, long after Lucius's breath had deepened to a slow, steady rasp in her ear. She flung down the makeshift washcloth, gathered her scattered garments, and dressed.

After a breakfast of unleavened bread, cheese and watered wine taken in the garden, Aurora paced the sunny patio until the sergeant of the household guard arrived.

"Hail, lady. I will take you to your companion."

"What, no escort? No dozen men to protect you?"

His face creased in a gap-toothed grin. "Nay, lady. The captain says you will not attempt escape without your friend, or offer violence."

Aurora frowned, but declined comment as she accompanied the burly soldier out of the commander's quarters and into the streaming sunlight. During the short walk to the stables, the thought teased her that Lucius Antonius was beginning to read her too well. He was playing with her mind as much as with her body. The urge to rock the Roman back on his heels grew with each step.

All thoughts of the captain fled, however, when she brushed past a guard and stepped into a small stone house near the stables. Sunlight filtered through shuttered windows and brightened the hut's single room, detailing its packed dirt floor, stone hearth and rough wooden benches. A single bed frame was pushed against one wall. The light also illuminated a solitary figure seated on a bench by the cooking fire.

"Charlie," Aurora called, moving forward. When her shadow fell across him, he jumped up, startled, and stumbled over the long chain anchoring his leg irons to the stone wall. Backing away as far as the small hut and chain would allow, her friend and copilot stared at her with wide, unfocused eyes.

"Charlie, please, don't be frightened. I ... I won't hurt you." Aurora forced the words out through an aching tightness in her throat.

"He cannot hear you, mistress."

Aurora swiveled, noticing for the first time the girl standing in a corner of the hut. She was young—in her teens, Aurora guessed—with the lank, dark hair and tanned skin of the desert tribes. She stood with one hand holding a woven basket and the other resting on her mounded stomach.

"Who are you?" Aurora asked. "What are you doing here?"

"I am called Jamille," the girl responded. "I was brought to care for this man when my belly became too big for me to pleasure the soldiers."

She spoke Latin with a low, guttural accent, but Aurora understood enough to feel an immediate rush of shocked sympathy. The girl was younger than some of her own nieces, whose most pressing concern was which shoes to wear with what outfit. Yet she was in the late stages of pregnancy, and her still, wary face reflected experiences Aurora prayed her nieces would never know.

"How long have you been with him?" Aurora's eyes darted back to Charlie.

The girl shrugged. "Since the night after he arrived."

So Lucius hadn't lied when he said Charlie had been cared for since the first days. Aurora felt a flicker of guilt, quickly stifled, at having doubted his word. "He's become used to me," the girl continued, "and will allow me close. I have bathed his shoulders with unguents as the physician directed, and cleansed his ears, but he has no hearing. He shakes his head often, like a dog with a tick."

The girl spoke with near-disinterest, as if the burden of caring for Charlie was just one more task in a lifetime of drudgery.

Aurora bit her lip, then settled herself on the wooden bench. She gave Charlie a gentle, coaxing smile and patted the seat. "Come on, sit down. Please."

He stared at her, eyes wide and wary.

"Charlie, I'm your friend. I'm Aurora."

Still he didn't move.

"Here, mistress, offer him food, and he will come to you."

Aurora's lips curled in distaste at the ripe figs in the girl's hand. The thought of bribing Charlie with bits of food, as if he were some starving, wounded animal, made her feel ill. She started to wave Jamille away, but stopped, hand lifted, when Charlie shuffled forward. His chains rattled with each hesitant step.

She held her breath as he neared, then reached out for the fruit. Jamille gave him a fig and passed the basket to Aurora. His eyes on the basket, Charlie sat down.

Aurora refused to give in to the feeling of hopelessness that enveloped her when she stepped out of the small hut an hour later. Although he'd given no sign of recognition, hadn't responded at all to her attempts to reach him, she was determined Charlie would recover. He would, she swore, striding through the narrow streets. He had to!

At least he wasn't frightened of her anymore. Aurora racked her memory, trying to recall what the flight surgeons had taught about shock and concussions during survival training. She knew enough to keep an injured crew member immobilized and warm after an accident, but long-term treatment was beyond her limited scope. Reluctantly she decided the captain's regimen for Charlie was probably the correct one. A quiet hut, constant care by this girl Jamille, and some exercise. Aurora would visit him daily and try to find some way to cut through the mists enveloping his mind.

Anxiety for Charlie made her short-tempered with Theodorus when he arrived later that morning, scrolls tucked under both arms.

"Please, mistress," he begged when she rose for the third time and began pacing the small room. "The captain wishes you to continue your studies. He wants you to know the calendar. You must be able to recite all the important festivals."

"I tell you I have no use for this knowledge. Besides, you've got so darned many gods and goddesses and holy days and festivals, I can't keep them all straight."

"But the feast in honor of Mars is tomorrow. 'Tis the fourteenth day of his special month. The captain says you are to attend the festivities. You need to understand the rituals. There will be many sacrifices, omens to be read, games in honor of the god."

Aurora stopped pacing and turned slowly toward the old man. Mars was the god of war, the deity most sacred to the Romans. He was so important to this race of soldiers that they'd named a month after him. March. So tomorrow was the fourteenth of March. It also just happened to be her birthday.

As if from a distance, she heard her brothers' hearty laughter, her mother's soft voice wishing her a year filled with happiness. The whole family had gathered to celebrate her birthday last year, knowing Aurora would be leaving soon for her assignment in Germany and wouldn't be home for her next one. It was the last time they had all been together. Aurora strained to capture the memory, to see their faces, but the sounds faded, the laughter dimmed. As if they had occurred in another lifetime. Another world.

At that moment, Aurora knew with absolute, gut-wrenching certainty that she'd never see her family again, that she wouldn't hug her parents, or loll on their wide sun porch with her brothers and sisters-in-law and a gaggle of nieces and nephews after a family gathering. That she was caught forever in another time, another place. For the first time, Aurora let the reality of her situation seep into her soul.

It was too much. First Charlie, and now this awful, shattering sense of loss. A small moan trembled on her lips. She pressed a hand to her mouth, holding it back.

"Truly, mistress, it will be a great feast. The games and races will last for several days, and—" The tutor's earnest attempts to capture her attention ceased at the sound of booted feet in the outer chamber.

She turned wide, stricken eyes on the figure framed in the doorway. The man she now thought of as Luke came forward and took her arms in a gentle hold.

"What ails you? Tell me, Aurora."

Shaking her head, she pulled back. His fingers tightened, and he gave her a little shake. "Why are your eyes filled with pain and whirling mists?"

Unable to speak, Aurora stared up at him. Her entire universe tilted on its axis, narrowing her life to this tiny space, this piece of time, this man. Everything she was, everything she knew, seemed to dance just out of her grasp, like dust motes drifting on sun-washed air. Aurora was afraid that if she moved, if she uttered any sound, the very light around her would shatter into a million crystalline particles and the world she knew would slip away forever.

Luke stared down at her, brows drawn together in a worried frown. Aurora could see her own reflection in his dark pupils, and she felt some of her panic subside. She was real. She existed. That was her image shimmering in his eyes.

"Come," he said abruptly.

Still shaken, she stumbled after him.

Luke flung open the door to his room and issued a low order to one of the guards, who sprinted off. Moderating his steps so that Aurora could keep up with him, he led her through the villa. Once they were outside, he pulled her to a halt at the bottom of the marble steps.

Aurora threw her head back, letting the sun beat down on her upturned face. Under its healing warmth, she felt the last of her frightened dismay melt away. The world righted itself, expanded. Gradually she assimilated the sounds of hobnailed sandals on cobblestone, the clatter of horses' hooves in the distance. The aroma of meat roasting for the noon meal drifted to her from the barracks area.

She opened her eyes to see Luke's dark head silhouetted against the blue sky. For a long, timeless moment, they stared at each other. Slowly, tentatively, he lifted one hand, and his fingers brushed her cheek in a light, soothing caress.

"Are you all right?"

Aurora ran her tongue over dry lips and nodded. As if suddenly becoming aware of where they stood, she looked around the busy square.

"Why are we here?"

"We're going to sweep the cobwebs from both our minds."

A low, rumbling roll of thunder punctuated his reply. Within moments, a pair of huge gray horses harnessed in tandem to a wooden chariot barreled around the corner and swept to a halt in front of them.

Aurora scrambled back up two steps as the horses skittered and danced on the cobbles. A soldier ran to hold their heads. The driver stepped down and handed Luke the reins. He mounted the chariot and wrapped the leather straps twice around one wrist, feeding the lines through his fingers, then held his other hand out to Aurora.

"Come."

"Uh-uh." She eyed the massive haunches and powerful hind legs of the nearest horse and backed up one more step. "If it's all the same to you, I'd just as soon go for a walk."

"Come, lady. You need to leave these walls behind and feel the wind whipping your face." One corner of his mouth lifted in a smile so full of devilment and daring, Aurora caught her breath. When he held out his hand to her once more, she knew she had to take it.

Edging away from the twitching hindquarters, she circled toward the back of the two-wheeled chariot. Placing her palm in his, she scrambled up. Luke moved her to the front, where she could grasp a wooden rail with both hands, and braced his body behind her.

"Are you ready?"

Her fingers clenched around the scrolled bar. "As ready as I'll ever be."

He flicked the reins, and the vehicle jerked forward. Jarring tremors shot through the plank floor of the chariot and tickled the soles of her feet as they moved over the rough cobblestones. For the first few minutes, Aurora concentrated on keeping her balance. By the time they'd traveled down the long avenue from the headquarters to the camp gates, she felt confident enough to dig her nails out of the wood where they'd embedded themselves. By the time the horses were clattering through the winding city streets, dodging animals and milling humanity, she'd found their rhythm and surged with, instead of bounced against, the pull of the vehicle.

When they left the city traffic behind and she felt the slap of dry desert air hit her face, she laughed in sheer delight. She was used to the sun dancing on her plane's silver wings and azure skies all around her. On her days off, she would put down the roof of her sports car and take to the roads. Confinement had eaten into her very being. Legs spread wide, arms braced against the rail, cocooned by Luke's massive strength, she felt the blood rush in her veins. Twisting her head, she shouted over the racket of wood and iron striking stone.

"Okay, big fella, open her up and let's see what this baby can do!"

Luke caught the excitement in her eyes, if not her words. His grin widened, and he slapped the reins against the horses' rumps. Aurora sucked in her breath as the perfectly matched grays lengthened their stride and the chariot flew over the road. They were heading west, into the afternoon sun. The basalt road stretched straight and endless before them, laid across the sands like a ribbon of black silk.

They slowed twice, once to maneuver around a slow-moving caravan, and then later as they neared a patch of dark green rising out of the desert sand. By then, Aurora's legs felt like rubber, and grit lined both her mouth and her eyelids.

"An oasis! An honest-to-goodness oasis!" she exclaimed through dry lips.

"Aye," he agreed, pulling the horses off the road, toward the towering palm trees. They needed little urging, having scented water and shade. "The caravan we passed will camp here this night. It's the first resting spot out of Dura, on the way to Palmyra.''

He reined in the horses beside a crystal-clear pool. Stepping down from the chariot, he put both hands around Aurora's waist and lifted her out. When her wobbly legs collapsed, she grabbed at his hands to steady herself.

"Here, sit beside the pool until the numbness leaves your legs.''

Luke settled her in the thick grass fringing the water, then tended to the horses. After they'd been unharnessed, watered and tied loosely to the chariot, he joined her. Aurora's brows rose as he stretched himself out on the grassy bank, hands behind his head. His short tunic inched up to reveal more muscled thigh than any one male had a right to.

"So where does this water come from?" she asked, more to divert her thoughts from the hair-roughened leg next to her than from any overwhelming interest in hydrology.

"It's fed by the Wadi Houran. Right now, the wadi is little more than an underground spring, but in the wet months it will become a raging river. This oasis is completely submerged when the rains come.''

Aurora surveyed the tranquil scene, trying to imagine the dry sand and the tiny pool under a torrent of swirling water. She leaned forward, cupping her hand to capture the cool wetness. With damp fingers, she wiped the corners of both eyes, then the gritty lines around her mouth.

"You're making mud of the dust," Luke drawled in lazy amusement. "You now have great circles around your eyes. You look like the little bears brought from the east.''

"Well, you're not exactly lily-white yourself, you know," she retorted. "You've got enough sand on you to qualify as a public beach.''

"We will rid ourselves of the sand." He rose with a smooth, liquid grace that only years of exercise and hard training could achieve. Before Aurora's startled eyes, he unbuckled his belt and let it slip to the grass. His light armor, tunic and loincloth followed in short order. Her stunned gaze traveled the length of his magnificent body.

Geez, the man was built! His thick ropes of muscles glistened with sweat under a light covering of body hair. The flesh of his belly stretched taut as he bent first one knee, then the other, to undo the straps of his sandals. Against his tanned skin, fading white lines marked what Aurora guessed were old battle scars. One ran halfway around his rib cage, another puckered at his elbow. But if the scars could be considered defects, they were his only ones, Aurora decided. When he straightened and grinned down at her, her throat closed.

"Shed your coverings and join me," he tossed over his shoulder as he headed for the pool. Watching his back and his trim buttocks, Aurora felt perspiration bead on her forehead.

"Come, Aurora. He who lives well, lives twice." At her confused look, he chuckled. "It's a saying, a . . ."

"I know, I know. A maxim," she muttered. "Probably something along the lines of 'Trust me, sweetie, I'll still respect you in the morning.'"

He submerged his torso inch by inch, until only his glinting brown eyes were above the water.

He was doing it again, Aurora realized suddenly. Laughing at her, toying with her. Adding more spice to the blasted bean pot. He planned to lure her into the water, play with her body, get her all hot and bothered and then bundle her back to the city with her blood pounding and her heart racing. Tonight they would mate, he'd promised. She knew, deep inside, that this time he meant to finish what he began. Tonight he would end their sexual skirmishing, and battle would be joined. Her pulse skittered at the thought.

Aurora's lips curved into a slow smile as she watched him cut through the water like a sleek, supple sea lion.

From her military training, she knew better than to let the adversary set the time and place to engage his forces. Senior Centurion Lucius Antonius had had things his way in their own particular battle of the sexes for too long. No longer would she wait like some timid second-century maiden for him to make his move.

She was here. He was here. This moment was as real as any would ever be for her. With a sense of having at last accepted what she could not change, Aurora rose.

Her fingers fumbled with the cord at her waist, then with the enameled pins that held her robe at the shoulders. The soft fabric fell in a pool of white at her feet, followed by her breastband and loin covering. She knelt to untie her sandals, then straightened, feet planted wide, toes curling into the grass. A sudden stillness in the pool told her she had the captain's attention. When she raised both arms to pull the gold ribbon from her hair and lift its heavy weight off her neck, the sound of his indrawn breath rippled across the water.

Slanting him her best sultry look, Aurora stepped into the pool. The water felt like liquid silk against her heated skin. Her eyes locked on his, she waded out until the water lapped at her chest. With a smooth, gliding breaststroke, she closed the distance between them. He treaded water while she circled him.

"I think you shall live twice this day, Senior Centurion," she said mockingly, throwing his own maxim back at him. "Mayhap even three or four times."

Beneath the sparkling surface, Aurora let her hands trail his body. Her fingers grazed his back, slid down, cupped his firm rear cheeks. She kneaded his flesh, discovering a previously unknown appreciation for that particular portion of the male anatomy.

Sliding one leg between his, Aurora ran her palms around his waist, along his lean rib cage, to his shoulders.

Her breasts flattened against his chest, and her pelvis rocked against his hips.

"Do you play with me, lady?"

"Oh, no," she breathed, taking immense pleasure in his clenched jaw and rigid muscles. "I'm not playing. This is for real."

"Is it the custom in your land for women to take the lead thus?"

"Sometimes," she murmured.

Her tongue darted out to lick the water from his neck. Following instincts she hadn't known she possessed, Aurora bared her teeth and nipped the muscle twitching at the juncture of his shoulder and neck. Buoyed by the water and her own mounting excitement, she rubbed her breasts and belly against him. When her nipples brushed against his wiry chest hair, a streak of white hot desire lanced through her. She bit back a groan and rubbed harder, closer. He jumped against her thigh.

She leaned back, far enough to look into his eyes. They flamed with pure, unadulterated male hunger. Yet still he held himself in check, his hands clenched at his sides, allowing her to explore and stroke and feather his skin with kisses. Aurora's half-playful desire to shatter his rigid control became a pulsing feminine need.

She kept herself anchored with one arm around the thick column of his neck while her free hand roamed at will. Her fingernails scraped against the flat pebble of his nipple, then pinched it gently. Aurora felt a flash of triumph when his eyes narrowed and his nostrils flared. Deliberately holding his look, she teased his nipple over and over, then slid her hand down the flat plane of his stomach. Muscles leaped under her hand when she combed eager fingers through the thick hair of his groin.

As if demanding attention, his shaft nudged against her hand. Aurora wrapped her fingers around it, marveling that it could feel smooth and silky and yet rock-hard at the same time. She continued to hold his hot, hungry gaze, but it took more effort now. Her hand slid up and down, shaping him, soothing him, squeezing him. Her head fell back and Aurora wet her dry lips with her tongue.

"End this game and mount me now, or I will take the reins myself." His voice rasped, low and urgent.

Panting, liquid with her own need, Aurora moved to comply. Evidently she didn't move fast enough. With an impatient grunt, Luke took control. Wrapping an arm about her waist, he raised her hips on his and positioned her over his probing shaft.

"Spread your legs, Aurora, goddess of light. Banish my darkness as you ride across the heavens."

Tightening his arm, he thrust her hips down. His member slid deep within her, stretching her, filling her.

The rough invasion startled Aurora out of her spiraling sensual web. Belatedly she realized that she'd lost control. And every shred of common sense. "Wait," she gasped. "Wait! I have no—no protection. We must—"

"I will protect you," he growled. He raised her a few tantalizing inches and held her against his chest.

"No, you don't understand. Luke... Lucius... Oh!"

In a swift, sure movement, he ground her hips down against his once more.

"This I understand."

Holding her in place, he began to move within her. Water sucked at her belly, splashed between her breasts. Aurora's eyes widened with startled pleasure. Her disjointed protests degenerated into a series of breathless gasps. Luke stilled even those, when he covered her lips with his.

With a helpless sense of inevitability, Aurora pushed aside all thought of birth control, of protection against disease. She doubted she could stop him now, even if she wanted to. Which she didn't. Heaven help her, she didn't. Breathing a tremulous sigh of surrender, she angled her head to take his kisses.

With a conqueror's sure instincts, he moved to take advantage of her capitulation. His tongue invaded her mouth in a dark dance that mimicked the rhythmic thrust of his hips. Keeping her lower body anchored to his with one strong arm, he used his other hand to tease and torment her breast. Her *small* breast. It appeared to fill his hand most satisfactorily, at least, and then his mouth. When his teeth rasped against a rigid, aching peak, Aurora flinched at the streak of raw sensation that shot through her. Immediately he soothed the afflicted spot with his tongue.

And still he ground his hips against her, lifting her, bringing her down against him, harder, faster. Aurora's legs churned the water around them as she fought for balance and then found his rhythm. Her heels kicked against the backs of his thighs, urging him on to an even more frantic pace. Her movements almost unbalanced them both and sent them toppling into the pool. He lifted his head and grinned at her.

"By all the stars, woman, you're like to drown us both. Come, I would finish this where my knees find some purchase and my hands can feel your every tremor."

Embarrassed by the little moan that escaped her when he slid out of her, Aurora buried her face in the warm skin of his neck. Even when he stretched her out in the thick grass, she refused to open her eyes. She didn't need to. Within seconds, he had claimed her again. His body covered hers, fitted itself to her as though they were two parts becoming one whole.

This time, however, his hand didn't leave once he'd guided himself into her. This time his fingers parted her, and he teased her as she had teased him. Finding the core of sensation buried within her folds, he rubbed and tugged and stoked her fires. Aurora felt flames flicker, low in her belly. They grew redder and darker and higher with each thrust, each stroke. She tore her mouth from his, panting, arching her back against the building pressure.

"Luke," she gasped. "I cannot...hold...back...."

"Then do not!" he growled, his voice hoarse. "Give yourself to me, Aurora. I will have all of you."

In her last rational moment, Aurora decided she didn't much care for his phrasing. As passionate declarations went, his could use a little work. And then she was beyond thinking at all. As instructed, she gave herself up to the feel of his hands, his body, the magic he worked within her. Waves of tight, sweet tension rose, receded, rose again. A long, low groan tore at the back of her throat.

She came in an explosion of light and pure molten sensation. Gasping, she arched her hips against his, seeking to ride the waves for a few seconds more.

Just when she thought her climax had peaked, Luke began to move toward his. Bracing both forearms beside her head, he dug his fingers into her hair. His kiss slammed into her with the same savage force as his lower body. Following instincts older than time, Aurora thrust her hips up to meet his, again and again. He stiffened suddenly, and then she felt him fill her. Aurora gained just enough conscious thought to wonder if her ribs would stand the pressure of his rigid, straining body before he gave a ragged breath and rolled off her.

Lying side by side in the cool grass, neither of them spoke for long minutes. At length Aurora opened her eyes to find him watching her, his head propped in one hand. A very satisfied, very male grin spread slowly across his face.

"As Sappho says, if the end is good, everything is good."

Aurora's own lips lifted. "Do you have a saying for everything? For every occasion?"

"Aye." He lifted his free hand to run a finger down her sternum. Taking one still-sensitized nipple between his thumb and forefinger, he tugged gently. "Shall I tell you what the poets say about breasts such as these?"

"No! Never mind! I'm not interested!" Aurora pushed his hand away from her aching, if not necessarily over-sized, breast and scrambled into a sitting position. She reached for her scattered clothing.

"What are you doing?"

"What does it look like? I'm getting dressed."

He plucked the linen loincloth out of her hand and tossed it over his shoulder. Aurora's mouth pursed in in-dignation as one of the horses plopped a large, dirty hoof right on the wrinkled fabric.

"Nice goin', big guy."

"You do not need clothes," he told her. "Not now. Not for many hours." His hands closed on her hips and slid her down in the grass again.

"Hey, doesn't it take some time to recharge your bat-teries? To rekindle your fires," she gasped in Latin, push-ing at the hands that spread her thighs.

"Aye, it does. Much time. And much effort."

Chapter 9

When they finally were ready to leave the oasis, Aurora couldn't find her loin covering, her breastband, or her gold hair ribbon. Either the horses had eaten them, having missed their dinner hour, or they'd sunk to the bottom of the pool during one of the captain's more innovative attempts to rekindle his fires. Aurora dressed in a haphazard way, hindered as much as helped by his roving hands.

The same caravan they'd passed many hours earlier topped the rise just as Luke lifted Aurora into the chariot. The outriders recognized them and galloped forward, wide grins splitting their faces at the sight of Aurora's tumbled hair and swollen lips. She was glad she couldn't understand their raucous gibes, which Luke tossed back with unruffled good humor. Only later did he inform her that he'd turned down two female camels that gave rich, sweet milk, and a mating pair of some other creature, in exchange for her favors.

Her legs ached from more than just the chariot ride by the time they reached the city's outskirts. Aurora discovered that what the vehicle lacked in modern comforts, like power steering and air-cushioned springs, it made up for in accessibility. Neither she nor Luke could resist the sensation of his arms wrapped around her breasts and her backside tucked against his loins during the long ride back. Aurora discovered that a moving chariot, while somewhat unsteady, held its own particular delights.

It was late afternoon by the time they topped a low rise and saw Dura laid out below them, bathed in the red-gold haze of the setting sun. Aurora leaned against Luke, reveling in the feel of his arms around her as they rode toward the city gates. A slow, delicious sense of lassitude filled both her mind and her body.

When they drove into the camp, however, Aurora's languor began to dissipate. The passing soldiers stopped to salute as their captain drove by. Their avid stares made her stiffen slowly. It was one thing for the caravaneers, or whatever they were called, to laugh and shout ribald catcalls in a garbled mixture of Latin and native dialect that she didn't understand. It was something else again for soldiers to smirk at her tangled hair and her disordered robes and nudge each other knowingly.

By the time they reached the steps of the villa, her cheeks were burning. The casual way the captain's hand brushed her bottom when she stepped down from the chariot upped her temperature several more degrees. The driver's wide-eyed stare didn't help, either.

"Go inside and take your ease," Lucius told her. "I have work yet that needs my attention."

That was it? A little afternoon delight in the desert, then back to work? The big, strong captain was going to go do "man" things, while she went inside to take her ease like some overwrought, stressed-out, totally worthless ... woman. Tight-lipped, Aurora lifted her skirts and turned to climb the stairs.

"I will join you later, for dinner."

The masculine complacency in his voice stopped Aurora in her tracks. Whirling, she placed both hands on her hips and sent the man who'd turned her insides to molten lava just a short half-hour ago a frigid look.

"I don't wish to go inside. I don't wish to 'take my ease.' And I don't particularly wish you to join me later. Or at any time in the foreseeable future."

Lucius stared up at the woman who stood on the step above him with hands on hips and eyes as cold and stormy as the seas that crashed against the coast of northern Britannia in the winter. A frown of genuine bewilderment flitted across his face.

What in Hades ailed the female? Not an hour ago, she'd opened herself to him, surrendered to him in the most elemental way a woman could to a man. Now she bristled like a spiny aloe plant and issued declarations in a tone that set his jaw. Mayhap it was the long ride that had set off her prickly temper, Lucius decided. She was no more used to charioteering than she'd been to riding astride a horse. Or to riding a man, he thought with a sudden, fierce stab of satisfaction. Her wild gasps of surprised pleasure had told him that clearly. He decided to overlook her sudden spurt of temper.

"What you wish in this instance matters not, lady," he replied, his tone light. "I have not time to dally further with you."

Her mouth sagged, then snapped closed. "Dally? You have not time to dally with me?" she repeated in a low, furious voice.

Lucius realized that his choice of words had perhaps been unwise.

She came down a step, her eyes smoldering. "Was that what we just did? Dally?"

"Look you, lady, 'tis not meet that we discuss such matters here, in the streets. Nor with such an interested audience," he added dryly.

She swung around, as if noticing for the first time the trooper holding the horses' reins, the charioteer, and the assorted members of the household guard who had come forth at their commander's return, all watching with openmouthed interest. At her furious glare, the men looked hastily away.

Lucius felt a smile tug at his lips. "Go inside, and I will join you later."

"Do not dare dismiss me as you would some lackey," she snarled.

Any inclination to smile Lucius might have had fled instantly. His jaw tightened.

"I've told you before to watch the tone you use with me. It appears your memory falls short, lady. I will deal with it, and with you, later. Go inside. Now!"

Her eyes flared with fury. Lucius met her look with a hard one of his own. Do not, he warned her silently. Do not challenge me further.

After a long, silent moment, she whirled and ascended the stairs with a decided lack of grace. She tripped over her long robe, grabbed her skirts in both fists and muttered a curse that she'd surely never learned from Theodorus before she stomped through the villa's portals.

Lucius issued a curt order to the sergeant of the household guard to ensure that the lady stayed within, then strode across the street to the headquarters, spurred by irritation and exasperation in equal measure.

By the sword of Mars, what *was* it about this particular female that made him want to peel off her clothes layer by layer and bury himself in her flesh one minute, and take the flat of his sword to her backside the next? When would she learn that she could not take that haughty tone with him, or contradict him in front of his men? Wherever and whenever she had come from, 'twas time she learned that such behavior was not permitted here.

He ignored the scribe who jumped to attention, and stalked into his office, slamming the door behind him. The thud of the iron-bound door hitting the jamb made him shake his head in disgust. Where was his vaunted patience now, he wondered? Where was the discipline he had always prided himself upon?

Gone, he admitted ruefully as he crossed to his desk. Tossed to the winds by a pair of rebellious gray eyes and a red, ripe mouth that tasted of honey and exotic spices. He paused, his eyes on the neatly arranged scrolls awaiting him, but his mind on the woman he'd taken into the desert. By Juno, she'd been wild and sweet and hungry. As hungry as he. For a few hours there, in that shady oasis, she'd flamed in his arms. This Aurora, this bringer of light and heat, had been all that he'd known she would be from the first moment he saw her sprawled in the desert sands. Lucius felt his irritation fade, to be replaced by a tight aching, low in his belly, as he remembered the scenes from the oasis.

His mouth twisted into a wry grin. He'd planned to reenact a few of those scenes this very night, if the gods and a hearty dinner gave him the strength. Now he'd have to deal with the lady's uncertain temper first. The thought daunted him more than he would have imagined it could just a few short days ago.

What was worse, he was damned if he knew just how to deal with either the lady or her temper. Any soldier who dared question a superior's orders risked flogging at best, or death at worst. Any native who rebelled against Rome's hand ended up in the arena or the slave market. Yet this stubborn, irreverent, disrespectful woman challenged him constantly. And he allowed it. Shaking his head, he sat down at his desk. Idly he toyed with the sharpened stylus the scribe had thoughtfully placed beside a fresh pot of ink.

What *was* it about this female? Lucius wondered again with some amusement. She was but a woman, after all, less beautiful than many, more headstrong than most. She was his to command. She awaited his pleasure even now. At the thought, a primitive bolt of satisfaction shot through him. The thick wooden stylus snapped in his hands.

A hesitant knock sounded on his door. Lucius laid the broken pieces aside.

"Enter."

His chief scribe stepped inside and peered at Lucius, as if uncertain of the captain's strange mood. "Do you wish me to summon the officers awaiting your return, Senior Centurion?"

"Who needs to see me?"

"The senior engineer. He would speak with you about the silver chariot he's retrieving from the desert. And about an aqueduct that has crumbled at the north end of the city. The quartermaster also needs your seal on the monthly pay vouchers. He's been waiting to see you since early afternoon," the scribe added, with seeming nonchalance.

Lucius knew well the man's words masked an intense curiosity. Never before had the commander ignored his duties to take an afternoon of play. Rumors were no doubt already circulating the camp about how he'd driven out with the flame-haired captive. And about how he'd ridden back in with that same captive tousled and half dressed.

"Show the senior engineer in," Lucius replied, ignoring the scribe's bright, inquiring look.

As he waited, Lucius settled behind his desk and pulled the stack of scrolls toward him. A few hours' work, he was convinced, would help him regain his perspective on this prickly female. Then he would deal with her tendency toward disrespect in a calm, dispassionate manner.

'Twas time they settled this matter of her uncertain temper once and for all.

It was time that she and a certain hardheaded Roman settled things once and for all, Aurora fumed. Who did he think he was? Just who the hell did he think he was?

Her skirts swirled about her ankles as she paced the captain's bedchamber from one end to the other. Hostility coursed through her veins with each angry stride. Where did he get off, ordering her about like some first-year plebe at the academy? Did he think she shook in her sneakers every time he barked an order? Did he think that he could just... just *use* her, then brush her off like some bubbleheaded, dewy-eyed twit? If he did, Senior Centurion Lucius Something had another think coming.

Aurora stopped in midstride, her hands curling into fists. Painful honesty licked at the edges of her anger. Why shouldn't he think he could brush her off? Why shouldn't he treat her like someone he'd picked up on Sunset Boulevard and taken for a little spin? She hadn't given him much reason to treat her differently. Cringing, she remembered the way she'd all but attacked the man at the oasis.

Vivid, startling images of those hours in the desert filled her mind and sent embarrassment and excitement pulsing through her in alternating waves. Her legs suddenly felt wobbly, and she groped for the chair beside the writing table where Luke kept his books and few personal effects.

Luke, her conscience jeered. She called him Luke, as though they were best buddies. Intimate acquaintances. Lovers. They were none of those, Aurora realized, swallowing thickly. Not even friends. With a sinking sensation, she realized she'd just made love to a man she didn't even like.

Well, she admitted with reluctant honesty, maybe there were one or two things she liked about him. That crooked grin, for starters. Those annoying maxims he whipped out on all occasions. And his buns. His neat, tight buns.

Aurora groaned and shook her head. She'd never thought she was the kind of a woman to be seduced by a man's posterior, even if the posterior in question happened to be pretty spectacular.

Her annoying innate honesty pricked at her again.

Okay, okay, so she hasn't exactly been seduced. So she was human. She was a healthy female in her prime, for Pete's sake. She didn't need to make a federal case out of the fact that she was attracted to a healthy male—a very healthy male!—in his prime. But, she decided, she did need to nip this attraction in the bud. So to speak.

Rising, Aurora began to pace once more. By slow degrees, grim reality set in. She couldn't afford to let herself get involved with this man, either physically or emotionally. She couldn't let him become her anchor to this world. Every seminar she'd ever attended on prisoner exchanges and hostage negotiations warned against becoming emotionally dependent on your captors. Every Vietnam-era POW who had addressed her class had stressed how vital it was to keep your inner core intact, to hold on to your identity. And one of the ways to do that was to stay in touch with other Americans in the same situation, if possible.

Her mouth set, Aurora whirled and headed for the door. She needed to see Charlie. Even if he didn't hear her, didn't speak to her, she could at least talk to him. In English! Suddenly, desperately, she wanted to hear her own language.

She threw open the door, intending to summon an escort. Two iron-tipped pikes clanked together in front of her face.

Aurora jumped back like a scalded cat. When she recovered her breath, she gave the guards a confused look.

"Why do you stop me? I wish to visit my companion, as I've done before."

"Nay, lady. The captain left orders that you were to rest this afternoon and not be disturbed."

Aurora drew herself up. "I don't wish to rest. I wish to visit my companion."

"Nay, lady."

"Summon the sergeant of the household guard," she ground out. "We'll settle this matter with him."

The legionary eyed her warily, but shook his head. "The captain's orders were very explicit. You are to keep within. He will attend you later."

Aurora stepped back and slammed the door.

When the chamber door opened some hours later, Aurora took the offensive. Lifting her chin, she met his steady gaze.

"I would that we settle my state, Senior Centurion."

His brows rose. After a moment, he inclined his head gravely. "That is my intention."

"Yes, well, I want you to know that...that I will not be treated as I was this afternoon."

The words came out sounding a bit more imperious than they had when Aurora rehearsed them.

His eyes narrowed. "Will you not?"

Oh, hell, she'd stepped in it now. Might as well wade all the way through. "No, I will not."

"How was it that you were treated that you object to?"

Aurora didn't care for the silky tone of his voice. It was too cool, too...unfriendly. Nor did she like the way his hand was toying with his silver belt buckle. If he thought that they were going to have a repeat performance of this afternoon...

As if reading her mind, he inquired, "Did you not like the manner in which we mated at the oasis?"

"What?"

"At the oasis, did you not find release? Your moans signaled otherwise to me, but mayhap I misheard them."

"No! I mean, yes." She took a deep breath. "Yes, I found release, and well you know it. That... that is not what I object to."

"Good."

When the silver buckle gave, Aurora's brows snapped together. Lucius caught his belt as it fell from his lean hips and slipped his scabbard off.

"Then mayhap it was the way we coupled during the ride home. 'Twas a rough ride, I'll admit. Did you object to the manner in which I took you in the chariot, with your—"

"Stop!" Red singed Aurora's cheeks. "'Twas not the ride home that I object to."

A muscle quivered on one side of his jaw. "Then it must be the scene you enacted when we arrived back at camp."

He turned to lay the scabbard on the small table. "I, too, found that scene objectionable. Most objectionable."

When he faced her again, the leather belt dangled from one fist. Aurora felt the hairs on the back of her neck rise.

"I've warned you before not to take a disrespectful tone with me. That you would do so, and in front of my men, angered me. Greatly."

The look on his face made Aurora decide that discretion might just be the better part of valor right now. She searched for the formal Latin phrases to signal a truce. "'Twas not well done, I admit."

"'Twas not."

"I apologize," she said stiffly.

His expression didn't soften.

"You angered me, as well, you know," Aurora added, goaded. As soon as she spoke, she saw at once that she'd spoiled the effect of her apology.

His lips thinned to a hard line. "It hangs by a hair here, woman."

"What hangs—?" She stopped, not sure whether that was another one of his blasted sayings or some crude sexual innuendo. She didn't much care either way. She'd had enough of big, bad Commander Luke and his Gestapo tactics. Crossing the room, she stood toe-to-toe with him.

"If you think you can intimidate me with that damned belt and some stupid saying I don't even understand, forget it." She gestured scornfully toward the leather strap. "And if you think to use that on me, go ahead and try. Give it your best shot. Otherwise, put the thing away and stop playing mind games with me."

He struggled with her words, then glanced down at the belt in his hand. His eyes held a distinct gleam when they lifted to Aurora again.

"If you wish me to flagellate you, I will," he offered with a small smile. "'Tis not one of my particular pleasures, but I know some women, as well as some men, crave it."

He raised his fist and wrapped the leather strap around it a few times.

"Hey, wait a minute."

"This will pain me as much as it pleasures you."

"No, wait!" Aurora scrambled back, both palms upraised, as he started across the room toward her. "Wait! You misunderstand me, Senior Centurion!"

"Do I?"

"Yes. I wasn't *asking* for the belt. Well, I was, but not in the manner you think. I don't wish...I don't crave..." Aurora stumbled to a halt. Her eyes narrowed in sudden suspicion. "Are you laughing? Damn it, are you laughing at me? You *are!*"

"Nay." His lips quivered. "Well, aye."

"Why, you damned chauvinist!" Her Latin failed her completely. "You sadistic, sleazy, evil-minded . . ."

His laughter erupted, full and deep-throated. If Aurora hadn't been so mortified, she might have appreciated the way his head went back and the way the rich, rolling sound filled the room. Her chagrin must have shone in her eyes, because after a moment Luke took her chin in his hand with a mocking smile.

"You should have seen your eyes when I offered to . . . stroke your passions."

"Yeah, well, I never claimed to be the most sophisticated person in the world," Aurora mumbled, embarrassed and just the tiniest bit breathless. It was only after he'd rubbed his thumb across her lower lip and taken the rest of her breath away that she'd realized what she'd done. Captain Aurora Durant, United States Air Force, had just confessed her naïveté to a man who'd never experienced television or flush toilets or chili dogs, let alone Madonna or the Grateful Dead.

His thumb stroked the outline of her mouth. "Nay, you are not sophisticated. Neither are you disciplined."

"I have been known to lose my cool on occasion," she admitted, shivering at his touch.

"Nor are you very wise."

"Look, let's not get carried away with this character analysis."

"I've debated this past hour and more how best to punish your disrespect this afternoon."

Aurora pulled back as far as the firm hold on her chin would allow. "Punish?"

"Aye."

She jerked her head free. "Punish?"

He met her outraged look with a steady stare. "Did you think I would let your behavior this afternoon pass, after having warned you on more than one occasion to moderate your tone?''

"But I've already apologized for speaking so."

"And that is supposed to end the matter?"

"Yes. Of course. In my world, an apology suffices."

Aurora felt a twinge of guilt at the blatant fabrication, but decided this wasn't the time to admit that in her world any creep with a grudge was just as likely to drive up alongside your car and blow your head off as apologize.

"You are not in your world now. You are in mine."

Aurora frowned at the implacable note in his voice. He was serious, she realized. The guy was actually serious.

"In my world," he continued evenly, "you are subject to my laws. And to me. I must see that you do not forget your place again."

She swallowed to relieve the sudden tightening in her throat. "Isn't this where we began this conversation? Let us discuss 'my place,' as you see it."

"There is naught to discuss. You have but one place. Remove your clothes and get you to it."

Aurora felt the blood drain from her face. "What?"

"Get into bed."

Stunned, she stared up at his face. There was no softening in his eyes, no hint that he was teasing her, as he had with that blasted belt a few moments ago. No trace of the man who had held her in his arms in a sun-warmed bed of grass.

"How . . . how can you speak to me so?"

"I may speak to you as I will," he said deliberately. "The same does not hold true for you. Slaves must guard their tongues, lest they lose them."

"Slaves?" she whispered. "Slaves?"

He frowned, as if impatient with her theatrics.

"You—" She struggled for breath. "You consider me a slave?"

Lucius drew in a deep breath, forcing himself to ignore the stricken expression in her eyes. He had begun this course. He would finish it. 'Twas time Aurora understood once and for all that she was his. For as long as he wanted her. In any way he wanted her. He hardened his voice.

"You know well what you are. And ere this night is done, you will know, as well, what you may expect at my hand if you again forget your place."

He took her arm to lead her to the bed. She stumbled against him, as though in a daze. When Lucius righted her, the stunned disbelief in her eyes made him pause. He swung her around to face him and grasped her forearms.

"What in Hades do you think you are, if not a slave?"

She stared helplessly up at him, searching for an answer.

"You cannot claim Roman citizenship," he reminded her harshly. "Nor can you prove that you are freeborn. I took you from the sands, from the companion who could not hold you. So what are you, lady, if not mine?"

"I . . . I'm an officer in the . . ."

He gave her a little shake. "Whatever you once were, you are no longer. When you passed into my hands, you became the property of Rome. You are mine. To use as I will."

She flinched. The little color left in her face faded away completely.

Lucius stifled a stab of compunction. "Listen to me, Aurora. From what you've told me, I know that you held a different status in your land. You did things no man who calls himself a man should have allowed you to do. But, for whatever reason, the gods chose to give you to me. They sent you from your world, to mine. 'Tis time you accepted that and learned what you must to survive here."

Hardening his heart against the bleak, lost look that filled her eyes, Lucius brought her closer to his chest.

" 'Tis time you took your place in this world. Tomorrow we celebrate the feast of Mars. I want you beside me at the banquet I host for the city dignitaries."

Aurora wet her lips. "You . . . you would display your slave."

"I would display my prize," he told her. "This gift the gods have given me."

"Your whore, you mean."

The bitterness in her voice lashed at him. "Nay," he replied firmly. "Not whore. Concubine."

"You'll excuse me if I fail to see the distinction."

Lucius hid a smile at the faint challenge in her tone. She did not lose her spirit for long, this Aurora.

"A concubine holds a respected position within a man's household. A position recognized in Roman law. Later, when I have the time and the inclination, I'll explain what rights you have, and have not."

She made no answer, only stared up at him with an indefinable emotion clouding her gray eyes.

Lucius drew her against him and tucked her head into his shoulder. " 'Tis not so terrible a fate," he said softly. "We discovered this afternoon how well we fit together."

She stood stiff and unmoving in his arms.

His lips brushed the top of her head. "I made you forget your world for a few hours this day. In time, I'll make you forget it completely."

And he would, he vowed silently as he bent and lifted her in his arms. He carried her to the bed, feeling the need rise in him to possess her, to claim her.

He laid her on the platform and stepped back. His gaze raked her long limbs and slender body. The primal urge to mark her with his scent and fill her with his seed swept through him.

"Roman," she said quietly.

He paused in the act of pulling off his tunic. "Aye?"

"I am not your slave." He frowned down at her.

"Nor will I play the whore for you, whatever you may call it."

"Aurora..."

"I choose who I will lie with. And I do not choose to lie with you this night."

Chapter 10

He should have taken her, Lucius thought savagely. By the sword of Mars, he should have taken her. He raised the goblet clenched in his right fist and took a long swallow. Sweet liquid fire slid down his throat and curled in his belly.

"By Jupiter, will you look at that!" Quintus nudged his commander with one elbow. His slightly slurred voice resonated with reverent awe.

Lucius followed his deputy's line of sight across the crowded banquet room and fastened on a pair of whirling, undulating hips. Colorful veils wreathed the sinuous flesh, flaring out with every twist and dip and turn. Silver bells attached to a jewel-encrusted belly band jangled a tempestuous rhythm, while tiny cymbals on the dancer's long, tapered fingers kept the beat. A dark-haired, doe-eyed girl of incredible beauty, she provided her audience with a feast for the ears, as well as the eyes.

Noticing the captain's attention, she danced slowly across the hall toward him, never missing a beat. Her feet, laden with silver anklets and bell rings on each toe, wove an intricate pattern on the brightly colored mosaic tiles.

Lucius watched her through half-lidded eyes and searched within himself for a response to the provocative, exotic movements of her slender hips.

None came.

Hell, he thought in biting self-disgust. He should have taken her.

"Captain." Quintus sloshed wine from his goblet as he gestured toward the dancer, now only a few feet away. "She dances for you."

He should never have allowed Aurora's cold, still face to weaken his resolve, Lucius thought. He shouldn't have let the memory of their hours in the oasis deflect him from his intention to remind her of her place. Nor, he thought with a wry grimace, should he have left her with the warning that she had but one day to reconcile herself to her fate. The *last* thing he should have given the blasted female was time to dig her trenches deeper and fortify herself against him.

"Captain." Quintus leaned toward him eagerly. "I think she wishes you to pluck the scarves from her belt."

Lucius glanced up. Above her half veil, the girl's dark eyes smiled an invitation. Lucius twisted his mouth upwards and reached out to grasp the end of a fluttering, floating scarf.

"Do you know what night this is, Charlie?" Aurora patted the hand resting loosely in hers. "It's the first of March. Well, maybe not exactly the first, but something pretty close to it."

Shadowed blue eyes met hers for a moment, then skittered away.

Aurora pressed her lips together. "Do you remember how you and a bunch of the guys from the squadron were going to take me to the officers' club to celebrate my birthday? To hear the country-western band in the downstairs lounge? You were going to bribe them to play 'Wabash Canon Ball' in my honor. In honor of my dad's days on the railroad. Remember?''

Her lanky copilot frowned.

Aurora held her breath, then let it out on a sigh when he hunched his shoulders and looked away.

" 'Tis no use, mistress. He does not speak.''

"He will," Aurora insisted. "He will.''

Jamille shrugged and went back to grinding corn in a shallow stone trough. Her arms moved awkwardly around the swollen mound of her stomach.

After another half hour of one-sided conversation, Aurora gave up. Resting her shoulders against the stone wall, she closed her eyes. Raucous shouts, and a high-pitched, drunken squeal, brought them open again. She glanced at the open doorway.

"It sounds like the party's just getting started," she commented.

Neither the girl nor Charlie responded.

"Do you not wish to join the feasting?" Aurora asked Jamille, feeling the need for some conversation, any conversation.

"Nay, mistress.''

"I can stay with my friend," Aurora offered, and wished with all her heart the words were true. If only she could stay here with Charlie in this small stone hut. For the rest of this night and every night, to come. Dread of what awaited her when she left the hut curled in her stomach.

"I would not join those pigs," Jamille muttered, breaking into Aurora's bleak thoughts. She spat in the dirt. "Those Roman swine, desecrating their bodies with their drunkenness.''

Aurora, who had been known to enjoy a cool beer or an occasional glass of wine, looked at the girl curiously. "Do you not drink ale or wine?''

Jamille gave her a closed, flat look, as if regretting that she'd said as much as she had.

"Do your people not drink the water of life?"

At Aurora's use of the Latin term for spirits, scorn flashed in Jamille's eyes. "Of course, but with moderation, as in all things. Only these Romans and the weak, decadent towns people they have corrupted indulge in such debaucheries."

At the distant sound of retching, Aurora could only agree with the girl's assessment of the Roman revelries. The feasting had gone on for hours and had spilled into the camp streets. More than one soldier would sport a sore head in the morning. She muttered a fierce hope that Commander Luke would be one of them. She hoped he was as sick as a dog. She hoped he couldn't even lift his head without feeling his eyeballs spin. Oh, God, she hoped he didn't have the strength to "end her woman's foolishness," as he'd promised to do.

Her hands shook as she recalled their confrontation last night. She swallowed, remembering how he'd leaned over her, his eyes hard and flat. He'd seen that she intended to fight him. With every ounce of strength she possessed. Her fingers had curled into claws. Her every muscle had tensed. She'd seen the calculation in his eyes as he decided what it would take to subdue her. At that moment, Aurora had realized that he really believed she belonged to him, that she was his to use as he would.

And then, incredibly, he'd backed off. He'd given her a night and a day to get her act together—or words to that effect. Aurora had until after the ceremonies in honor of Mars to accept the fact that she was his toy, his little sex slave. He would excuse her from the games and the feast, but when he returned from the festivities, he wanted her there, in his bed, this foolishness behind her.

At another drunken shout, Aurora wondered wildly how long this Mars business lasted.

"Tell me about your people," she asked Jamille desperately. She needed something, anything, to take her mind off the confrontation to come.

The girl shrugged. "We are of the desert."

"Where are their lands?"

Jamille sat back on her heels. "We are of the desert, mistress. We have no lands. We have all lands."

"That must make it tough for the mailman," Aurora murmured in English. At the girl's confused glance, she went on in Latin. "So where then is your home? How would you find your tribe?"

The first hint of a smile softened the girl's face. "Anyone of the desert knows how to find their tribe. I herded my father's camels from the time I could walk. I know how far they can travel in summer, when they must water every four days. I know how far they travel in winter, when they water but once a month or less. I can tell their hoof marks from all others and track them across the desert, even in the midst of a great herd."

Genuinely curious now, Aurora leaned forward. "Are your father's camels part of a great herd?"

All traces of softness melted from the girl's face. "The Romans killed my father, in the same raid in which I was taken."

"I'm sorry. Have you no family now?"

Jamille's chin lifted proudly. "I am of the al Azab lineage. My family traces its line back from my father, to my father's father, and unto his father and beyond. My brother, Talib ibn Salem al Azab, now rules our tribe. These Romans calls him the fox of the desert."

A tentative idea formed at the back of Aurora's mind. "Could you find his camp?"

Jamille studied Aurora's face for long, silent moments before responding. "The Romans destroyed his camp some weeks ago. They killed many of my uncles and cousins, and used the women most shamefully."

A sick feeling curled in Aurora's stomach. Vaguely she recalled Theodorus telling her that Luke—that Lucius Antonius had led a retaliatory strike against a desert raider. Had he 'used' this girl's relatives shamefully? As he intended to use her?

"But they didn't take al Azab," Jamille said with low, vicious satisfaction. "He yet lives, and builds his strength in a corner of the desert no Roman has yet found."

Aurora knelt in the dirt. The idea had now blossomed into a full-fledged plan. Her heart pounding, she grasped the girl's arm. "Could you take us there, to your brother? You and me and Charlie?"

Jamille's eyes narrowed on Aurora's face. After a long moment, she nodded slowly. "Aye."

"Gather bread, and what water you can carry," Aurora whispered. "We leave tonight."

The girl's face lost its blank mask. Incredibly, she grinned. "We don't need to carry water, mistress. I know where to find it. At this time of the year, the desert abounds."

Using both hands, she pushed herself awkwardly to her feet.

"Oh, boy," Aurora murmured. In her gathering excitement, she'd forgotten all about the girl's condition. "When is your baby due?"

The girl shrugged. "When the gods will it."

Ignoring Aurora's small groan, she turned and took Charlie's hand. He rose like a docile puppy and followed her to the back of the hut. She stretched to wrap a length of cloth around his thin shoulders, then pull it up to drape his head.

At least Charlie's chains had been removed, Aurora thought thankfully. It was going to be difficult enough to make her way through the camp with a pregnant woman and a shuffling, vacant eyed man in tow. The chains might have been a little too hard to explain.

She picked up a shallow bowl, and the silver urn she'd brought in the vain hope that Charlie might want to celebrate her birthday with her. Motioning to her traveling companions to stay far back in the shadows of the hut, she took a deep breath, then sauntered to the door.

"Soldier."

The legionary pushed himself off the wall where he'd propped his shoulders.

Aurora gave him a small smile. "I thank you for escorting me here this night, when I know you would rather be with your friends, celebrating."

"I will celebrate when I return you to your quarters, lady." He eyed her hopefully. "Are you ready to go back?"

"Aye." Aurora sighed, then lifted her face to the dark, moonless sky. "Nay. Not yet."

A burst of laughter in the distance brought both their heads around.

"Here, take a bowl of wine with me," she offered, holding out the urn. "Let us share a few moments before I must return to my cell."

If the trooper thought the captain's luxurious villa was not quite the equivalent of a cell, he was too well trained to say so.

Leaning her shoulder against the rough wood of the hut's doorjamb, Aurora splashed wine into the shallow bowl and held it out. He eyed it dubiously.

"'Tis from the captain's own stores," Aurora told him innocently. "Fine, rich red, from the Thracian slopes, or so I'm told."

Aurora could see duty warring on his face with a desire to join the revelry. Duty lost, or at least got put on hold. He reached for the bowl.

"I wish you good health, lady." He saluted her, then raised the silver dish to his lips.

"And I wish you good-night," Aurora muttered, just before her fist slammed into his stomach. She dodged sideways as wine spewed out of his open mouth. Eyes round with surprise, he doubled over. A chop to the back of his neck finished the job. Aurora caught his arm as he went down, and swung him through the hut's open door. She spun around to peer out the door, afraid one of the revelers dancing the streets might have seen or heard the takedown.

"They would not hear the heavens crashing down on their heads this night," Jamille whispered in her ear. "Here, put this on, quickly."

Aurora ducked for the girl to throw a ragged length of cloth over her head. It settled over her shoulders serape-style and hid almost every inch of her pristine white robe.

When Jamille's hands moved over her face, Aurora jerked back. "Ugh! What *is* that?"

"Mutton fat mixed with ashes. Be still."

When they stepped out into the night air a few moments later, Aurora was nearly gagging. With every step she took, the noxious stench that clung to her face and hair wafted into her nostrils. She sure as heck didn't have to worry about being molested by any drunken soldiers. When they smelled her, they'd probably trip over their own feet getting out of her path.

As it turned out, the soldiers they encountered were too busy with willing women of their own to molest anyone. Despite her nervousness, Aurora could only gape when she saw what was happening in the fountain that graced the center of the plaza. Raucous laughter floated on the night air, along with shouted encouragement from several women to the grinning trooper who was impersonating— or trying to impersonate—Neptune cavorting with the sea Sirens.

"Ha, Gaius! You must stiffen your trident!" a feminine voice called.

Using the shadows for cover, Aurora led her charges past the bawdy group. She drew in a shallow breath as the sounds of their revelry faded, only to have it catch immediately in her throat. A door opened just ahead of them, spilling light out into the street, and a big, barrel-chested legionary stumbled out. Even with the huge haunch of roasted meat he waved in one hand and the silly grin he wore on his face, Aurora recognized him immediately. The sergeant of the household guard.

She pressed back into the shadows, gesturing violently to the others to do the same. Thankfully, the door slammed shut behind the sergeant, closing off the light. Aurora closed her eyes in a silent prayer that he was too drunk to notice them. Opening them slowly, she watched him fumble under his tunic at his loincloth, obviously intending to relieve himself. Evidently the task was too difficult to manage one-handed. He tore off a healthy bite, then tossed the joint of meat aside. Chewing contentedly, he watered the wall.

Aurora felt sweat break out on her forehead while she waited for him to finish. The man had the kidneys of an elephant. When he was finally done and turned to reenter the house, she sagged in relief. But then the man stopped suddenly and stood stock-still.

He couldn't have seen them, Aurora thought in panic. They were too far back in the shadows. Her fingers curled into fists.

He gave a funny, choking cough, then bent over. Two beefy hands came up to claw at his throat. He sank to his knees, wheezing and choking.

"Now," Jamille whispered sharply. She darted past Aurora, Charlie in tow. "Come now, while he's down."

Aurora felt her way along the dark wall opposite the choking man. Two steps, three, then he was behind her. She turned to follow the dark shadows ahead of her. Hoarse, tortured gasps seared her ears with every step.

She couldn't do it. She just couldn't do it. "Wait!" she called out softly. Turning, she raced back to the helpless and now nearly comatose sergeant. Wrapping both arms around his middle, just below his rib cage, she clenched her fists into a hard ball. Jerking upward with all her might, she drove them into his diaphragm. It was the first time she'd ever used the Heimlich maneuver in a real-life situation, but it worked. By God, it worked, just as her instructors had assured her it would.

The gasping, wheezing sergeant sagged in her arms and dragged air into his starved lungs. He recovered more quickly than Aurora would ever have dreamed possible. Before she could unwrap her arms, he grabbed her forearm for support and slewed around on his knees.

"I thank you," he croaked, peering up at her in the darkness. "I know not what you did, but I—" His eyes narrowed. "*Domina?* Lady Aurora, is that you?"

"Oh, hell."

Aurora didn't waste another moment. For the second time in the space of a few heartbeats, the sergeant slumped to the pavement.

"Why didn't you let the swine choke?" Jamille hissed as she rejoined her and Charlie.

"I have no quarrel with these soldiers," Aurora shot back. Only with their commander, she added silently.

"Bah!" The girl spat onto the cobbles, clearly disgusted but aware that this was no time to argue. "Come, this way!"

"The gates are the other direction."

"The gates are too well guarded. We'll have to climb the wall."

Aurora glanced down at the girl's bulging stomach. Yeah. Right. Climb the wall.

"Come!"

Jamille tugged Charlie down a side street. Aurora shook her head and followed.

The streets narrowed, slanting upward toward the highest point of the camp. The sounds of revelry grew fainter and farther behind them as they headed toward the parapet that overlooked the river Euphrates. Charlie stumbled every few steps, unable to keep his balance. Aurora caught him as he pitched forward, almost tumbling Jamille to the cobbles. He must have severely damaged his inner ear, Aurora realized with a sinking feeling in the pit of her stomach. Wonderful. She was going to climb a wall with a pregnant woman and a man who'd lost his sense of balance.

They were all breathless and panting by the time they reached the wall. Jamille especially seemed winded, bending over to drag in long, slow breaths. Aurora crouched beside her, thankful that the barrier was lower than she'd feared. She could boost the other two over, then scramble over herself.

Sentries marched along the wall in the distance, the sound of their hobnailed sandals striking stone just carrying over the laughter and shouts that rang through the camp.

Aurora eased her shoulder out from under Charlie's and stretched up on tiptoe to peer over the edge. The sight that greeted her sent the breath back down her throat. Aghast, she turned to face Jamille.

"It must be three hundred feet straight down!"

"It is the only way!" The girl pressed a hand to the side of her belly. "We must climb down to the river and follow its course."

Aurora risked another look over the parapet. Far below, the Euphrates gleamed like a silent ribbon of silver. "It's too dangerous for you. We must find another—"

The sound of footsteps cut through her whisper.

"The sentry!" Jamille's eyes were narrow slits of ebony. "We must go, mistress. Now, or not at all."

"It's too dangerous."

"Please!"

"No. No way. You can't make it down that steep slope."

"I can," Jamille insisted in a fierce whisper. "If it means my freedom, I can."

Aurora saw the desperate urgency in the girl's eyes. "Okay, okay. We'll go for it."

She eased over the wall on her stomach, wishing air force survival training had included a session on mountain climbing. With her breath lodged in her throat, Aurora planted a cautious foot on the narrow ledge of earth beside the wall. The ground sloped sharply, then dropped away into the night.

Lowering herself to a sitting position, Aurora groped for a handhold. Sharp rocks cut into her palms, then her fingers clutched the smooth curve of a wind-sculptured tree root. She slid a few feet on her bottom, then transferred her grasping hold to another root. Peering down the steep slope, she saw it was dotted with scrubby bushes.

They might make it, Aurora thought as she slid a few more feet. They just might make it.

They might have—if Charlie hadn't overbalanced just as he reached for a handhold. He missed the tree completely. His hand waved wildly in the empty air, and then his body skittered down the sheer, rocky surface.

"Charlie!" Aurora held on to a root with one hand and grabbed desperately at his ragged tunic with the other. She caught a corner of the material just as he slid past.

For long, heart-stopping seconds, his bare feet scrabbled for purchase. His weight pulled the fabric inexorably from Aurora's frantic fingers.

"Jamille! Help!"

The girl slithered past.

"I . . . I have him, mistress."

Disoriented, his balance completely lost, Charlie twisted and flung himself sideways. He landed square atop Jamille.

"Ah!"

The girl's involuntary cry of pain cut through the night. She held on to Charlie with both hands.

Aurora's arm wrenched as their combined weight pulled at her hold on the thick, stubby root. She clutched at her copilot's tunic, praying as she'd never prayed before. Miraculously, the fabric held. With Jamille clinging to him like a limpet, Charlie found a handhold. The pressure on Aurora's shoulder socket eased, and she sobbed with relief.

They lay in the dark, gasping, panting, shivering in delayed reaction.

"Who goes there?"

At almost the same moment the guard's cry rang out some distance away along the wall, Jamille gave a low, guttural groan.

"Come on," Aurora panted, slipping an arm through Charlie's. "We've got to get farther down, into the shadows, before we're discovered."

She slithered a few feet down the slope, tugging Charlie with her. "Jamille!" she whispered. "Come!"

"Nay, mistress." The girl's breathless pant barely carried to Aurora.

"Who goes there?"

The guard's shout was closer now, almost directly above them.

"Jamille, you must come. Now."

"I...I cannot." Jamille sucked in a sharp breath, then met Aurora's eyes helplessly. "The baby comes."

"What?"

"You go, mistress. Go to my brother."

Aurora scrambled back up the few feet separating them. "Are you crazy? I'm not leaving you!"

Charlie crawled past her. He crouched beside the girl, his face screwed into stark lines of fear.

"Go," Jamille panted. "Go to my brother. Follow the river north until—" She grunted. It was a long, low animal sound that raised the hairs on Aurora's neck. "North...until...until the sun's shadow at midmorn... falls across an outcropping of rock that looks...that looks like a lion's head. Go straight into the sun thence. My...my brother will find you."

"I'm not leaving you." Jaws tight, Aurora reached for the girl. Charlie brushed her hands aside and pulled Jamille into his arms.

The sound of an iron-tipped striking stone just a few feet away sent them all into an instinctive crouch.

"Who is down there? Speak!" Even before the echoes of the guard's call had died away, his shout cut the night. "Sergeant! Sergeant! Come at once!"

"Go," Jamille urged Aurora in desperation. "Go!"

Another spear clanged into the rocks beside them.

"Charlie..."

Her copilot neither saw nor heard Aurora's low call. With Jamille cradled in his arms, he rocked back and forth as much as his precarious perch would allow.

"Go, mistress," Jamille panted. "I will care for your friend as best I can. Go! Now!"

Chapter 11

"They were on the west escarpment, Captain, halfway down to the river."

The lean, weathered sergeant cleared his throat, obviously nervous about interrupting the senior centurion in the midst of his sumptuous banquet for the city's dignitaries.

"They would have made their escape, had not the girl's cry alerted us."

As he surveyed the prisoners, Lucius felt his jaw clench so tightly that a muscle spasmed in one cheek. Behind him, a buzz of excited murmurs gave evidence of the crowd's avid interest.

His officers fanned out in a semicircle on either side. They glanced from him to the small patrol, then back to him again, as though unsure of his reaction. Invited guests peered over the officers' shoulders and craned to see. Slaves huddled together at the far end of the hall, frightened yet morbidly fascinated by the drama about to be

enacted. They knew all too well Rome's brutal response to
any who tried to escape her hold.

A low groan sliced through the hum. Lucius turned
stiffly to face the native girl. Held in a legionary's hard
grasp, she was bowed with the weight of her belly. Sweat
pearled on her pallid face. The male prisoner strained
against the ropes that bound him, leaning toward her.
Confusion and concern sharpened the dull glaze in his
eyes. When the girl grunted and rose up on her toes, he
jerked against his guard's hold and tried to go to her. The
soldier cuffed him viciously on the side of the head, sending him to his knees.

"Do that again and your arm comes back a stump!"
Aurora snarled.

All eyes in the room swung to the filthy, tattered, blazing creature. Lucius clamped his teeth together so hard his
jaw ached. By all that was holy, did the woman not realize
the precipice that yawned at her feet? Could she not exercise one ounce of discretion? Could she not keep her
mouth shut this once?

The sergeant cast her a wary look and stepped forward.

"We came close to skewering them to the mountainside
with pikes, Captain. I planned to leave them for the vul-
tures to feast on as an example to all, but I recognized the
woman as your... uh, as the one who..."

He trailed to a stop. A dull red crept up his leathery
cheeks. "I knew you would wish to decide their punishment yourself," he finished lamely.

The hushed silence behind Lucius told him the rest of the
crowd recognized the woman, as well. Despite her ragged
coverings, and the odoriferous muck streaked down her
face and neck, there was no mistaking her. None other had
such a tumble of wine-red tresses. None other would stand
with arms bound behind her and yet threaten a guard in so
fearsome a tone.

"Aye," Lucius ground out. "I will decide the punishment myself."

Conscious of the crowd at his back, he cursed silently, savagely. As Rome's senior administrator, he had a duty to enforce the laws and see that justice was dispensed equally to all. Yet every man in the room knew that this was the captive he kept within his chambers. The one he used for his private pleasures. They waited now, his officers and the city fathers, to see if he would put his own interests before Rome's. His own desires before his duty.

As he fought to subdue his fury that she would dare try to escape him, Lucius felt his old, original suspicions come flooding back. Where had she been going? Who had she been fleeing to? Was Aurora not the unwilling traveler from another time she claimed to be, but an enemy in disguise?

The object of his furious thought jerked in the guard's hold. "Release me. I wish to speak."

The fool! She would force the issue here, in front of everyone. Before Lucius could order the prisoners taken away to await his decision, she called out in a loud, clear voice.

"Senior Centurion! These two with me are innocent of any intent to escape. My companion knows not what he does. In his confused state, I convinced him to go with me. The girl was forced to come with us under threat to her person. If there is to be any punishment, it is mine, and mine alone."

When—*if*—he got her back to his chambers, he would skin her, Lucius decided. He would beat her within an inch of her life, and teach her once and for all to keep her damned tongue still.

"Do you know what Rome's punishment is for escaped slaves?" he asked, his low voice vibrating in its intensity.

She blinked at his tone, her foolish bravado slipping for an instant. Recovering almost immediately, she gave him a look filled with scorn. "I can imagine."

He would flay her. He would peel every scrap of clothing off her body and— A trickle of sweat rolled down one of his temples.

"Nay, you cannot imagine. You cannot begin to imagine."

He'd sheltered her too much these past weeks, Lucius realized grimly. He'd protected her and shut her away from too much of the camp. Well, she was about to learn in the most brutal way possible that life outside her small room was not all books and tutors.

"If a simple infraction like spilling the master's wine or overcooking his dinner can earn a beating, what do you think happens to those who attempt escape?"

"I...I don't know."

His fist shot out and grabbed the front of her tattered covering. The guards fell back as he hauled her within inches of his face.

"What do you think the punishment is?" His eyes blazed down into hers.

"I...I don't know!"

She was frightened now. He could see doubt, and the first tendrils of fear, curling in her pupils. Good, he thought viciously. He drew in a deep breath, then immediately wished he hadn't. By the gods, what had she rolled in? He released her abruptly, and she stumbled backward.

Lucius could feel the eyes boring into his back. Every person in the room waited avidly to see what he would do. For a moment, he hesitated. The gods help him, for a moment he actually hesitated. But then he squared his shoulders and prepared to pronounce her sentence.

"Captain!"

A raspy voice at the back of the hall halted the words on his lips. Eyes narrowed, he watched the crowd shuffle aside to allow the soldier who had just entered to come forward.

"Captain, may I speak?"

Lucius kept his face impassive as he studied the bedraggled legionary before him. Never before had he seen the sergeant of his household guard in anything less than a spotless uniform and polished armor. Now the man looked as though he'd been dragged backward through a pigsty. Wondering what in the name of Jupiter the man had to do with the events of the night, Lucius nodded.

The sergeant stood at rigid attention. "I would ask that I be allowed to take any punishment you decree for this lady."

Ignoring the wave of excited murmurs that rose behind him, Lucius stared at the man. "Explain yourself."

"She saved my life," the sergeant said simply. "She was fleeing, yet she stopped and dislodged a piece of meat that was stuck in my gullet."

He gave Aurora a grateful look, then lifted his lips in a broad, gap-toothed grin. "I would have thanked her then, but she knocked me senseless."

Laughter erupted around him, easing the tension of a few moments before.

Lucius felt his own sharp supicions fade. Only Aurora would stop to save the life of a soldier as she fled. She was not escaping *to* someone. She was escaping *from* someone. From him, and the ultimatum he had given her.

"I would take her punishment," the sergeant finished, "in return for my life."

"Your offer does you credit, but 'tis not necessary."

"Captain, I would not see her—"

"Hey," Aurora interjected, "I can fight my own battles."

He would flay her! "Be silent!" he roared. "Speak not another word!"

Her eyes widened to great silver pools.

Satisfied that she was silenced, at least for the moment, Lucius faced the crowd. "Know you all that this woman is mine. I have claimed her as concubine. She has slept in my bed, taken my seed."

Every eye in the hall turned toward the dirty, disheveled woman. Under her coating of filth, a wave of red washed up her neck. She stiffened and sent Lucius a glare that would have sliced through his heart, not to mention his manhood, had it been a sword. For the first time since the guards had hauled their prisoners into the hall, he smiled.

"Since she is mine, under the law I am responsible for her actions. All her actions. Any punishment she has earned, I will take."

Excited babble burst out behind him. Roman officers, bejeweled city elders and awed slaves alike were astounded.

"I belong to no man," Aurora said, scowling. "I fight my own battles!"

Lucius reached for her with both hands. He'd take a whip to her! He'd—

A sobbing, gasping moan made him whirl. The native girl sank to her knees. Her guard looked down at her doubled-over body in stunned surprise.

"What ails the wench?" Lucius snapped.

"I—I know not, Captain," the man stuttered.

The girl groaned again.

"You ying-yangs!" Aurora shouldered her way toward the girl. "She's having her baby!"

Aurora leaned against one wall of the cell, wishing with all her heart and soul that she could help. That she could melt into the little crowd surrounding Jamille and assist her, somehow, some way.

Okay, so she wasn't the handiest person to have around at a birthing. So she'd never seen any of her nieces and nephews until they were scrubbed and wrapped in pink or blue blankets and held up by nurses behind a glass partition. So she wasn't exactly sure whether Jamille's low, rolling grunts indicated pain or imminent birth. That still wasn't any reason for Charlie to elbow her out of the way as he paced the cell with Jamille or for the midwife to ignore her every tentative offer to help.

Aurora folded her arms across her chest defensively. She was a woman, wasn't she? She was supposed to have instincts about things like birthing and babies. She wanted to help. She needed desperately to help. To assist Jamille. And to keep her mind off the hours that crawled by.

The small group took another turn about the cell, Jamille panting with the effort it cost her. Charlie held one arm, his face fierce with concentration. The midwife held the other while she crooned an ancient incantation. They didn't have much room to maneuver. The cell was similar to the one Aurora had occupied when she first arrived, devoid of all furnishings except a pile of straw on the floor and a trough that served for sanitation. The bags and bundles the midwife had brought were stacked in one end, next to two crouching female slaves who would assist her at the birthing.

Jamille stumbled, then righted herself and continued her dogged, determined pacing. Above her head, the barred window showed the first hazy pink streaks of dawn.

Aurora tore her eyes from the drama before her to stare at the small square of light. The goddess she was named for was just beginning her chariot ride across the sky, she realized with a start. Bringing light after darkness. Bringing hope after despair. Surely, with the daylight, Luke would come.

Where was he? she wondered. What was he doing? Why hadn't he summoned her or spoken to her after that scene in the great hall so many hours ago? Why had he sent them here, to this small cell, and provided the midwife and her assistants, but not come himself? What was this punishment that he had insisted he would take for her?

Aurora had spent a good portion of the long night regretting her rash escape attempt and wondering what the penalty would be. In the time she'd been at Dura, she'd hadn't seen any mistreated slaves other than those in the stables. But she knew from the history books that Rome wasn't exactly known for their humane treatment of prisoners. Hazy tales of brandings and of slaves being fed to lampreys kept in huge tanks rose to haunt her.

As Aurora watched the window fill with dull, grayish light, one potential horror after another flitted through her mind. Her flesh cringed at the thought of what Luke would face in her stead. Anger at the savagery of the times burned in her stomach. Gradually her innate honesty forced Aurora to acknowledge that Rome wasn't the only empire with a history of abusing its captured peoples. The United States had had a pretty dismal record in its early days. The treatment of POWs during the Vietnam era was another modern low. No, Rome didn't have a corner on cruelty. Not by a long shot.

A long-drawn-out grunt from the other side of the room broke into her gruesome thoughts. She watched as Jamille sank to her knees. Panting, the girl placed both palms on the floor and rocked back and forth, back and forth. Her head hung down between her shoulder blades. Her black hair, unbound and slick with sweat, brushed the stone floor. Suddenly she stiffened and arched her back. A low keening whistled from her lips.

"'Tis time, little one," the midwife crooned, kneeling to wipe Jamille's red, straining face. "'Tis time."

Charlie knelt beside her, his eyes grim and determined. The two slaves opened the baskets and began to lay out cloths and implements that Aurora could only guess at the use of.

When the birth liquid gushed out moments later, Charlie and the midwife positioned themselves behind Jamille's widespread knees. Grabbing a soft, clean rag, Aurora rushed to the girl's side.

Evidently she had some woman's instincts, after all. Each time Jamille arched her back and strained, Aurora felt her muscles clench and heave in sympathy. Her breath shortened to small, panting gasps that matched the frantic rhythm of the girl's. She wiped Jamille's face. She whispered meaningless words of encouragement. And she felt a wrenching within herself when at last the baby moved.

Hours later, the clang of the bolt being drawn back shattered the stillness of the small cell. Aurora scrambled up, her heart pounding. She waited while the guards stood aside and a helmeted, cloaked figure strode inside.

"Ave, domina."

A crushing wave of disappointment washed through Aurora. *"Ave,* Centurion Quintus."

"The captain sent me to see how the girl fares."

"He . . . he would not come himself?"

"Nay, he would not. He battles in the arena in a few hours, and would not drain his strength."

Aurora felt the blood leave her face. "In the arena?"

"Aye."

"You mean...you mean, he battles with a gladiator? Is this the punishment I would have faced?"

"A gladiator?" The blonde shook his head in amusement. "Gladiators are highly trained fighters. They don't waste their skills on mere slaves. Nay, you would have faced a beast."

"A beast?" Aurora gasped. "A beast? As in lions or tigers?"

"Or mayhap a panther." The deputy shrugged. "The prisoner never knows until the gates open."

Her jaw sagged at his casual unconcern. "You don't sound very worried," she snapped when she recovered.

He glanced at her in surprise. "Why should I be worried? Here at Dura, at least, the prisoners who take part in the wild beast fights are allowed a weapon. The captain stopped sending unarmed slaves to the arena the first day he arrived. Allowing them a weapon makes the game more sporting."

"A game? You think facing a panther in the arena is a game?"

She'd never understand men, Aurora thought furiously. She'd spent her childhood surrounded by brothers and her adult life in a predominantly male environment, but she was continually surprised at what the masculine portion of the species considered amusement. The thought of Luke facing a lion or a panther did not amuse her. Not in the least.

"He could be hurt!" she shouted. "Maimed for life!"

"Not the captain," Quintus scoffed. "He trains every day with sword and spear. I once saw him and one other take down a charging bull elephant."

A tiny wail from the far side of the cell interrupted their argument. Guilt at having awakened the child warred with soaring anxiety as Aurora followed Quintus over to where Jamille lay in the straw, her baby at her breast. At their approach, Charlie scrambled to his feet. Balling his fists, he placed himself protectively in front of the girl.

Quintus eyed him thoughtfully, then turned back to Aurora. "His eyes are sharper, less confused, than they were before."

"Yes, I guess so."

"Mayhap he regains his senses."

Aurora waved an impatient hand. "Yes, yes, mayhap."

At any other time, Aurora would have latched on to this confirmation of her own hopes that Charlie might be recovering. At this moment, however, she had other things on her mind. Things with claws and fangs.

"Centurion, when does the captain go to the arena?"

"Within the hour, I would guess," he replied. "He needs time to exercise and oil his body."

"I want to see him. Please, take me to him."

"Nay, lady. I told you, the captain does not wish to see you now. He must conserve his strength."

"And speaking with me would drain his strength?"

Quintus sent her a wry look. "I don't believe it was speech that he planned to have with you. I believe he mentioned that, were he to see you before the contest, he would wear out his arm beating you. Or his..." He made a small gesture. "His..."

Aurora choked. "I get the picture!"

"Just so."

His expression told Aurora that he believe she deserved whatever she got. And then some. Aurora lifted her chin.

"Will you see him before the games?"

"Aye."

"Tell him... tell him..."

"What, lady?"

"Oh, hell, I don't know." She raked a hand through her hair. What in heaven's name were you supposed to say to a guy about to wrestle a lion or a tiger for you. "Tell him that I read something in one of the scrolls Theodorus brought. It said that luck is the companion of courage."

One blond brow arched. "A maxim, lady? You begin to sound like the captain."

"Great," she muttered. "Just what I needed to hear right now."

His eyes softened at her obvious distress. "Worry not. The captain has courage aplenty. He doesn't need luck."

He turned toward the door, then paused, eyeing Aurora silently for a moment. "But if aught should happen, if some mischance should occur, know you that Senior Centurion Antonius has prepared the documents conferring citizen status on you. Not that anything will happen," he added at her stricken look.

What time was it?

Aurora leaned her crossed arms on her knees, pressed her shoulders against the rough stones and stared at the small window high on the opposite wall. She tried to judge just how far the dying sun had moved across the window opening. Since Charlie and Jamille and the baby had been removed from the cell and taken back to their own hut, she'd lost all track of time. Surely it must be late afternoon or early evening by now. Surely the games were over!

Why didn't Lucius come?

Why didn't Quintus, at least, come?

What time was it?

God, she wished she had her watch.

Vaguely Aurora recognized the irony of her sudden preoccupation with time. Somehow the fact that she hadn't been able to measure the passage of time these past few hours seemed worse, so much worse, than the fact that she had defied time altogether.

She squinted up at the window, pretending not to notice the way the sun's last rays painted the stones a bright red. Bloodred. Closing her eyes she blocked out the color, but it danced on her lids, surrounding her, filling her mind with images that made her heart pump with slow, leaden beats.

No! Not Luke! He was in excellent shape, as Quintus had stated and she herself could personally attest to. He had an athlete's smooth coordination and lightning reflexes. His arms and legs were roped with muscles that had the tensile strength of steel. Aurora should know. She'd felt them around her often enough.

She rested her head against the stones and tried to analyze the fluttering ache in the region of her chest. It was more than fear that he might be hurt, she acknowledged. It was a slow, agonizing dread that he might die. That he might be lost to her, after she'd crossed eighteen centuries to find him.

Aurora groaned and covered her face with both hands. She couldn't believe she'd fallen in love with a hardheaded, muscle-bound barbarian. One who would fight for her, even when she didn't particularly want him to. One whose most tender, sharing moment was when he ordered her to give herself to him.

But give herself she had, Aurora acknowledged painfully. Sometime between wrestling with him in the desert sands beside her plane and facing him across the crowded banquet hall, she'd given more than she would ever have dreamed possible to this man. This arrogant, chauvinistic male who made her pulse race and her blood sing whenever she looked at him. This warrior who even now battled some wild beast for her.

Oh, God, what time was it?

Chapter 12

When at last she heard footsteps echoing in the hall, the light outside her window had faded completely and Aurora was a shivering, shimmering bundle of nerves. She whirled to face the door, fists clenched, heart pounding.

The iron bolt screeched in protest. The heavy wood panel crashed open.

He was bloodstained.

All but naked.

Magnificent.

He stepped into the cell. Across the room, his eyes gleamed with a feral light. Aurora's glad cry of welcome died in her throat.

A blood-streaked arm reached out for the door. The hinges groaned, and then the timbers slammed against the lintel.

"Luke..." she began hesitantly, unable to interpret the look on his face.

"Do not," he growled, moving toward her with the slow, sinuous grace of a jaguar. "Do not say a word. I swore when this was over I would teach you once and for all to hold your tongue."

"But what happened? Are you badly hurt?"

He grabbed her forearms.

"Do not..."

Her shoulders struck the wall.

"...speak..."

His body crashed into hers, pinning her against the stone.

"...a word."

His mouth took hers in savage possession.

Aurora couldn't breathe, much less speak. She could only feel his hard flesh against hers. And touch his warm skin. And taste his hungry male need. Her fingers curled against the bare planes of his chest, burying themselves in hair matted with blood and sweat.

His hips ground against hers. His tongue thrust past her teeth, hot and fierce in its demand. Aurora gave a fleeting prayer of thanks that she'd washed the noxious grease from her face and arms, then opened her mouth to his. When he dragged his lips from hers, it was to bury them in her neck. Aurora felt his teeth rake her skin. Keeping her pinned to the wall, Luke lifted one hand to her shoulder. With a swift, hard pull, he shredded the tattered material she still wore as a mantle over her stained robe, then ripped off the robe itself.

With a flash of insight, Aurora understood his rough, urgent need. The twentieth-century woman in her rebelled for an instant, then wavered. Her half-formed protest stuck in her throat. He had fought for her, had battled some fearsome beast for her. Now he would claim his prize. In his world, he'd won the right to her. In his world, she acknowledged that right. Something primal, something deep and elemental, surged within Aurora. She arched her back, offering her body up to him.

"Luke..." She breathed his name on a half moan.

He raised his head. His dark eyes glinted with golden lights. "By all that is holy, woman, you will learn to hold your tongue if I have to have you on your knees to do it."

Aurora's primitive instincts vanished. In the space of a heartbeat, she was transformed from a willing, submissive female into a woman who'd darn well have some say in how this game was played. Angling her head, she gave him a narrow-eyed glance.

"You want me on my knees, big guy? Well, if you think you can handle it..."

Wedging her arms against his chest, Aurora opened some space between them. Slowly, feeling every stone and rocky protuberance, she slid down the wall.

Lucius grabbed at her hair. "Aurora!" he snarled. "Do not toy with me!"

"To paraphrase a general of my time," she murmured, "I have not yet begun to toy."

Slicking her hands down his thighs, Aurora drank in the feel of his taut, corded muscles. Eyes closed, she trailed a wet track down his belly with her tongue. The salty tang of sweat and what she knew must be blood tingled on her lips.

"Aurora!" His fingers tightened in her hair.

She blew against the skin of his stomach, stirring the wiry hairs of his groin. "Aye, Lucius?" she crooned.

"By all the gods, I—"

His harsh words ended on a strangled note as her lips closed over his straining arousal. They slid down his satiny length, feeling every ridge, every pulsing vein. Cupping her hands around his buttocks, Aurora brought him fully into her mouth.

With a low groan, he arched toward her.

Her fingers curled into his firm flesh. Holding him steady, she worked her magic on his eager, leaping member. Her wet lips stroked him, shaped him, drew him to greater length and even more rigid hardness.

He groaned again, then used the fingers still tangled in her hair to tilt her head back. "This changes naught," he ground out. "When this is done, we will yet settle matters."

Teasing, tasting, tracing his length with her tongue, Aurora slipped a hand between his legs to cup his tight sack. "When I finish with you," she promised, rubbing her lips against the velvety head, "you won't have the strength to settle anything."

She was wrong on at least two counts.

Aurora didn't quite get to finish with Luke before he stopped her. And he had more than enough strength left to reach down and pull her upright. Bracing her against the wall, he used one hand to lift her bottom, then slid into her wet, welcoming channel. Aurora wrapped a leg around his hips and both arms around his neck.

"Now," he whispered hoarsely in her ear. "Now you may finish. Finish us both."

As if she needed his permission! Just the feel of him within her was enough to make the muscles low in Aurora's belly clench. She squeezed her thighs, let them slacken, then squeezed again, giving herself up completely to an intense, compelling rhythm. Her rasping pants mingled with Luke's thick, labored breathing. While she could still form a coherent thought, Aurora wondered why it sounded as though they were engaged in some desperate struggle. Then she realized that it was a struggle. An ancient battle. The most basic, instinctive drive of any being. She and Luke strained and panted and ground against each other with the urge to mate, to meld with one another, to make two into one. Aurora had never felt this primitive, this raw, before. There was only her. And Luke. Locked together in their need.

She tightened her arms, drawing his head down to hers. Hungrily she explored his mouth, seeking, demanding, giving. Aurora hoped he could taste himself on her, as she had tasted him.

Luke braced one closed fist against the wall. A roar filled his ears, louder and more urgent than the noise of the arena had ever been. With his good hand, he pulled Aurora forward against his chest so that the stones wouldn't abrade her back. He wanted to feel her breasts flatten against his chest, her pelvis fit into his. He was desperate with the need to fill her with his life force.

Legs spread, his arm wrapped around her waist, Luke supported her while she moved against him in a mating dance that brought her to a shuddering, gripping climax. He gave a low, savage groan, then thrust upward, impaling her on his shaft. Once, twice, his leg muscles straining, his stomach clenching. And then he poured himself into her. For the first time since the moment the guards had pushed their three bedraggled captives into the great hall, Lucius felt a measure of relief. Holding Aurora tight, he sank to the stone floor.

When her rippling waves of pleasure finally ebbed, Aurora stretched out beside him and rested her head on his chest. The furious thundering under her ear made her smile with feline satisfaction. They lay intertwined for long, quiet moments. Idly Aurora wondered if they were ever destined to make love in a bed. She trailed her fingers across his chest, then grimaced when they encountered dried blood. He couldn't be very seriously injured, she reasoned. Not the way he had just performed. Still, the blood worried her. Propping herself up on one elbow, she ran her hand lightly down his body. When her fingers passed over a series of crusted ridges, she swallowed.

"Was it very bad?" she asked softly.

"Nay," he mumbled, his eyes closed. "It was good. Very good."

She gave a choking laugh. "In the arena, you dope. Was it very bad?"

He opened his eyes and sent Aurora a slumbrous look that almost made her forget she was lying naked on a cold, bumpy floor. She wet her lips. He smiled and reached up to trace the path of her tongue.

"Oh, my God."

Aurora jerked her head back, staring at his hand in shock. What she'd taken for blood-encrusted scratches were deep, lacerating wounds.

"What did you fight? What did this? A lion?"

"A bear," Lucius told her casually, peering at his hand. "A particularly evil-tempered one, too. The thing must have been starved for weeks before being let loose in the arena. He came close to having me for dinner."

Appalled, Aurora pushed herself up and sat cross-legged on the stone. Cradling his hand in both of hers, she bent to examine his hurts. The back of his hand was criss-crossed with claw marks, and when she turned it over she saw that the palm was even worse. At least the wounds had been stitched, with thick black thread. Aurora swallowed and raised her eyes to his.

"I'm sorry," she whispered. "I'm so sorry that you were hurt because of me."

He gave a rueful, self-deprecating laugh that only added to her anguish. "I was hurt because I grow too old and too slow to be battling bears in the arena." He paused, then continued in a low voice. "I trust I won't need to do so again on your account?"

Aurora met his steady gaze. With a feeling that she was committing herself to far more than she realized, she shook her head. "Nay, you won't have to battle in the arena on my account again."

Fierce satisfaction flared in his eyes, until she added the kicker. "As long as you don't try again to keep me in my 'place.'"

He groaned and flopped back on the floor. "Would that I could."

Aurora ignored him as she bent over his injured hand once more. To her relief, she saw that the stitches were covered with a thick protective salve. At least he'd had that much medical attention.

"Why in the world didn't the doctor bandage your hand when he cleaned these wounds and set the stitches?"

"He wished to, but 'tis my sword hand. I cannot manage a weapon with my hand bandaged."

"Are you crazy? These cuts could get... They could..." Aurora didn't know the word for *infection* in Latin. She wasn't even sure there was one. "The cuts could become putrid," she finished.

"I've been a soldier too long to worry about my wounds. I'll recover, or not, as the gods will."

"Wrong!" Aurora released him and scrambled to her feet. "Get up. Come on, get up. We're going to go back to your chambers and wrap that hand."

She bent to gather the scattered remnants of her robes and threw them on haphazardly, concerned only with covering herself and getting Luke back to his chambers. Holding up her long, trailing skirts with one hand, Aurora turned in exasperation. He stood still and unmoving, his expression unreadable in the dim light.

She planted a hand on either hip. "What? What is it? Oh, Lord, you're not going to give me another maxim now, are you?"

Lucius couldn't have voiced any quotation at that moment, even if he'd been able to think of one. The emotion that suddenly gripped him precluded rational thought. He stood stiff and still, surprised by the intensity of the feelings coursing through him. The physical battle in the arena and the wild coupling with Aurora should have drained every vestige of his strength. Yet seeing her there, illuminated by the hazy glow of the rising moon, he felt it return in slow, pumping waves.

She was smeared with dirt from her forehead to her bare toes, and with what he suspected was his blood, as well. Her robe hung in tatters about her slender frame, while her hair could have housed a nest of field mice without anyone being the wiser. A faint aroma of rancid mutton fat clung to her skin, although he'd been too driven with the need to mate with her earlier to notice it. Yet Luke was sure he'd never seen or smelled anyone more vibrant and desirable than this woman who even now glared at him. If he didn't ache in every corner of his body, he'd lay her back down on the stones and bury himself in her once more.

It was all he could do to grin and take her arm in his one relatively undamaged hand. "Nay. No quotations. There are none I can think of appropriate for the moment."

"Well, that's a first!"

It was only after they'd repaired to Luke's villa, tended to his hand, bathed each other and tumbled exhausted into bed that Aurora realized they'd never really gotten around to settling her status. She nestled against Luke's side, listening to the soft, even rustle of his breath in the darkness. From the confused collage of emotions that she'd experience these past twenty-four hours, Aurora extracted two.

While sleep tugged at the edges of her consciousness, she mulled over the fact that Luke had arranged with his deputy to give her citizenship status if anything happened to him. Her fingers tightened convulsively around the arm she nuzzled against. Nothing had happened, she reminded herself sternly. At least nothing that he wouldn't recover from. But she made a silent pledge to remind him of the arrangement in the morning.

She'd need citizenship, Aurora decided. She'd need equal status in his world, since she seemed to have committed herself to it. With her unspoken promise not to attempt another escape, she had acknowledged Luke's hold over her. Just as she had earlier acknowledged to herself that she loved him. Aurora stirred, not exactly sure what her newfound feelings meant for her or for Luke.

She was too tired to figure them out tonight, though. This business of being in love was too confusing, too exhausting. And, she suspected, too one-sided just yet. She'd have to do something about that, Aurora thought sleepily.

A faint smile curved her lips as she snuggled closer to Luke's warmth. If he thought he'd had his hands full with that bear in the arena, he was in for a big surprise. The poor man didn't know that he'd just grabbed a tiger by the tail.

Aurora awoke the next morning to an empty bed and a sense of purpose. For the first time since she'd stumbled into the past, she'd decided that she'd have a role in it. She just had to figure what that role would be. First things first, however.

Knowing that Luke wouldn't allow his wounds to keep him from his military duties, Aurora threw back the bed coverings and wrapped a mantle around her shoulders. With a newfound authority, she tripped to the door and flung it open.

"Send a runner to the baths," Aurora told the guard imperiously. "If the senior bath attendant is available, ask her if she would come to me."

Closing the door on the guard's surprised face, Aurora whirled. She let the mantle drop and stretched her arms above her head. If she was going to enter into Roman life, Aurora decided, she'd do it with style.

It took several hours to get rid of the last traces of her grime. The senior bath attendant, summarily detailed as Aurora's personal assistant, washed and scrubbed and pumiced and painted with a will. She attacked Aurora's hair with creamy shampoos, hot oils and stiff brushes until it crackled with life. Once they'd regained their glossy shine, however, the unruly tendrils stubbornly defied the maid's earnest attempts to confine them with golden ropes. She finally gave up and drew the thick mass back from Aurora's face to anchor it with gold combs at her temples.

The older woman, Sulline by name, sent the bewildered guards scurrying on one errand after another. Maids entered the captain's chambers in a steady stream, carrying pots and jars and soft, scented linens. A gawky young trooper staggered in under the weight of a huge square of steel, polished until it could serve as a mirror.

"Put it there," Sulline ordered, pointing to a table in the corner.

Luke's orderly, who had been summoned by the household guard, protested. "That is the captain's campaign desk. 'Tis where he works at night."

The maid glanced down at Aurora, who was sitting on a stool in front of the desk, a small smile on her lips. The older woman snorted and brushed the orderly aside.

"He'll not be working this night, nor any other in the near future." She gathered up the scrolls stacked neatly on the desk's surface and thrust them into the orderly's arms. "Here, take these away. I need room for my jars and brushes."

By the time she emerged from the captain's chambers, Aurora glowed with the confidence of a woman who knew she looked her best. Better than her best, actually. With her busy flying schedule and irregular hours, Aurora had rarely had time to pamper herself in her previous life. She couldn't remember ever spending several hours just bathing and doing her face. Of course, she'd never had a small army of eager women helping her with the task before, either.

Lifting the rose-hued skirts of her robe, Aurora opened the door and sashayed out into the corridor. The guards glanced at one another, then fell back in obvious relief as the sergeant of the household guard came down the hall.

He stopped in front of Aurora and inclined his head respectfully. "*Ave, domina.* Do you wish to go out?"

Aurora eyed him for a long moment. "Yes," she answered finally. "Are you here to try to stop me?"

His lips parted in a rueful grin. "Nay. I would not be so foolish."

"Are you here to escort me, then?"

The man shook his head and stepped aside. "The captain says you no longer need escort."

Aurora's heart leaped. Giving the sergeant a brilliant smile, she gathered her skirts and brushed past him. Freedom thrummed in her veins. For the first time in weeks, she was free of guards, of constant watching.

She stopped for a moment on the steps of the villa and lifted her face to the sun. The warmth washed through her, and the sounds of the busy camp drifted into her consciousness with a reassuring sense of familiarity. A chariot clattered by, its iron-bound wheels ringing on the cobbles. Horses neighed, and the slam of a blacksmith's hammer against an anvil sounded a distant counterpoint to a centurion's crisp commands as he drilled troops in a small square in front of the barracks.

Aurora smiled and made her way unerringly through the streets to the small hut that housed her friend. She found Jamille sitting on a stool by the doorway, weaving rags into a small blanket, and Charlie at the back of the hut, rocking the baby in his arms. Greeting the girl, Aurora passed her the pile of soft linens she'd brought for the babe, then joined her friend to coo and make faces at the baby.

"Look, Charlie! She smiled at you!"

The tiny being flailed the air with two little fists and gurgled up at them. Her wrinkled face was scrunched into an expression that only someone who had been present at her birth could have construed as a smile.

"She knows you," Aurora insisted.

Charlie grinned and nodded absently, his entire attention focused on the child in his arms. Aurora caught the movement of his head out of the corner of one eye. She swiveled slowly on her stool, feeling hope thump wildly in her chest. Had he heard her? Had he actually heard and responded to her?

"Charlie?" she asked tentatively. "Can you hear me? Do you know who I am?"

When he refused to be distracted from his play with the baby, Aurora tugged at his arm. "Can you hear me?"

He swung his head toward her and frowned.

Aurora's heart jumped into her throat as she saw comprehension replace the confusion in his hazel eyes. Her hands balled into fists.

"Do you know who you are? Lieutenant Charles Everett? United States Air Force? Remember?"

As if sensing the sudden tension in the room, the baby let out a tiny, hiccuping cry. Jamille looked up, then crossed the room to take her from Charlie's arms. She carried the child to the narrow cot and settled down to nurse her.

Aurora wet her lips and tried again. "Charlie?" she whispered. "Do you know me? I'm Aurora. Aurora Durant."

"Aurora?"

The word was little more than a croak. His voice sounded dusty from misuse. But it was strong enough to make Aurora give a wild cry and throw herself off his stool and into his arms.

"Aurora?"

Wild tears of joy threatened to smudge the charcoal lines Sulline had painted on Aurora's lids. She blinked furiously and swallowed the ache in her throat. Leaning back in Charlie's arms, she managed a shaky grin.

"It's me, pal. Don't let this piled-up hair and long dress fool you."

"I . . . I don't . . ." He shook his head, his eyes clouding with confusion once more.

Aurora gripped his arms. "Don't force it. Let it come back to you slowly. You'll remember," she promised fiercely. "You'll remember me. You'll remember us. How we were before."

" 'Twould be better if he didn't."

At the harsh words Aurora spun around in Charlie's arms.

Luke stood framed in the doorway. When Aurora saw the expression on his face, her instinctive retort faltered on her lips.

Luke's eyes were hard and flat as they swept from Aurora's face to the arm resting loosely on her hips.

" 'Twould be better if he never remembered that he once had you. 'Twould be better if he knows only that you are now mine."

He stepped into the hut. His shoulders blocked out the light, but Aurora had still seen the way his hand reached instinctively for his sword. His injured hand, she remembered.

"Oh, for Pete's sakes," she muttered, pushing herself out of Charlie's slack hold.

If that wasn't just like a man. He'd bristle and strut and ruffle up his neck feathers in some atavistic male-of-the-species nonsense and probably tear every stitch out of his hand. She marched across the room and took his wrist in a firm hold. Ignoring his start of surprise, she twisted his arm around to the light and bent to examine the his palm.

"Aurora?" Charlie's hoarse call barely penetrated her consciousness. "What's . . . what's happening?"

Luke stiffened at the sound of her copilot's voice. He threw the lanky Texan a glance that made Charlie swallow nervously.

"Aurora?"

"It's okay," she called, torn between her copilot's confused state and the sluggish blood seeping from one of the lacerations in Luke's palm.

"I knew it," she declared grimly. "You've torn open the stitches with this macho act of yours." Gathering her skirts in one hand and Luke's arm in the other, she turned toward the door.

"I'll be back later, Charlie."

"Aurora..." Luke growled.

"Aurora!" her copilot called.

"Look, we'll sort this out later, guys. But first we have to get Humpty-Dumpty here put together again."

Chapter 13

Aurora perched on the edge of Luke's desk and peered down at his hand as the physician cleansed and restitched the wounds.

"And so, lady," the *medicus* finished, "you tie the knot thus." He made a loop in the black thread, slipped the curved needle through and pulled the knot tight. With a small knife, he trimmed the thread close to the skin.

Aurora was impressed. This guy obviously knew his business. She probed the swollen, inflamed area with a tentative finger, earning a flinch and a hostile glare from Luke and a warning shake of the head from the uniformed physician.

"Don't touch it until we dust the wound," the bushy-haired man advised her. He snapped his fingers to summon his assistant, then rummaged through a small chest fitted with bottles and vials. "Ah, here it is."

He straightened, preening just a bit at Aurora's deep interest. "'Tis my own mixture, a tincture of iron rust and verdigris scraped from old bronze implements. It works every time. We'll dust the cuts with this to dry them, then smear on more salve to keep the surrounding skin supple." Aurora leaned forward, watching intently as he worked on Luke's hand. "Shouldn't it be bandaged?"

"Aye, it should," the physician responded tartly, "but some persons in the camp are more stubborn than others."

"Bandage it."

The doctor hesitated.

"Aurora . . ." Luke began warningly.

"Bandage it," she repeated.

His gray brows rising, the physician glanced from Aurora to the captain. Whatever he saw in Luke's eyes when they met Aurora's brought a small smile to his lips. He waved another assistant forward, then open the carved wooden chest the trooper held. Still smiling, the *medicus* began to wrap clean linen around the captain's torn, scarred flesh.

Lucius sat back in his chair, wondering just when he'd lost command.

Since the moment Aurora swept him out of the small hut, she'd been in charge. She'd marched him back to the headquarters like a new recruit. Ignoring his protests, she'd sent his scribe scurrying for the physician. While Lucius struggled to unclench the jaws that had locked the instant he saw Aurora in her Char-Li's arms, she'd pushed him into the chair behind his desk, swept several stacks of maps and scrolls to the floor and planted herself on its polished surface.

Lucius barely felt the pain of the physician's needles in his fury over finding Aurora in another man's embrace. The tall, wiry foreigner would never know how close he'd come to being thrown in a dank hole, never again to see the light of day, he thought grimly. The only thing that had saved him was the way Aurora brushed aside his remarkable recovery in her concern over Luke's wounds. A visceral satisfaction that she'd chosen him over this Char-Li surged through Lucius's veins. Involuntarily he clenched his fist.

"Oh, for Pete's sake!"

"Captain!"

At their irate looks, Lucius relaxed his hand once more. He restrained a grimace as Aurora poked and probed at his wound with more interest than tenderness. Her hair slipped forward over her shoulder, drawing his gaze. Lucius stared at its lustrous shine, letting his fascination with its dark fire gradually soothe what he now recognized as raw, untempered jealousy. By the gods, he thought ruefully, Aurora as she was today was enough to send any man into a jealous fit.

He'd barely recognized her when he first saw her there in the hut. Nor could he keep his eyes from her now. Not only was this Aurora a dazzling, glowing portrait of womanhood, but she exuded a confident, purposeful air that was as compelling as any physical beauty. There was no trace in her this morning of the dirty, defiant woman the guards had hauled into the great hall. Nor of the panting, musk-scented female who had writhed in his arms after he returned from the arena. Luke wondered if he'd ever come to know all the different sides of this creature he'd plucked from the sands.

At that moment she glanced up and flashed him a quick look from her luminous gray eyes. When the physician reclaimed her attention, Lucius sucked in a slow breath.

Not in this lifetime, he told himself wryly. He'd not begin to know Aurora in this lifetime, or the next. He wondered if any man ever really understood the woman he took to his heart.

The thought made him stiffen and glance around, half-afraid one of the medical assistants had read his thoughts. He wasn't ready to acknowledge to himself, let alone to anyone else, how deeply this woman had affected him.

"Aren't you done yet?"

Aurora's head came up at the sound of his gruff voice. "I knew it. You're in a lot of pain, aren't you? You should have let the doc give you a drug before we started, instead of trying to act like a big, tough-as-nails cowboy."

Lucius saw the senior medical officer's brow furrow as he struggled with her reference to a male cow person. Lucius himself had given up all attempts at literal translations of Aurora's words. It was enough for him to recognize her cocky, irreverent tone to know 'twas time to rein her in.

"Nay, I'm not in great pain," he replied, rising. "Just weary of having half the camp hovering over me."

"Wait a minute! We're not done here. We need to take a look at your other hand. And then I want to talk to the doc about Charlie."

"I thank you, Physician. You are dismissed."

Pursing her lips, Aurora crossed one knee over the other and drummed her fingers on the polished surface of the desk. She waited while the medical officer and his technicians gathered their equipment and left. With a curt order to the scribe outside to stay out until he was summoned, Lucius slammed the door in his face.

When he turned to face her, she had assumed the mantle of her newfound authority. Lifting her chin, she sent him a firm look.

"There are matters that need to be resolved between us, Senior Centurion."

"Aye, there are."

"First, there's this citizenship deal that Quintus told me about. I wish to know exactly what it entails. You may have your scribe provide me with the written documents."

"I may?"

She ignored the touch of sarcasm in his voice. "Second, I want you to understand once and for all about Charlie."

"Yes, let's discuss this Char-Li." The sarcasm deepened to an outright sneer.

"He is my lieutenant. My subordinate, not my lover!"

Lucius stepped forward until his belt buckle brushed Aurora's knees. She was forced to plant both hands behind her on the desk and lean backward to look up into his face.

"Every time I've found you with this man, you've been in his arms. 'Tis not the custom in the Roman army to embrace subordinates."

"Well, it's not the usual custom in the United States Air Force, either," Aurora sputtered indignantly, "but you have to understand the circumstances."

"Nay, I do not have to understand. Nor do I have to tolerate his hands on you. From this day hence, you will not embrace him, or any other man except me."

Aurora's eyes narrowed. "Which brings us to the third point I want to talk to you about, big guy. This relationship of ours."

His hands settled possessively on her knees. "There is naught to talk about. You are mine."

She drew in a deep breath. Her lashes fluttered down, and for a long moment she stared at the scarred hands resting on her knees. Lucius felt his stomach clench at the expression in her eyes when she lifted her gaze to his.

"Aye, I'm yours."

His head snapped back.

"Well, don't look so surprised. I'm woman enough to admit that you...you turn me on. As a matter of fact, you all but turn me inside out. I've never met a man such as you, Senior Centurion," she finished softly.

"Aurora—" he got out on a strangled note. His hands tugged at her legs, separating them. A need to possess her swept through him, strong and hot and urgent.

"Wait! We must settle this between us."

"We've settled all." He surged against her.

She gasped and tried to scoot backward on the desk. "Not...not quite! I will give myself to you, freely and without reservation."

"'Tis all I ask."

"At night! But during the day, I'll not sit idly by. I would have... Luke, stop it! Listen to me!"

Gently Aurora grasped the hand that fumbled with the pins holding her gown at the shoulder.

"Listen to me. I will be your...your woman." She stumbled over the word, then gritted her teeth and pressed on. "But I'll not be your concubine. I won't sit on my hands, waiting for you to come to me when your duties permit."

Through the raw need roaring in his ears, Lucius heard the determination in her voice. His thighs quivered with the need to press into Aurora's open, vulnerable core, but he refrained. His throat was dry with the effort, and he dared not look down at where their bodies nearly joined.

"I would have some occupation," she told him, her eyes on his. "Some useful role in the camp to fill my days."

She was serious, Lucius realized with an inner groan. Aurora wished to talk of occupations, and he wished to...

"Please, Luke. This is important."

He straightened painfully. By the gods, would he ever understand her? She'd just admitted that she was his. In any other woman, such a declaration would have been accompanied by melting surrender. But Aurora, his stubborn, independent Aurora, gave herself to him and then wished to talk of occupations. With a feeling of wry resignation, Luke fought to control his raging need. Stepping back, he put some distance between their bodies.

"What is it that you would do?"

She pushed her skirts down to cover her knees with a hand that trembled just a bit. Lucius noted the faint tremor with a grim satisfaction. For all her air of cool command, she was not as unmoved as she would have him believe.

"I've been thinking about this all morning," she said slowly. "I've been well trained in self-defense. I could work with your men, showing them the moves."

Lucius grappled with a sudden, vivid image of Aurora training his men. He shook his head emphatically.

"No."

She bristled at his arbitrary refusal. "No? What do you mean, no? You had a taste of my skills yourself. As I recall, I tossed you on your head a few times. You know how good I am."

"I fear I'm not willing to see you, naked and glistening with oil, wrestling with similarly unclad soldiers."

"Wait a minute. Aren't you the guy who insists on bathing with half the camp in that darned *frigidarium* of yours? What's with this sudden modesty?"

"Bathing is one matter. Wrestling is another."

"Oh, for—" Aurora slid off the desk, her air of cool authority gone. "Look, they could wear G-strings or something, if it bothers you so much."

"No. You'll not wrestle, with or without these strings."

She folded her arms across her chest, obviously irritated by his lack of cooperation. "Well, I have to do something."

Her lips pursed, and Lucius almost gave in to the urge to cover them with his own.

"I suppose I could work with your cavalry," she said after a moment. "I spent some time as an air liaison officer with a tank battalion. I could instruct them in the art of fast, mobile attack. Yeah, that would work."

Lucius felt his lips quivering. "Aurora," he said gently, "I doubt my cavalry officers would take instruction from you. They've seen you astride a horse."

She began to pace the room. "I don't believe this! I spent four years at the air force academy, two years getting a master's degree, and more months than I care to remember in advanced technical training, and I haven't got a single skill that's useful here. There must be something I can do."

Lucius let out a long breath. "If you're set on performing some task..."

"I am."

"Then we must find you one that matches more closely your woman's disposition."

Aurora swung to face him, her eyes narrowing. "Careful, fella."

"You could govern my household," he said slowly.

As soon as he spoke the words, Lucius sensed their rightness. The idea of Aurora in his home, seeing to his wants, triggered a fierce, masculine need, one he hadn't felt since he first took a bride so many years ago. The pallid lust he'd felt for the girl he'd never met until their wedding, and never missed after their divorce, was nothing compared to the raging desire he felt for Aurora. He wanted this woman in his home, in his bed. Warming to the idea, he ignored her disgusted expression.

"Mayhap the wife of Centurion Quintus would take you in hand. She could show you how best to order a Roman household."

"And mayhap you could take a flying leap." She faced him, hands on hips. "You still don't get it, do you? I'm not into cooking and cleaning. My rooms are a perpetual mess, and my favorite meal is microwave popcorn, although leftover pizza runs a close second."

"Aurora, speak in words I understand."

She waved an impatient hand. "I'm not trained in household skills. I don't know how to order a Roman home, nor do I wish to learn."

Lucius's vision of a smiling, smoky-eyed matron who waited for him each evening with her hair perfumed and his meal spread on the serving tables faded slowly. "If you don't wish to manage my domestic affairs, you need not," he replied, somewhat stiffly.

She gave a little snort. "Thank you."

"But you must find some other occupation than wrestling men to the ground or instructing the cavalry. Tell me what it is that you do best."

"I fly airplanes! I'm a pilot. A damn good one, too. Or at least I was, until I plowed my plane into the desert floor," she added on a dejected note.

Lucius hesitated.

"What?" She tilted her head. "What are you thinking?"

"I see a precipice at the front," he murmured, "and hear the wolves behind."

Aurora gave a low groan. "Great! Just great! We're talking about the rest of my life here, and you're worried about being between a rock and a hard place. What, exactly, is your problem?"

Lucius knew well what his problem was. This irritating, fascinating, vital woman wanted a task to keep her busy, a task she had the skills for, and he had it to give. Yet something within him resisted.

With a start, Lucius realized what that something was. Selfishness. Base, instinctive selfishness. He wanted to deny Aurora all reminders of her world. He wanted her to realize that she was here now, and here she would stay. He would have banished this Char-Li in an instant to the northernmost reaches of the Empire if he weren't convinced that Aurora would set out immediately to retrieve him. Fiercely, possessively, Lucius wished her to forget where she'd come from, what she'd done before she came into his arms.

But the mounting frustration in her swirling, mist-filled eyes tugged at his soldier's soul. Were he in her place, he, too, would chafe at inactivity. He, too, would want to be busy at that which he knew, that which he'd trained for.

Like the goddess she was named for, Aurora was too vital to keep confined, too vibrant to restrain her energies.

Nor, Lucius admitted grudgingly, would he have her any other way.

"I have a task that needs doing," he said at last, his mouth twisting into a wry grin.

Forty-five minutes later, Aurora wiped the grit from her eyes with a corner of her robe and forced her rubbery legs to step down from the chariot. She hadn't quite gotten the hang of pounding over rough cobbles in a two-wheeled wooden vehicle yet.

Glancing behind her, Aurora saw the city lying somnolent in the afternoon heat, far below. They'd driven hard, up a steep incline, pushing the horses, until they reached this high, windswept plateau. A rocky prominence at the edge of the plateau jutted out over the city. Aurora turned slowly to survey the huge, many-poled black tent atop the slab of rock.

"What is this place?"

Luke ignored her question, as he had the others she'd thrown over her shoulder during the long ride.

Aurora pursed her lips, deciding she'd just about had enough of this silent treatment. Just then, a middle-aged officer came hurrying toward them.

In an undertone, Luke identified him as the senior engineer, one Marcellus Petronius by name. He returned the man's salute, waited while the officer gave Aurora a courteous, if curious, greeting, then nodded toward the tent. "How goes the work, Marcellus?"

"Well, Captain," the man responded, "we have got the vehicle in its temporary quarters, as you see."

He fell in beside Luke, and the two men strolled up the incline. Aurora was left to pick up her skirts and trudge up the freshly graded dirt road after them. Her nose wrinkled as a familiar scent teased at her nostrils.

"We've yet to design a permanent mounting. I'm working on a mounting that will secure—"

"I smell gas!" Aurora's surprised exclamation cut off the engineer in midsentence. "Aviation fuel! JP-4, to be specific!"

The two men turned in surprise.

Eyes wide, she stared at the billowing sides of the tent. "Just what the heck have you got in there?"

Without waiting for a reply, Aurora hiked up her robe and darted past them. Rounding the corner of the structure at a run, she stumbled to a halt. Openmouthed, she gaped up at the cone-shaped nose of her plane. Sunlight slanted over her shoulder, painting its long, sleek fuselage a molten silver. Stunned, Aurora raised a shaking hand to the sun-warmed metal. For a long moment she was transported to another time, another place. To a world where she'd taken this craft into the sky, and seen the sun dancing on its wings. A pain lanced through her for this crippled bird, and for the world she'd never see again.

As though from a great distance, she heard the two men come to stand behind her.

"How . . . how did you get it here?" she whispered, turning.

At the captain's nod, Marcellus cleared his throat. "'Twas not difficult, lady, once we understood the balance of the craft's weight. Slaves dug trenches until the wheels were clear, then we harnessed specially reinforced slings to the metal legs. Camels in tandem pulled it to this spot."

His calm, measured words penetrated Aurora's utter stupefaction. They'd dug her plane out of the sucking sand! They'd dragged it for miles along the rough, cobbled road. Tucking her skirts into the cord wrapped around her waist, Aurora ducked under the wing. Like a horse trainer examining a prize filly's fetlock, she ran a hand down the hydraulic cylinders that raised and lowered the landing gear. They were gritty with sand and grease, but she didn't feel any cracks in the metal casings. Swiveling on one heel, she examined the other strut. Relief, and a healthy dose of respect, coursed through her. Scooting out from under the plane's belly, she beamed at the officer.

"You did good, Senior Engineer. Real good."

The man colored slightly. "'Twas not so difficult. If you would like, I will show you the drawings of the slings and harnesses."

At Luke's nod, he strode toward a flat stone surface that doubled as a workbench. Aurora turned to face the man beside her.

"Why? Why did you bring my plane here?"

"I wanted to examine it."

With a wave of her hand, she indicated the high, desolate plateau. "But why here? Why not bring it to the camp?"

Golden lights gleamed in his dark eyes. "I thought at first it might be a horse."

She stared at him, uncomprehending. "A horse? Okay, I'll bite."

"I feared it might be a ruse," he explained, smiling, "like the fabled horse of Troy. A hollow vehicle to convey an enemy inside the camp. Until I was sure of it, and you, I did not want it inside. Nor did I want you to have access to it."

A little niggle of hurt pierced Aurora's simmering excitement. "I'm not your enemy," she protested. "I never was. Well, maybe when we first met. You did scare the you-know-what out of me when you tried to peel off my flight suit. But I didn't really mean you any harm." Her gray eyes filled with remorse. "Even if I did almost make bear bait out of you."

He laughed and lifted his bandaged hand to stroke her cheek. "Nay, little one, I know you meant no harm."

The wind ruffled his hair and sent a dark strand whipping across his forehead. Aurora sucked in her breath, drinking in the harsh beauty of his face. Her eyes met his, and she saw a smile in their brown depths that filled her with a love so strong and powerful, she ached with it. She rested her cheek in his cupped palm, feeling the rough bandages against her skin. For a long moment, there was only the two of them, alone on a windswept plateau, caught between the earth and the sky.

"Here, lady. Here are the sketches for the excavation."

Luke's hand brushed down her cheek, then fell away. Aurora felt its loss all the way down to her toes, but she managed to nod and murmur appreciatively at the engineer's animated explanations.

"And here is the rough design for the temple."

She leaned forward as he unfolded another parchment and held it in both hands against the stiff breeze.

"What temple?"

"The temple that will house the vehicle."

Openmouthed with surprise, Aurora examined a sketch of a long, low-roofed structure supported by marble columns. The building was just wide enough and high enough to accommodate her plane, which the artist had drawn in with a fine, precise hand.

"You're...you're going to build a temple for my plane?" she asked weakly.

Her mind boggled at the thought of some twentieth-century archaeologist digging through the ruins at Dura and uncovering a temple that housed a C-21 cargo jet, complete with two turbofan engines, USAF markings and a hold full of electronic components.

Luke grinned at her obvious astonishment. "Nay, he's not going to build it. You are."

"Me?"

"Aye. Who better to build it, and dedicate it to the goddess whose name you bear?"

"Wait. Wait just a minute. Let me make sure I have this straight. You want me to construct a permanent building?"

"Aye."

"Out of marble?"

"Aye."

She whirled, sweeping her hand in a wide arc that encompassed the desolate promontory. "Up here?" Her voice rose to an incredulous squeak.

A crooked grin tugged at Luke's lips. "'Twas only after we got it halfway back that we realized the damned thing wouldn't fit inside the city gates unless we dismantled its wings. I didn't want to take your chariot apart, Aurora of the skies, and I didn't know what else to do with it."

Aurora's mind began to whirl. The logistics of the project overwhelmed her. Intrigued her. Made her want to grab a pencil and start making lists.

She'd need to do a complete site survey.

She'd have to devise a method of anchoring the plane to the rock so that the wind wouldn't sweep under the wings and stress the joints.

She'd need architects and stonecutters. And Charlie. He could help her clean the plane and restore it as much as possible to its original condition. If she was going to leave a monument for some future generation to uncover and exclaim over, she wanted to make darn sure it did credit to the United States Air Force.

Whipping around, she went to examine her plane again. "The port wing sliced through a sand dune," she told the engineer worriedly. "The engine intake must have sucked up half a ton of sand. I hope it didn't destroy the blades. Come on, Marcellus, let's take a look."

The engineer's face held blank confusion as he disappeared around the silver tail in Aurora's wake. He'd be even more confused by the time she was through with him, Lucius thought, his grin deepening. The gods knew she kept *him* in a constant state of confusion. And turmoil. And raw, aching need.

Well, at least she'd be occupied and out of trouble for some months to come. Mayhap by the time the temple was finished and dedicated, Aurora would chafe less in her new world. Mayhap by then she would have discovered a more conventional, more womanly, outlet for her energies. Mayhap by then, he thought with a sudden, fierce stab of desire, she'd be swollen with his child and content to take her place in his household.

Lucius shook his head at his own fantasies and strolled forward to join the others. Somehow he doubted Aurora would ever slip into an accepted niche in his life. But searching for it would likely prove interesting, if not exhausting, for them both.

Chapter 14

"Let me up." Aurora tried to unwind the heavy arm that lay over her waist and tucked under one armpit. "Luke, let me up."

The arm tightened slowly. Aurora squirmed against the hold, feeling his solid chest against her back.

"Come on, let go."

"'Tis not yet dawn," he mumbled in her ear.

Aurora hunched one shoulder as his warm breath stirred the fine hairs just above her ear. "Yes, I know, but I've got a ton of stuff to do."

"We can sleep yet another hour."

"*You* can sleep yet another hour. *I* need to get it in gear."

Aurora managed to unwrap the dead weight of his arm and lift it off her waist. Sliding her hips to the edge of the bed, she sat up and stretched. The predawn cool raised goose bumps on her arms and puckered her nipples. It was a welcome contrast to the dry, suffocating heat that would come later. Arching her back, she let the invigorating air bathe her body while she made a mental checklist of her tasks for the day.

She needed to consult with Theodorus, who was newly freed and established in his own household, with a score of fresh-faced pupils to instruct. He'd promised to research several different texts for an appropriate inscription for the south wall of the hangar/temple that would house her plane.

And Marcellus was supposed to meet her and Charlie on-site, together with the master stonecutter who was shaping the pediment that would support the roof.

And she'd promised the quartermaster she'd give him a list of—

A warm hand on her back made her jump. The hand slid down to cup her bottom.

"Come back to bed."

"I can't. I've got too much to do."

Strong, sure fingers began to knead her flesh. "Lie with me, Aurora, bringer of light. Banish my darkness before you ride your chariot across the sky."

She rose, laughing. "As I recall, I banished your darkness twice last night. And once earlier this morning, when the sentry's call woke you. I'm surprised I have the strength to crawl out of bed, with all the banishing I've been doing lately."

Lucius propped himself up on one half-healed hand and watched through heavy-lidded eyes as Aurora knelt to light a twist of straw at the tiled hearth. The fire's dim glow washed over her long, lean flanks and painted her skin a pearly pink. When she rose, shielding the straw with one hand, Lucius felt the last vestiges of sleep vanish instantly. Propping his head on his crossed hands, he watched her move across the room.

She lit an oil lamp, then groped through the clothing scattered on the floor for the strips of linen that served as breast and belly bands. She found one, held it up to the light to inspect it, and frowned at the gaping tear in it.

"You've got to go easier on my clothes, fella," she commented, tossing the torn strip to the floor.

The discarded wrapping fluttered down to join the other garments strewn across the tiles. Lucius's gaze roamed the once-austere chamber, taking in the evidence of Aurora's presence in every cluttered nook and cranny. He no longer had access to his desk. It was covered with an array of pots and jars and brushes and other implements he dared not ask the use of. The rack that had previously held his armor was now heaped with robes in jewellike colors. A lyre hung crookedly from a peg on one wall, while sketches and drawings of her project covered the other.

Books and scrolls from Aurora's continued studies with Theodorus spilled off the table onto the floor. One in particular caught Lucius's attention. 'Twas the work she'd stumbled upon just last week, a treatise by the poet Ovid on the amatory arts. He grinned at the memory of Aurora, bound parchment in hand, eyes wide, straddling his chest as she attempted one of the positions recommended as a means of keeping a lover. Ovid certainly knew whereof he wrote, Lucius thought with a painful tightening in his groin.

When she bent to tug a robe out of the jumble that had slipped off the overloaded rack, the pain sharpened into piercing, aching need. Lucius swallowed at the sight of her trim posterior, outlined by the transparent linen. By the sword of Mars, what ailed him? He had only to look at this woman, to see the flash of her cocky grin or hear the sound of her teasing, irreverent voice, and he hardened. He'd thought himself long past the age of such uncontrolled response to any woman.

But Aurora wasn't just any woman, he reminded himself. She was like no other woman of his world. This Aurora, this creature who had tumbled from the skies and landed in his arms, was unique unto herself. She'd turned his world upside down with her laughing, breathless pas-

sion and her whirlwind energy, and she kept the entire
camp agog to see what she'd do next. Just yestereve, she'd
abruptly risen from the banquet table, banished the dancing girls who had been hired at great expense, and treated
his astonished guests to a version of a dance she called,
incomprehensibly, New Age hip-hop.

Remembering how she'd moved in the dance, Lucius
threw off the wool coverings and padded across the room.

"You know," she mumbled, "I wish to heck Levi
Strauss had lived a couple of thousand years earlier."

She struggled with the voluminous folds of her sky-blue
robe, holding them in place with one hand while she tried
to wrap a silver cord around her waist with the other. Lucius had tried to convince her to call in serving women to
help her dress, but Aurora felt ill at ease with personal
slaves. She would let none attend her except the woman
Sulline, whom Lucius had freed at Aurora's request.

She twitched her hips to settle the offending fabric and
sent him an irritated glance. "I don't know why you're so
hardheaded about me wearing my flight suit. It'd be a lot
more comfortable than these silly layers for the ride out to
the site."

"You will wear the green suit only at the workplace, as
you promised. You startle the citizens of Dura enough
without riding through town in that strange garb. They're
not used to seeing women without veils, nor those who
have the freedoms I've allowed you."

"Excuse me?"

"The freedoms you've taken unto yourself," he said
with a grin.

"That's better. You know, if we work on you for a few
more months, I think we'll be able to promote you from
chauvinist first-class to semisensitive and almost-with-it
nineties male."

He reached out and wrapped his hand around her waist. "Nay, I think not. You know what 'tis said about old soldiers being slow to learn new ways."

"I think that's 'old dogs' and 'new tricks.'"

He drew her forward. "I fear it will take years for you to teach me these new tricks."

"Luke..."

Spreading his legs, he cradled her against him. "Decades, mayhap."

"Oh, for Pete's sake!"

"Someday," he murmured into the tangled, fragrant hair beneath his lips, "you will tell me who is this Pete you refer to on so many occasions." He bent, burrowing under the silken mass to nuzzle her neck.

"It's a saying. A maxim, just like you're always—Ouch!"

Lucius soothed the tender lobe he'd just nipped with his tongue. Aurora started to protest, but when he buried his tongue in her ear, her words ended on a breathless gasp. She slid her hands up his chest and circled his neck.

"Come back to bed," Lucius murmured some moments later.

"Nay," she whispered back, arching into him. "I can't make it that far."

It was well past cockcrow by the time Aurora woke once more. Sated, satisfied, her earlier energy drained, she watched Luke rise and dress for morning parade.

His stiff-faced, disapproving orderly, who carefully avoided looking at Aurora or at the chaotic disorder of the room, brought in his armor. Drawing the covering up to her nose, Aurora smiled into the scratchy wool as Luke wrapped his loincloth around those incredible buns. With quick efficiency, he pulled on his tunic and donned his sandals, then lifted his arms for the orderly to strap on his breastplate, with its bronzed eagle crest. He'd go to the baths later, Aurora knew, at the close of the duty day, to be scraped clean and shaved and massaged. If she arrived back in time, maybe she'd join him. She had—almost!— shed her inhibitions about communal bathing.

Late that afternoon, Aurora eased her tired body down onto a rock beside her equally exhausted copilot. "So, what do you think, Charlie? Can we power up engines for the big ceremony?"

He glanced at the small, sleek jet, which still sat under its tent canopy. A few yards beyond it, at the highest point of the promontory, stood the outline of the white, roofless temple that would house it permanently. Lacking only the rear wall that would be added after the roof was on and the plane rolled inside, the temple was within weeks of completion.

"I don't think we should risk it, Aurora."

"We've still got time to work on it. Don't you think we could get the engines working by then, at least long enough for one big roar?"

Charlie shoved a hand through his short brown hair. "I took the engine cowlings apart and cleaned out most of the sand. The turbo blades rotate okay now, but I don't dare reconnect the starter to the auxiliary battery. Without any instruments or warning indicators, I could overcharge the cells and blow us all up."

Aurora nibbled on the corner of her lower lip. "Couldn't we rig up a remote starter? We've got all those spare electronic components in the back."

Charlie swiveled on his rocky perch to face her. Perspiration glistened on his forehead, and he'd rolled the sleeves of his flight suit up to bare his forearms. They'd been working on the plane since early afternoon, and had both generated a healthy sweat. Aurora was glad to see the ruddy color in his face. He'd finally lost the pallor and the dazed look that had frightened her before. He still occasionally had trouble with his balance, but he showed no other visible signs of his ordeal.

"Why is it so important to you that we fire the engines for this big ceremony?" he asked.

Aurora rested her chin on her drawn-up knees. She let her gaze drift to the city sprawled far below them, hazy blue in the heat, banded by a narrow ribbon of silver that was the Euphrates.

"I don't know," she said finally. "I guess I just want to send her off in style. Once we roll her inside and finish the temple, she'll be trapped forever in a marble cage."

As if to underscore her words, the sound of a hammer chinking against marble carried on the afternoon air. The master stonecutter, carving the final decorative figures on the pediment for the temple.

Charlie gave her a keen glance. "Are you sure you're talking about the plane here, Aurora? Not about us?"

She angled her head toward him, resting one cheek on her knees. "Do you feel trapped?"

He shrugged. "At first I did. When I realized what'd happened, I felt trapped and disoriented and scared."

"And now?"

"Now, whenever I wake up sweating in the night or crave the taste of a greasy hamburger, I hold on to Jamille or the baby." The expression in his hazel eyes softened. "I didn't leave a whole heck of a lot behind in our world, Aurora. I found them in this one."

"I know your parents are dead, Charlie, but isn't there anyone you miss? No cousins or great-aunts? No girl-friends?"

"Nah, not even a cocker spaniel. The air force has been my home for the last dozen years, ever since I was seventeen. It was all I had. Now I have Jamille. What about you, Aurora? Do you miss home?"

She gazed out at the city once more. "Yes. A bunch. I think about my family a lot. But not as much now as at first. Not since Luke and I...since we, uh..."

"You don't have to spell it out. I noticed the guy can't seem to keep his hands off you."

The dry note in Charlie's voice brought a flush to Aurora's face.

Despite her best efforts, she hadn't been able to lessen the animosity between the two males in her life. Luke wouldn't quite buy the concept of a friendly relationship between a man and a woman, a relationship based on business. On the few occasions he and Charlie had met in recent weeks, he'd made it a point to demonstrate—blatantly, arrogantly—that Aurora was his. The two men had eyed each other with unconcealed hostility, and only Aurora's most forceful, provocative, exhausting efforts had wrung from Luke the concession that Charlie could work with her on restoring the plane. As long as they did so in broad daylight. In the company of the soldiers. And returned to their separate quarters immediately afterward.

She really had to work on that possessive streak of his, Aurora mused.

"It is kinda weird when you think about it," Charlie admitted, breaking into her thoughts. "We both had to cross time to find someone." He paused, then eyed her hesitantly. "Do you think it was fated? I mean, I'm not real up on philosophy or religion, but it does sorta feel like this is all part of some big cosmic scheme."

He gave Aurora a shamefaced look, as if worried that his image as a tough air force pilot might somehow be tarnished by his talking about such deep subjects.

"I don't know. Luke and I have talked about it, though."

"And what does Commander Luke think about our little trip through the ozone?"

Aurora shrugged off his sarcasm. "He's read much more than I have, particularly about ancient Eastern philosophies. According to him, many people believe that a person's essence—his soul, or his spirit—passes to another upon death. In a form of reincarnation, I guess. Sometimes it happens right away, sometimes it may be centuries before that person is reborn. If a person's essence can go forward in time, perhaps it can go back, as well. Do you think that's what happened to us?"

"Beats the hell out of me."

Aurora sat up, her laughter joining Charlie's. Out of the corner of one eye, she caught sight of a veiled figure trudging up the steep incline, her arms laden and a heavy bundle on her back. A tall, brawny soldier strode along beside her.

"Look! Isn't that Jamille?"

Charlie squinted at the black-robed figure. "Damn it, I told her I didn't want her coming all this way." He stood up, brushing off the seat of his flight suit. "She said she was going to bring us out something to eat if we didn't get back early. I told her not to, but she insisted."

Aurora hurried along beside him. "Doesn't she know the quartermaster sends provisions every day?"

"Yeah, I told her, but she says I don't eat enough. According to her, I weigh too little for my height."

"Ha! She ought to try dragging you out of a plane sometime."

"Well, if you'd ever learned how to fly the blasted things, you wouldn't have had to drag me out."

They were both laughing again by the time they reached the girl. She greeted them breathlessly and passed her bundles into their arms, then swung the baby off her back. The soldier saluted Aurora and left to join his companions.

Aurora noted the sheen of sweat on the girl's forehead. "Are you all right, Jamille?"

"Yes, mistress," she replied, her gaze darting around the site.

"I wish you wouldn't call me 'mistress,'" Aurora muttered. "It makes me think of black leather and whips."

Aurora had tried several times to convince Luke to free Charlie and his little family and move them into better quarters. But while Luke had agreed to housing them more comfortably, he'd so far refused to grant Charlie the same freedoms he'd given Aurora. She was working on him, though.

"Here, let me take the baby."

Jamille took a quick step away from Charlie's outstretched hands and clutched the child to her breast. "Nay, I'll keep her."

Both Charlie and Aurora stared at her in surprise. Usually she was happy to share the burden of care for the infant.

"'Tis...'tis time to feed her."

Charlie bent to peer down into Jamille's bright, glittering eyes. "Hey, are you okay? You look like you might have caught a fever. An illness."

She pulled her veil across her face to shield it, but not before Aurora caught a glimpse of white, strained lines at either side of her mouth. "I have no illness."

"Look, it was crazy for you to come all the way out here," Aurora said. "Sit down and rest. Charlie and I will get changed, then take you back to town."

Jamille's hand plucked at her sleeve. "Nay, mistress. Truly, I'm fine. I but need to catch my breath."

"We'll get changed," Charlie said firmly, "then have something to eat. When you're rested, we'll go back to town."

Using the aircraft's cabin as a changing room, Aurora struggled back into her robes. Charlie changed when she was done. They left their gear in the plane, then strode together across the windy plateau to rejoin Jamille.

As they approached the stiff, silent figure, a strangled shout broke the stillness of the afternoon. Before either Charlie or Aurora could react, the girl dropped like a stone, the baby cradled protectively in her arms.

"Down!" she shouted. "Get down!"

"What the hell—"

Aurora whirled as another shout split the air, then a wild series of yells. Her disbelieving eyes saw the stonecutter crumple over the marble block he'd been working on, a long spear protruding obscenely from his back. A ribbon of bright red trailed down the white marble.

"Get down!" Jamille tugged at Charlie's tunic with one hand, and sent Aurora a frantic look. "Stay low until it's over!"

"What's over?" Aurora's voice rose to a screech. "What's over? Jamille, what's happening?"

The sound of iron ringing against iron brought her head whipping around. The troop of soldiers detailed to the project had pulled their swords from their scabbards and were defending themselves against a swarming, screaming horde that seemed to have sprung up from the very stones that dotted the plateau.

"Oh, my God! No!" Aurora shouted. "No!"

She lunged forward, intending to grab a sword and rush to the soldiers' aid. Jamille thrust out a foot, tripping her. Sharp rock ripped at her palms and dug deep gouges in her knees.

"They are my people!" Jamille screamed.

"Call them off!" Curling her knees under her, Aurora sprang up. "Charlie, tell her to call them off!"

She raced toward the thronging mass. Two cloaked warriors turned at her wild approach. Aurora dodged one, but the other grabbed her arm and twisted her around, away from the melee. Aurora's hand doubled into a fist. Pivoting on one heel, she swung with all her might.

Her blow never landed. Something slammed against her temple with blinding, shattering force, and she crumpled to the ground.

Chapter 15

As late afternoon melted into night, and night slowly gave way to gray, hazy dawn, Aurora slowly discovered that she disliked camels even more than she did horses. The ungainly beast she was riding loped along with an uneven gait that added to the pounding pain in her temple and kept her feet dangling so far from the ground that she was afraid she'd get a nosebleed.

What was more, it stank. It didn't just smell. It reeked. The shaggy coat under her high-pommeled saddle gave off an odor strongly reminiscent of dead rats and an old, moth-eaten raccoon coat she'd once found in her grandparents' attic.

The creature didn't have the greatest personality in the world, either. When Aurora tried to turn the beast and head back to Dura, it had craned its neck, nipped at her thigh with huge yellow teeth and blasted her with a waft of breath so foul she'd gasped for air. The stubborn animal had stayed right in line with the other, ungainly mounts, carrying her farther and farther into the desert. Farther away from Luke.

Wearily Aurora shifted in the high saddle and wondered for the thousandth time where they were heading and when she could climb down off this shifting, lumbering beast. She ached in parts of her body she had never known existed, her head hurt, she was freezing in the cold night air, and she wanted to go home. The fact that she now thought of Dura as home didn't even faze her.

When at last the shadowy figures in front of her began to slow, she almost sobbed in relief. Her own mount altered its gait to a teeth-jarring canter, then an awkward amble. Finally, mercifully, it stopped. Aurora clung to the pommel with both hands while muted sounds drifted back to her. A dim, robed figure materialized out of the darkness, grabbed her mount's bridle and whacked it on the shins. Aurora nearly tumbled out of the saddle headfirst as the beast tilted forward on its front knees. She held on to the pommel desperately, then slammed back in the saddle when the creature tucked in its rear legs and sank to the sand.

The robed figure reached out and took Aurora's arm in a firm hold. She lifted her aching leg over the pommel and slid to the ground. He released her immediately and stepped back. Aurora peered up at him, trying to make out his features, but the headdress he wore kept his face in shadow.

He said something in a low voice, his words flowing in an smooth, rhymthic cadence. Aurora shook her head, not understanding a word.

Pushing aside the flaps of his long, heavy cloak, he rested his hands on his hips. Moonlight glinted on the long, curved blade of an evil-looking scimitar. Aurora swallowed and took a step back.

Jamille came rushing out of the darkness. "Don't be afraid," she called breathlessly. "This is my brother. This is al Azab."

Jamille and the tall, intimidating figure carried on a hurried dialogue, while Aurora waited for the feeling to flow back into her numb legs. She'd already guessed that Jamille had known, somehow, of the attack. Her visit to the site had been too unexpected, too perfectly timed, to be a coincidence. But that al Azab, the very raider Luke's patrols scoured the desert for, would dare strike so close to the Roman camp stunned her. No wonder Luke's men called him "the desert fox."

Aurora stepped toward the man. "Do you speak the Roman tongue?" she asked boldly.

He flicked her a glance of pure contempt and snapped something to Jamille.

"He would not lower himself to use the tongue of his enemy," she translated. "Nor should you address him without permission, mistress. My brother is a great chieftain."

Aurora gritted her teeth. And she'd thought a certain Roman captain was arrogant!

"Well, tell your brother for me that he's made a mistake by taking us. A big mistake."

The girl shook her head. "'Twas no mistake, mistress."

"Look, Jamille, I understand that they would come for you, that you would wish to go back to your people. But he shouldn't have taken me, as well. Nor Charlie. The Roman captain will come after us."

Privately Aurora suspected Luke would just as soon let Charlie vanish into the desert, but she wasn't about to admit that to this raider, whose eyes suddenly gleamed with a dark, savage glow.

"Aye," Jamille nodded. "The Roman will come after you."

"If your brother releases us..."

"He will not release you, nor the man I now claim as husband. The one who birthed my child."

Aurora's mind reeled with this new complication. Before she could sort through all the ramifications of Jamille's pronouncement, the girl gripped her arm.

"Do you not understand? My brother did not come for me. He would not risk his men for a woman who has lain with the Romans, even against her will. I heard whispers of the raid in the marketplace, and came to the site on my own."

"But—"

"You! You are the prize! You are the bait that will lure the Roman to his death!"

"What?"

"He will come, with his legionaries, these men that know not the desert ways. 'Twill take some days for them to march this far, but they will come. And when they do, they shall not return."

"Do you think 'tis their camp?"

Lucius's eyes narrowed against the glare. Heat rose in shimmering waves, blurring the image of the black goathide tents in the distance. Slowly, scarcely stirring the folds of cloth dusting his cheeks, he shook his head.

"There are too few tents for this to be the main camp."

"But the tracks led here. I swear we did not take a false trail, Captain."

He sent the young tracker a reassuring glance. "Nay, we did not. I, too, think these are they whom we seek. But the main body of their troops is elsewhere."

"What now, Captain?" the younger man whispered.

Lucius burrowed into the sand, pulling the concealing headdress about his face. "We wait."

He lay in the sand for long, sweltering hours, cocooned in his borrowed desert garb. His eyes burned with the effort of watching the distant camp, of straining to catch a glimpse of a familiar face or figure. He was too far away to make out anything except the hazy figures of tall, robed men wearing desert headdresses and a few heavily veiled, black-robed women tending cookfires. Try as he might, Lucius couldn't tell if any of the women was the one he sought.

Was she there? Lucius wondered time and again. Was Aurora one of these women who moved about the camp with apparent freedom? A sudden knife blade of doubt twisted in his gut. Had she escaped him once again, after lying in his arms and whispering soft words of love? Had he misread her so completely? Become so beguiled by her wide, smoky eyes and soft lips that he'd forgotten his original suspicions?

Nay, not Aurora, he told himself fiercely. Not the woman who'd laughed and teased and flamed with passion in his arms. Not the woman who planted her hands on her hips and defied him time and again. She would argue with him and rail against his strictures, but she would not watch while his men were cut down and then vanish into the desert. Not Aurora.

The sun was flaming in a bright orange ball when at last he caught sight of a figure he recognized instantly. A man emerged from one of the goathide tents and stood still, his body taut. Even from this distance, there was no mistaking the one called Char-Li's tall frame. Lucius's stomach clenched into a tight, hard knot.

She was here. Aurora was here, Lucius was sure of it. With this Char-Li. This companion she had once bartered her body for. This "friend" she worked with daily. Once again doubt—and something darker, something fiercer— pricked at Lucius's soul. His jaw hardened. He reminded himself yet again 'twas Aurora he'd come for. At that moment Aurora herself threw up the flap of the tent and stalked out. Her hair was fiery nimbus, a cloud of wine- colored red in the last of the sun's rays.

Sweat ran down Lucius's cheeks in rivulets as he fought the urge to sweep down into the camp. Every one of his instincts screamed for him to draw his sword, to challenge whoever it was that sheltered her, to reclaim her. But he was too seasoned a soldier to give in to the wild, roaring need. Exerting a rigid discipline over his emotions, he signaled to the tracker to stay low and watched her through narrowed eyes.

Aurora's chin jutted up at a ferocious angle. "Charlie, I'm telling you I won't let them use me like this."

"And I'm telling you there's nothing you can do about it."

"Talk to Jamille! Tell her that I must speak with her brother."

Charlie raked a hand through his hair. "I've talked to her. She doesn't understand why you're so upset. Hell, you were the one who suggested we escape in the first place?"

"Me?"

"The first time. The night Jamille had the baby."

"That was different!" Aurora shouted. "That was . . . that was before!"

"Before what?" Charlie shouted back. "Before you got the hots for this Roman? Before you let a set of pecs make you forget you're an officer, sworn to resist the enemy?"

Aurora rocked back on her heels, stunned by Charlie's attack. "Luke's not the enemy," she choked out after a moment.

"Not yours, at least," her copilot retorted, sneering. "He didn't put you in chains. He didn't let his men use you like they did Jamille."

Hurt and angry, Aurora could only stare up at him.

"I've seen a different side of things from you," Charlie reminded her brutally. "The Romans are conquerors. They invaded this land. You can't blame Jamille's people for wanting to drive them out."

"You're on their side?"

"She's my wife, Aurora."

"Since all of yesterday!"

"Yeah? Well, at least—" He broke off abruptly.

"At least what?" Aurora voice rose. "At least she isn't just sleeping with you for fun and games, is that what you were going to say? At least she respects you enough to make an honest man out of you, is that it?"

Charlie met her glare with a fierce one of his own. They faced each other, nose to nose, until the absurdity of her words sank in. Aurora was the first to back off, biting her lip. The angry glitter in Charlie's eyes faded.

"Aw, hell, Aurora, I'm sorry. Anyone can see the jerk's crazy about you."

"Yeah, sure."

"How many men have wrestled a tiger for you lately?"

"It was a bear," she muttered, plucking at the black robe that swathed her from head to toe.

"Whatever." His voice sobered. "So you see why Jamille's brother won't let you go? All Dura knows that the Roman claims you as his. The word got out through the desert equivalent of a grapevine. Al Azab knows that Luke will bring his armies and try to take you back."

She laid a hand on his arm in a gesture of reassurance and reconciliation. "He'll take us both back, Charlie. He won't leave you in the desert."

He shook off her hand. "I'm not going back."

"You can't be serious!"

"Why not?"

"Because . . . because we're a crew, and crews stay together. Because the plane is at Dura. Because . . ." She stumbled to a halt, realizing that her arguments didn't carry any weight with Charlie. He wasn't the same person who'd taken off from Saudi Arabia so many weeks ago, any more than she was.

He gripped both her arms, his face grim. "Aurora, listen to me. There won't be anything for you to go back to, either. Jamille's brother has gathered all the tribes of the desert. He meeting with the chiefs now, just a few leagues away. When Luke comes for you, al Azab will be ready. He'll kill the Roman commander, then sweep down on Dura and destroy the garrison."

"No!" She wrenched herself out of his hold. "No! Luke's too smart to be drawn into a trap like this."

"He'll come for you. It'll take a while for him to get here, but he'll come for you."

Lucius made his move two hours after midnight.

With a silent signal to the tracker, he began a wide circle that would bring him to the west of the camp. The younger man faded into the darkness in the opposite direction.

When he judged himself to be in position, Lucius dropped to his belly. Inching forward in a slow, torturous crawl, he moved toward the tents. They were dim patches of black against the dark sky, barely visible to his straining eyes. Every few seconds, he lifted his head to test the direction of the wind and to scan the blackness ahead of him for roving sentries. He spotted one guard only seconds before he was sure the man would have seen him. Lucius left him staring sightlessly up at the night sky.

He crawled to within yards of the tent he'd seen Aurora emerge from. His heart pounding, he flattened himself in the sand. A minute dragged by. Two. Sure that discovery would come at any moment, he forced himself to wait.

He jerked when a dog barked furiously in the distance. A sentry called out a sharp question. One or two of the hobbled camels lifted their heads at the disturbance. Lucius watched as dark shapes rushed toward the sound of the yapping dog.

Dagger in hand, he sprang to his feet, his muscles tensing for the dash across the open space toward the tent. His straining eyes caught an undulation in the hide wall, then a shadowy movement at its base. Lucius dropped like a stone. 'Twas one of the dogs, he thought grimly. He'd hoped the ploy of sending the tracker upwind with a false scent would draw them all out of camp, and most of the defenders with them. Evidently this low, slinking beast was too old or too lazy to chase the spoor. Lucius palmed the dagger until his fingers gripped the blade. He'd silence the creature before it caught his scent.

The beast moved toward him, a dark shadow barely visible against the moonlit sands. His arm drew back.

Before his startled eyes, the creature reared up on its hind legs. It ran past him a few yards away, never seeing him in the dark. But he saw enough to recognize Aurora's white, strained face under the black mantle she'd pulled over her head and shoulders.

His senses whirling, Lucius absorbed the astounding fact that the woman he'd come to rescue was rescuing herself. He shook his head, rose to a low crouch, and followed her.

Not wanting to startle her and cause her to cry out, he closed the distance between them slowly. The camp was well back behind a screen of dunes when she stumbled over her trailing robes and went to her knees. Moving swiftly, silently, Lucius came up behind her. He slapped his palm over her mouth and jerked her head back against his chest.

"Aurora," he whispered, "do not—ooopmh!"

Her elbow hit his stomach with the force of a battering ram. Lucius clenched his muscles, sucked in a quick breath, and hung on. Her teeth closed on his hand.

"Great Jupiter, your bite is sharper even than the bear's," he ground out.

Her rigid body slackened immediately. Thankful, Lucius felt her teeth loose their hold. Muffled squeaks rose from under his palm.

"Be silent," he warned her, easing his hand from her mouth. As though she ever would, he thought with a wry grimace.

"Luke!" she cried, spinning around. She had enough presence of mind at least to keep her voice low as she flung her arms around him. "You came!"

Tremors racked her body. He allowed himself ten precious seconds to hold her, to feel her warmth against his, to stroke her tangled hair. "Of course I came," he murmured.

She pulled back. "How could you be so stupid!"

Lucius saw the silvery track of tears on her cheeks before she dashed a hand across them. "It's a trap. Couldn't you see that!"

"Aye, I saw it."

She snuffled and wiped her nose on her sleeve distractedly. "No, you don't understand. They knew you would come. Al Azab has gathered a huge army. Your men will never make it out of the desert alive."

She picked up her skirts and turned. "We have to get to your camp immediately and organize a retreat. When they find me gone, they'll come after me. They'll sweep down on your men, overwhelm them."

"Aurora," he told her gently, falling in beside her. "There are no men."

She stumbled. "What?"

"Just me, and a tracker." He took her arm, tugging her along. "Come, we must move quickly."

"Just you?" she echoed, her voice faint. "And a tracker?"

"I knew I could not hope to lead a squadron into the desert undetected. I also knew I had to strike swiftly, before they expected it, or I'd have no chance of reclaiming you."

As he spoke, Lucius eased them into a loping run.

"You came here alone?" Aurora panted. "Knowing an army was lying in wait for you?"

"Aye. Save your breath. You'll need it before this night is through."

"For me?"

"Aurora..."

She stumbled to a halt. "You came across the desert alone? For me?"

"Did you think I would not?" he asked, exasperated. At any moment he expected to hear the drum of camels' hooves behind them.

"Why, Luke?"

"Aurora, for the love of all the gods!"

"Why?"

"Because you are mine." He snagged her arm to haul her along.

She resisted, digging in her heels. "Not good enough. Why, Luke?"

"Aurora," he snarled, "when I get you safely home, I will—"

"Why! Tell me why! I need to hear it! These may be the last words I ever hear, and they'd better be good."

He gave a savage oath, swept her into his arms, and covered her mouth in a bruising, punishing kiss. When he pulled his head back, his eyes were blazing.

"Because you are mine! Because I will allow no man to take you from me. Because I cannot imagine life without you. Now move, before I knock you senseless and carry you out of here over my shoulder."

As declarations of undying devotion went, it could use a little work, Aurora decided. But it would do. It would definitely do. Besides, she realized grimly, the odds were pretty good that neither one of them would live long enough to work on his delivery technique.

Holding her skirts up with both hands, she raced beside him through the night, expecting to hear the sounds of chase behind them at any moment. The sand sucked at her feet. Her breath sliced at her throat. Just about the time she decided that Luke planned for them to run all the way back to Dura, he grabbed her arm and dragged her to the ground. Aurora's heart somersaulted in her chest. She flung herself face down, tensing every muscle and sinew against the feel of an arrow or a spear. It took her a few moments to realize that Luke was on one knee beside her, sniffing the air.

"Come." He pulled her upright. A few more stumbling steps brought them into a shallow bowl, protected on all sides by high, sloping sand dunes.

"Captain!" A dim shape materialized out of the darkness. White teeth flashed in the darkness. "It worked, just as you said. I led the dogs well away from the camp with that wolf's pelt."

"You did well," Luke murmured, pushing Aurora toward a dark, rounded rock in the center of the bowl. She put out a hand, leaning gratefully on the rock, then gave a small shriek when it moved.

Luke appeared at her side. "Quickly, climb on. 'Tis the fastest racing camel in the city."

Aurora gave a little groan and clambered into the saddle. Luke mounted behind her, jerked the camel's head up and kicked it into motion. With the tracker beside them, they flew across the desert.

For a few short hours, Aurora thought they might make it.

The camels were incredibly fast. Uncomfortable, aromatic and jarring, but fast. The miles and the hours slid by. After what seemed an eternity, the darkness around them edged into purple, then became a deep, violent red.

"Red sky in the morning, sailors take warning," Aurora said wearily. Great, just great. As if the sand and the bone-jarring ride weren't enough, it looked as though they

might have to slog through one of those violent desert
storms, as well.

Her eyes straining, her throat parched, she scanned the
horizon for some sign of life, of aid. Although the sun
wasn't visible when it finally rose, enough light filtered
through the scudding clouds for her to see the vast, empty
tract ahead of them. Numb from the waist down, Aurora
grasped the pommels and tried to take comfort in the feel
of Luke's hard arms around her. She remembered another night, another ride, when he'd first taken her to
Dura. It seemed so long ago, now.

"Captain!" The tracker's urgent voice cut through her
haze of fatigue. "Look!"

Luke threw a glance back over his shoulder and swore
viciously. Leaning precariously in the swaying, jolting
saddle, Aurora peered around him. What she saw almost
made her fall out of the saddle.

The weak sun illuminated the sky behind them just
enough for her to see a roiling cloud of dust rising from the
desert floor. It billowed upward, stretching across the horizon for miles. Aurora swallowed, knowing the impend-
ing storm wasn't stirring up these clouds. These were made
by men, mounted and moving fast.

"How long yet to Dura?" Luke shouted to the dark-
skinned tracker.

"Two hours, or more."

The two men exchanged a grim look, then turned their
faces forward. Luke's arms tightened protectively around
Aurora as he urged the camel to even greater speed.

The beast lunged forward, its sides heaving. Foam
spotted its flanks. It raced valiantly, but the distance and
the double burden proved too much for the creature. It
stumbled once. Luke held on to Aurora with one hand and
the reins with the other, swearing. The camel recovered,
then plunged on.

By the time it stumbled the third time, Aurora knew they wouldn't make it.

She could see the faint blue smudge in the distance that had to be the hills east of Dura. But behind them, closer by half, was the rolling, thundering cloud of al Azab's army.

They wouldn't make it. There was no way they could make it. The desert warriors would have fresh mounts. Theirs were tired, wheezing with every step. Al Azab would overtake them, then sweep down on the city. The soldiers and the peoples of the city would have no warning. No chance to organize their defenses. They'd be slaughtered.

Aurora thought of Theodorus. Of the sergeant of the household guard. Of Marcellus, with his charts and sketches and plans for the temple.

Her eyes flew to the high promontory that loomed in front of them. They'd ride right past it. Right past the roofless temple perched atop it. Right past her plane.

Aurora tore aside her veil. The wind whipped it out of her hands. She leaned forward, her eyes on the jutting mound of rock. The wind and flying sand teared her eyes, but she could see the incline leading upward, the one cut especially to haul her craft to its lofty mooring.

Their camel stumbled once again.

"Luke, stop! Let me down."

He either didn't hear her or chose to ignore her. She grabbed the tasseled reins and sawed back on them with all her might. The beast jerked its head upward and slowed. The tracker threw them a confused look as he raced by, then drew his beast around.

"Aurora, what—?"

Luke's surprise gave her the chance she needed. She ducked out of his hold and launched herself from the saddle. She let her body fold into an awkward roll when she hit the ground to lessen the shock of the impact.

Stunned, Luke fought the exhausted, frightened camel to a plunging, protesting halt.

"You won't make it with me riding double!" Aurora shouted, holding her wildly whipping hair out of her eyes with one hand. The wind had gathered strength and a touch of fury. "Go!" she screamed. "Go to the city!"

He threw his leg over the pommel and slid off. Holding on to the reins with one hand, he tried to reach her, but the animal backed away.

"Aurora! Mount this beast! At once!"

"No! He can't make it with both of us!"

"Get on!"

"No, Luke!" she cried desperately. "Go on without me."

He turned and yanked at the reins with both hands. The camel danced backward, its eyes rolling. Luke's curses battered Aurora's ears with more force even than the wind.

"I'm going to the temple," she shouted, pointing up toward the promontory. "To my plane! There are arms aboard. Flares. A gun."

She saw from the fury and desperation in his eyes that he didn't understand her words. Afraid that he would let go of the camel and come after her, she backed away.

"I'm an officer, a soldier. Like you. There's equipment aboard my plane that only I know the use of. I can help. I *will* help."

"Aurora!"

"Go! If you love me, go! Save the city!"

She whirled and ran.

Chapter 16

Aurora raced up the incline toward the tent that sheltered her plane. Silhouetted against the gathering storm clouds, the black tent billowed, straining the ropes that anchored it to the rocky surface. Under its temporary hide covering, the sleek jet sat poised at the top of the incline. Marble blocks and the harnesses that the senior engineer had designed held it in place.

Frantically Aurora ran through an inventory of the objects inside the plane. She had the flares that she'd dug out a few weeks ago and set aside for use at the dedication ceremony. The jumble of electronics gear. Her sidearm, the nine-millimeter Beretta, which she'd hidden in one of the zippered seats when she was allowed back in the plane. She hadn't been quite ready to show it to Luke or explain it to his engineers. One clip of rounds wouldn't stop the hordes that were bearing down on Dura, but it sure as heck might create a little confusion in the front ranks.

She was halfway up the incline when she heard footsteps pounding behind her. Her heart in her throat, she whirled and dropped into a crouch. The sight of a bronzed warrior racing toward her, sword in hand, made hers eyes widen in shock.

"Luke! What—what are you doing here?" Her rasping cry barely carried over the roar of the wind.

He stopped beside her, his chest heaving. "Think you I would leave you to face the hordes alone? Nay, Aurora, my bringer of light. We face then together."

She pushed her wildly whipping hair out of her eyes with a trembling hand. "But the city? The camp?"

"I sent the tracker ahead with orders to Quintus. He will have the camp's defenses mounted. Come, show me what you plan."

"But your duty to Rome! You must—"

He grabbed her arm and spun her around, pulling her with him as he ran up the hill. "My duty is to assist you in whatever mad scheme you plan. Come!"

"Luke!"

"Someday," he shouted, "I will teach you to obey my orders."

Aurora didn't have either the heart or the breath to remind him that they were fast running out of somedays. But the ache in her heart slowly gave way to a fierce rush of joy. Whatever came, whatever happened, she and Luke would meet their fate together.

They stumbled into the shelter of the tent. The wind poured in, but at least they could communicate without screaming.

"What is your plan?"

"I'm going to give them the scare of their lives," she panted. "I'm going to pull the chocks…to release the craft from its restraints and roll it down the hill as the enemy approaches. I have flares … firesticks to shoot across the front ranks."

"You plan to scare them?" he asked incredulously.

"I plan to create chaos, confusion. To turn their front lines," she snapped. "The idea was to give you time to reach the city."

His eyes narrowed. "And if the line did not turn?"

"Then I'd have one heck of a last ride."

"Show me what you want me to do."

In the midst of her pounding fear and roaring adrenaline, Aurora felt a burst of sheer satisfaction. For the first time, Luke accepted that she was an officer, a warrior of her own time. For this moment, for the brief time they had left together, they were equals.

"Cut the ropes holding the tent, then the woven leather harness attached to the struts. When I give the signal, push the marble blocks away from the tires . . . the wheels."

Without another word, Luke whirled and stepped to the side of the tent. His sword swung in a vicious arc, slicing through the ropes. The hide flapped in the wind. He crossed to the other side, and the tent blew backward, clearing the wings.

As she pulled open the hatch at the side of the plane, Aurora sent the black, foaming clouds a nervous glance. The last time she climbed into a plane and got swept up into this type of weather, she'd come down in a different century. Swallowing, she realized that this was probably the last time she would climb into a plane, in this or any other century.

The dim interior cut off much of the storm's gathering fury and surrounded her in a familiar cocoon of metal and plastic. Her pounding fear faded, and a cool, ruthless efficiency took over. This was her plane. She was in charge. For however many hours or minutes she had left, she was in command.

The idea of actually firing the engines didn't occur to her until she stumbled over her boots and her neatly folded flight suit on her way to the cockpit. She lifted one foot to kick the suit out of the way, then stopped abruptly, her foot drawn back. Then she remembered that she was an aviator. Why roll her plane down the hill? Why not taxi it? Hell, why not fly it?

Charlie said the turbofan engines were in working order, as far as he knew. The auxiliary battery still held a charge, enough to power up. The danger was that Aurora wouldn't be able to tell how much power flowed from the battery when she engaged the starter. Without the cockpit indicator, she might overcharge the cells and blow the engines completely. The blades might explode out of their casings, sending deadly slivers of metal through the fuselage, the wings, the fuel tanks. And then again, they might not. Well, an explosion would sure as heck be a lot more impressive than shooting off a few flares, she thought with a shaky grin.

It took her less than a minute to tear off her robe and zip herself into her flight suit. Hopping from one foot to another, she tugged on her boots. She slipped into the pilot's seat a few moments later.

Her fingers curled around the wheel, reacquainting themselves with its feel. Instinctively Aurora's mind conjured up a preflight checklist. When she realized what she was doing, she shook her head. There weren't any checklists for this flight. Feeling much like Wilbur and Orville must have on their first attempt to defy gravity, she glanced out the window to the tall, muscled man standing beside the nose of the plane. Her hand hovered over the instrument panel. Then she drew in a long breath and released the ground brakes.

Pushing open the side window, Aurora gave Luke a thumbs-up. "Now!"

His shoulders strained with the effort. Tendons corded into ropes of steel. Veins rose in his neck. Every muscle stood out in stark, savage relief as he pushed against the massive block in front of the nose wheel. Slowly, inch by painful inch, he edged it aside. Without stopping to draw a breath, he raced toward the rear wheels.

When the last chock gave, inertia held the plane still for long, heart-stopping seconds. Long enough for Luke to climb aboard. Ducking his head, he stumbled through the cabin. Bracing a hand on either side of the cockpit door, he stood behind her.

Aurora felt a film of sweat break out on her forehead. It was now or never. If she was going to do it, she had to do it now. She had to power the engines before the plane began rolling wildly out of control, or she'd just send them into a spin. Biting down on her lower lip so hard that she tasted the coppery tang of blood, Aurora pressed the starter.

The starboard engine caught on the third try. Through the howl of the wind, Aurora heard its muffled choke, then a low whine as the blades began to turn. She gave a sob of pure, unadulterated relief and kept her finger on the starter. The whine grew to a dull roar. She used her ear, her experience, and the sheer terror coursing through her veins to tell her when the engine reached full power. Her hand shook when she flipped the switch that would start the port engine. To her stunned amazement, it caught immediately.

Easing back on the throttle, she gave the craft its head. Metal creaked. The tail shuddered and skittered sideways. The wings stressed with the contrary winds. Slowly, painfully, the plane began to move.

She speared the silent man behind her a quick look. "Sit down, strap yourself in, and don't ask any questions. You're about to go for the ride of your life."

They were halfway down the incline when lightning split the skies. Aurora flinched, then widened her eyes in shock at the scene so briefly illuminated.

Al Azab's army filled the horizon to their east. As far as she could see, black-robed figures leaned forward in their saddles to lessen the pull of the wind as they galloped toward them and the city below.

"By the sword of Mars." Lucius's oath ripped from his throat. His head swung to the right, and he searched the swirling sand and dark clouds for some sight of an armored column, of a cavalry formation. Although his rational mind screamed that the tracker could not yet have made it to the camp, that his troops could not yet have any warning of the horde sweeping down on them, still he searched.

Aurora eased back on the throttle, increasing their speed.

"Luke! I'm going to take her up!"

"What?"

"I'm going to fly this baby."

He swallowed convulsively.

"Hang on!"

She let the plane gather speed, until it was careening down the last of the incline. The engines roared, deafening them both. Her hands were slick with sweat on the wheel.

She sent Luke a last, desperate look, took courage from his strained grin, then pulled the throttle back.

The wheels bounced and jarred for a few agonizing seconds. Then, incredibly, unbelievably, the plane lifted into the air. Aurora gave a whoop and worked the flaps.

Black, whirling clouds surrounded them immediately.

"Reach under your seat," she yelled. "There's a flare gun and a box of flares. I don't know how long I can keep us in the air, probably only long enough for one or two passes. I want to give them everything we've got."

With grim shouted instructions to Luke to open the side window and cock the flare gun, she rolled them into a slow bank. Luke flattened himself against the seat and clutched at the armrests. Sweat ran down his cheek, but he didn't say a word. After a few seconds, he released his death grip on the armrests and picked up the flare gun.

Aurora saw the calm manner in which he inspected the unfamiliar weapon. Her heart leaped into her throat at the bravery of a man who would trust his life and his fate to a winged vehicle and a woman who came from another time.

"Senior Centurion Lucius Antonius! If ever again I have to go into battle, I would have you beside me."

Across the small space separating them, Aurora saw golden lights leap into his eyes.

"And I you, Aurora."

She flashed him a wild grin. "Hang on, big guy. Here we go."

They got only one pass. But it was enough. More than enough. Flying as low and as slow as she dared with no airspeed indicator to guide her, Aurora swept down out of the clouds. They broke into the open just a few hundred feet from the vanguard of the onrushing army.

For as long as she lived, which probably wasn't going to be very much longer, Aurora thought grimly, she would carry the vivid kaleidoscope of images from these few seconds.

Camels dancing sideways in fright.

Stunned faces turned up to the apparition that swept out of the clouds.

One mounted warrior swerving, then crashing into the man next to him, bringing him down, and the dozens who followed.

A red flare exploding at the side of the plane, and white, burning light arcing earthward.

And Luke, a second-century warrior, calmly reloading the flare gun as though he'd handled such weapons every day of his life.

Craning her neck, Aurora watched the melee as they swooped past. Al Azab's front line crashed in on itself. Camels ran wildly in all directions. Men flung themselves off their mounts and threw themselves on the ground, their hands over their heads.

"Whooeee!"

Aurora whipped her head around in wild elation. At that precise instant, a violent wind shear threw her plane upward, out of control. In the next moment, her worst nightmares came true. Once more her plane was sucked into a dark, whirling vortex. Once more it tumbled through the sky like an wounded bird.

Only this time, when the heaving maelstrom spat it out and threw it toward the earth, she couldn't bring it down safely. This time, when the ground rushed up to meet them, a wing tipped into the earth and sent the plane cartwheeling through space. And this time Aurora couldn't fight the blackness that took her when the nose plowed into the hard earth and the windshield shattered into a thousand splintering pieces.

"Aurora."

As if from a great distance, she heard him calling.

"Aurora, come back to me."

The voice faded, edged out of her consciousness by pain.

"Open your eyes, my love."

That got her attention. Aurora rasped her tongue across dry, sandpapery lips and waited until the black, heaving wave inside her head subsided before trying to open her eyes. Her lids felt as though they were glued shut.

The support under her neck shifted, lifting her head to cradle it against a warm, hard surface. The deep, rich voice vibrated in the chest pressed against her cheek.

"I never thought to hear myself say this, but I beg you, open your eyes and speak to me."

Aurora pried open one lid and squinted up at his blurred face.

"I thought that might bring you back," he murmured.

She struggled to sit up. A sharp pain lanced through her skull, and she fell back in Luke's arms, gasping.

"Wh-where are we?"

His eyes swept the horizon, then smiled down at her. "In the desert. Somewhere."

That was when she noticed the blood. It covered one side of his face. It streaked his neck and trailed down his shoulders in wide, smeared tracks. It covered the front of her flight suit.

She grabbed his arms, pulling herself upright. "Oh, my God! Luke, you're hurt!" Panic laced her voice.

"Aurora, take your ease."

She pushed herself away from his chest, running her hands frantically over his torso in search of the source of all that blood. "What injury did you sustain?"

"Only minor ones, I swear. The shards cut my face, and tried to finish the job the bear began on my hands, but the wounds are not serious."

Aurora fought down waves of panic as she examined his face. The cuts were superficial, she saw after a moment. The blood had already dried on most of them, although several would require stitching to close cleanly. Ignoring the pain in her head, Aurora shifted sideways and drew his arm from around her waist. Her horrified gaze fastened on the blood-soaked linen strips that covered his hand from wrist to fingertips. With a low moan, she took his hand in both of hers and cradled it against her breast.

Luke managed not to wince. Easing his hand out of her hold, he slid it around her back and used his forearms to press her close against his chest.

For long, healing moments, they clung to each other. Her breath warmed his skin. His stirred her hair. The terror of the last hours receded slowly.

"We have to get up," she mumbled at last into his chest. "We've got to go through the plane, gather what survival gear we can."

"I pulled what I could from the pieces," Luke told her gently.

"Pieces?"

She gaped at him a moment, then struggled upright once more. Luke supported her while she stared over his shoulder at remnants of her plane.

The cockpit had miraculously remained intact, which had probably saved their lives, but most of the fuselage was broken into huge, grotesquely shaped pieces strewn across the silvery sands. The starboard wing had sheared off completely. It lay about a hundred yards behind the main body of the wreckage.

"Well, so much for leaving it at the altar for posterity to ooh and aah over," Aurora said, fighting back a sudden rush of tears. Embarrassed by this unexpected weakness, she pushed herself shakily to her feet. Luke rose to stand beside her.

"Do. . . do you have any idea where we are?" she asked after a moment. "Does anything look familiar?"

He made a slow circuit, his eyes narrowed and piercing as a hawk's. "Nay, nothing. We could be anywhere between Palmyra and Circesium."

Aurora squinted at the horizon. She put up a hand to shade her eyes, then lowered it a moment later.

"Luke." His name came out as a strangled croak. "I think we may be somewhere between Cairo and Baghdad."

She pointed a shaking finger toward the sky. Far off in the distance, a faint white line traced its way toward them.

"If I'm not mistaken, that's a vapor trail." Her voice gathered in intensity and excitement. "It is! Luke, that's a jet up there! That's a jet!"

"Aurora, speak in words I understand."

She whirled, then winced at the sudden movement. Raising wide, brimming eyes to his, she took his arms in both hands.

"Uh, I'm not quite sure how to break this to you, Senior Centurion, but we seem to have left your world. You're in mine now."

Luke's face whitened under its smear of blood. His eyes grew hard and flat. Not a muscle moved. Except the small one at the side of his jaw that began to twitch spasmodically.

Knowing there was nothing she could do to cushion his shock, Aurora bit her lip and turned to watch the sky. If her caculations were correct, the last time she'd put her plane down it had been in what would become Iraq. She hoped to heck that this time she'd brought it down someplace a bit friendlier. Like in Saudi. Or Israel. Egypt would be nice.

Shading her eyes with one hand, Aurora strained to identify the low-flying plane that zoomed toward them. When she identified the huge black letters on its tail, relief washed through her in great, rolling waves.

"He's one of the good guys!" she shouted, waving both hands over her head with wild abandon.

A black shadow raced across the ground toward them. A roar split the skies.

Aurora shrieked in joy.

Luke dropped into an instinctive crouch. His hand groped for his sword.

Waving frantically, Aurora jumped up and down. "Isn't that the most beautiful sound you ever heard? Look! He's wagging his wings! He'll circle again to give us another once-over and then call for help."

She danced in the sand, kicking up huge sprays. Her shouts of laughter spilled into the air. She rushed over to Luke, who straightened slowly.

"Luke, we're safe. We're safe."

"We are also in a different world," he growled. "One I know not."

The jet roared overhead again, without warning. Even Aurora hunched her shoulders that time. When she saw the expression on Luke's face, compassion feathered her wild exuberance. She laid a hand on his arm.

"Kinda weird, huh? Are you frightened?"

"Aye." His bloodied fingers closed over hers. "Were you?"

She nodded solemnly. "Scared out of my gourd."

Despite himself, Luke felt a smile tug at his lips. "Nay, not you, Aurora. You fought me and challenged me from the first moment we met, and turned my world upside down."

"Just wait until you see what you do to my world," she told him, laughing.

He glanced up at the silvery streaking plane. "Aye, 'twill be an experience."

Aurora's singing euphoria left her like air rushing from a deflated balloon. He was right. Oh, God, he was right. It would be an experience. More than an experience. It would be a nightmare. When the scientists and the historians, not to mention the press, got hold of Luke, he'd become a specimen. The man she knew, the proud, strong warrior she loved, would be turned into a laboratory rat. They'd keep him under observation, probe his brain, draw his blood, measure his electrical impulses, test his reactions to all kinds of stimuli. He'd lose all privacy, all right to his own choices. They'd never leave him alone.

No, damn it, no! He was hers. She'd traveled through time to find him. She wouldn't give him up now.

"Luke, do you trust me?"

"Nay, woman, not when you get that gleam in your eyes. It has boded ill for me since the moment I met you." His lips twisted in the crooked grin that never failed to make her breath catch somewhere in the middle of her chest.

Aurora felt an answering laugh bubble to her lips. "You ain't seen nothin' yet, big guy. Wait right here."

She raced to the pile of gear Luke had pulled from the plane. Digging through it frantically, she found what she was looking for and gave a shout of triumph. Within moments she was back, a wadded green bundle and a pair of black boots clutched to her chest. She dropped the boots in the sand and shook out Charlie's flight suit. "Here, put this on."

Luke stared at the green bag as though it held a nest of vipers in its zippered pockets.

"Come on. We don't have much time. The choppers could be here at any moment. Put it on."

"Why?"

"Because, as of this moment, you're Lieutenant Charles Everett, United States Air Force."

"Aurora, are you mad? I know naught of this force you speak of, nor of your world. I cannot be that which I'm not."

"You're a soldier, aren't you?" she said fiercely. "A warrior? You have courage, and heart, and spirit. You can do this."

She grabbed his wrist and turned the palm up. "You battled a wild beast with these hands. You saved my face and my eyesight and probably my life with these hands when the windshield shattered. And, coincidentally, you destroyed any hope of getting a clear set of prints."

"What do you speak of?"

"Never mind." She freed his wrist, then stepped back, gnawing on her lower lip.

"You're Charlie's height, your eyes are close enough to hazel as to qualify in my book. His hair's a shade or two lighter, and his nose doesn't have that interesting lump, but by the time we get you bandaged, no one's going to see your face."

"Aurora . . ."

"Look, they'll take you to a big air force hospital to treat your wounds. No one will know you, at least not right away. They'll fly in Charlie's medical records, but we'll claim that . . . that someone else's records were misfiled in Lieutenant Everett's folder. His are lost. It happens all the time," she assured him. Her mind raced with plans and pitfalls.

"And you won't have to talk. The lightning went through your earphones. You lost your hearing and your memory, just like Charlie did. You can't answer anyone. Not until I have time to teach you the language."

"Aurora . . ."

"I'll be with you the whole time," she assured him. "I'll tutor you in our ways, as you and Theodorus did me. You're my crew member, they'll expect me to stay with you. It'll work," she insisted when she saw his disbelieving look.

"No one could believe I am this Char-Li for very long."

"It doesn't have to be for very long. Just long enough to buy us some time. Time to ease you into this century. Time to come up with a rational explanation for you. One that won't land you in the zoo."

He stared at her, his eyes fathomless.

"Luke, it's the only way. We can pull this off." She drew in a deep breath. "As the philosophers say, 'It is certain, because it is impossible.'"

The stark planes of his face softened imperceptibly. A golden light gleamed in his eyes. "A maxim, Aurora?"

She grinned idiotically. "Whatever works."

His rich, welcome laughter joined hers. Shaking his head in resignation, he reached for the silver buckle on his sword belt.

"Here, let me do it."

She made short work of the belt and clutched his sword to her breast while he shrugged out of his tunic. She'd have to bury the sword and his clothes, she thought regretfully, remembering how frightening it was to go unarmed into the unknown.

She felt an even deeper twinge of regret when he unwrapped his linen loincloth and tossed it aside. She'd definitely miss that particular article of his clothing. He wouldn't find anything that suited him half as well in this century.

With a lean, lithe grace, he stepped into the green bag. Thank heavens Charlie was so long and lanky, she thought, setting aside the sword to help him with zippers at the ankle. Luke's more muscled frame just fit into the flight suit, although his wide shoulders strained the seams. The seams would hold, Aurora knew from personal experience. They'd hold.

His fingers hesitated on the front zipper. It wasn't pain that stayed his hand, she guessed shrewdly, but a reluctance to clothe himself in garments strange to him. A fear that he would lose his identity. She waited, still bent on one knee, her heart slamming against her ribs, for him to make a move. To take that first step into her world. Slowly, awkwardly, he tugged at the metal tab. Aurora let out the breath she was holding.

Rising, she dusted the sand from her hands. "We have a lot to get done before a rescue crew arrives. Get it in gear, Lieutenant."

He looked up, startled at the crisp command.

Aurora had been waiting for this moment for a long, long time. She tapped the set of silver tracks on the shoulder of her flight suit.

"Lesson number one. I'm a captain. You're a lieutenant. I outrank you. In this world, men take orders from women who are their superiors. Now move it."

Luke's eyes narrowed, but he zipped up the flight suit without another word.

Hiding a smug grin, Aurora turned to retrieve the boots. Before she'd taken half a step, a hard arm wrapped around her waist. In one swift move, Luke hauled her up against his chest.

"I think we shall have to find a world of our own," he told her. "One somewhere between yours and mine."

His lips met hers in a kiss that promised passion and simmmering excitement and a love that would span all time.

Breathless, Aurora raised shining eyes to his. "I think we just found that world, Senior Centurion."

* * * * *

JINGLE BELLS, WEDDING BELLS:
Silhouette's Christmas Collection for 1994

Christmas Wish List

*To beat the crowds at the malls and get the perfect present for *everyone,* even that snoopy Mrs. Smith next door!

*To get through the holiday parties without running my panty hose.

*To bake cookies, decorate the house and serve the perfect Christmas dinner—just like the women in all those magazines.

*To sit down, curl up and read my Silhouette Christmas stories!

Join *New York Times* bestselling author Nora Roberts, along with popular writers Barbara Boswell, Myrna Temte and Elizabeth August, as we celebrate the joys of Christmas—and the magic of marriage—with

JINGLE BELLS, WEDDING BELLS

Silhouette's Christmas Collection for 1994.

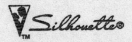

JBWB

MILLION DOLLAR SWEEPSTAKES (III)

No purchase necessary. To enter, follow the directions published. Method of entry may vary. For eligibility, entries must be received no later than March 31, 1996. No liability is assumed for printing errors, lost, late or misdirected entries. Odds of winning are determined by the number of eligible entries distributed and received. Prizewinners will be determined no later than June 30, 1996.

Sweepstakes open to residents of the U.S. (except Puerto Rico), Canada, Europe and Taiwan who are 18 years of age or older. All applicable laws and regulations apply. Sweepstakes offer void wherever prohibited by law. Values of all prizes are in U.S. currency. This sweepstakes is presented by Torstar Corp., its subsidiaries and affiliates, in conjunction with book, merchandise and/or product offerings. For a copy of the Official Rules send a self-addressed, stamped envelope (WA residents need not affix return postage) to: MILLION DOLLAR SWEEPSTAKES (III) Rules, P.O. Box 4573, Blair, NE 68009, USA.

EXTRA BONUS PRIZE DRAWING

No purchase necessary. The Extra Bonus Prize will be awarded in a random drawing to be conducted no later than 5/30/96 from among all entries received. To qualify, entries must be received by 3/31/96 and comply with published directions. Drawing open to residents of the U.S. (except Puerto Rico), Canada, Europe and Taiwan who are 18 years of age or older. All applicable laws and regulations apply; offer void wherever prohibited by law. Odds of winning are dependent upon number of eligibile entries received. Prize is valued in U.S. currency. The offer is presented by Torstar Corp., its subsidiaries and affiliates in conjunction with book, merchandise and/or product offering. For a copy of the Official Rules governing this sweepstakes, send a self-addressed, stamped envelope (WA residents need not affix return postage) to: Extra Bonus Prize Drawing Rules, P.O. Box 4590, Blair, NE 68009, USA.

SWP-S994

The Loop™

Is the future what it's cracked up to be?

This September, tune in to see why Jessica's partying days are over in

GETTING IT RIGHT: JESSICA
by Carla Cassidy

She had flunked out of college and nearly out of life. Her father expected her to come crawling home, and her friends expected her to fall off the wagon…but Jessica decided she'd rather sell her soul before she screwed up again. So she squeezed into an apartment with some girls she barely knew, got a job that barely paid the bills and decided that things were looking up. Trouble was, no one knew better than her that *looks* could be deceiving.

The ups and downs of modern life continue with

GETTING REAL: CHRISTOPHER
by Kathryn Jensen in October

GETTING PERSONAL: BECKY
by Janet Quin Harkin in November

Get smart. Get into "The Loop!"

Only from

Silhouette®

where passion lives.

LOOP2

SILHOUETTE ®

Shadows ™

MORE GREAT READING FROM
BARBARA FAITH

If you enjoyed Barbara Faith's DESERT MAN, you'll want to join her in November as she visits the dark side of love with DARK, DARK MY LOVER'S EYES, Silhouette Shadows #43.

When tutor Juliana Fleming accepted an assignment in Mexico, she had no idea the turn her life would take. Kico Vega—her solemn, needy student—immediately warmed to her presence, but Kico's father, Rafael, showed her nothing but contempt. Until he took Julie as his bride, ravishing her with his all-consuming desire—yet setting in motion Julie's worst nightmare.

Take a walk on the dark side of love with Barbara Faith—only in **SILHOUETTE SHADOWS**

INTIMATE MOMENTS®

™ *Silhouette*®

You've met Gable, Cooper and Flynn Rawlings.
Now meet their spirited sister, Kat Rawlings, in
her own installment of

THE WILD WEST

by Linda Turner

Kat admitted it—she was once a spoiled brat.
But these days she focused all her attention
on making her ranch successful. Until
Lucas Valentine signed on as her ranchhand.
Sexy as hell, the bitter cast to his smile pointed to
a past that intrigued her. The only problem was
that Lucas seemed bent on ignoring the sparks
between them. Yet Kat *always* got what she
wanted—and she was readying her lasso,
because her heart was set on Lucas!

Don't miss KAT (IM #590), the exciting
conclusion to Linda Turner's Wild West saga.
Available in September, only from
Silhouette Intimate Moments!

And now for something completely different....

SPELLBOUND

R O M A N C E

In October, look for
ANNIE AND THE OUTLAW (IM #597)
by Sharon Sala

Gabriel Donner rode into Annie O'Brien's life like an outlaw—and an angel—saving her from the gang who threatened her safety. Yet the fight of Annie's life had only just begun, and bad-boy Gabe would move heaven and earth to save her again.

Don't miss ANNIE AND THE OUTLAW, by Sharon Sala, available this October, only from

Premiere

The stars are out in October at Silhouette! Read captivating love stories by talented *new* authors— in their very first Silhouette appearance.

Sizzle with Susan Crosby's
THE MATING GAME—Desire #888
…when Iain Mackenzie and Kani Warner are forced to spend their days—and *nights*—together in *very* close tropical quarters!

Explore the passion in Sandra Moore's
HIGH COUNTRY COWBOY—Special Edition #918
…where Jake Valiteros tries to control the demons that haunt him—along with a stubborn woman as wild as the Wyoming wind.

Cherish the emotion in Kia Cochrane's
MARRIED BY A THREAD—Intimate Moments #600
…as Dusty McKay tries to recapture the love he once shared with his wife, Tori.

Exhilarate in the power of Christie Clark's
TWO HEARTS TOO LATE—Romance #1041
…as Kirby Anne Gordon and Carl Tannon fight for custody of a small child…and battle their growing attraction!

Shiver with Val Daniels'
BETWEEN DUSK AND DAWN—Shadows #42
…when a mysterious stranger claims to want to save Jonna Sanders from a serial killer.

Catch the classics of tomorrow—*premiering* today—
Only from

Silhouette®

PREM94